ADVENT of ANTICHRIST

A Tale of the Time of the End

Advent of Antichrist

A Tale of the Time of the End

T. Steven Brown

Other books by T. Steven Brown
The Science of Building
The Elephant in the Atrium
ABACUS

FOREWORD

The advent of antichrist means that the time of antichrist, or even THE Antichrist has arrived. We are admonished to not even speculate on the time of Christ's Second Coming, and hence, the Rapture and the Tribulation. But we are told that we shall know the *Season*. I believe we are in that *Season*. Biblical scholars tell us that all prophecies leading up to the *Blessed Hope* have been fulfilled, so that event could come at any time. This fictional account speculates about what the time just before these events might be like, and a fictional account of the Rapture itself is described. **This story may very well approximate how history will unfold during the next few years.**

Who can deny that we are in a time of antichrist? Events, such as the drive toward a one-world government, and rapidly advancing technology, and even the abolition of organized religion, or a new ecumenism is not apparent? If the author is right, it behooves everyone to learn about what we may soon be facing.

Much of the paraphernalia required for the literal fulfillment of the Prophesies is already present, such as worldwide television networks, satellites, and super-computers. Other developments, such as a practical working tokamak are imagined, but are not necessarily required by prophecy.

The time span covered in this tale is about ten years, and therefore requires the *telling* of parts of the story; else the story would require hundreds of more pages of *showing*.

As background research for this novel, I have used the *Golden Rule of Biblical Interpretation* originally postulated by Dr. David Cooper. That means that wherever possible, the Prophesies are taken literally. The majority of Biblical scholars seem to have adopted this standard for themselves, but as any student (such as I am) knows, one should not be dogmatic about any interpretation of these matters.

Those familiar with socio-economic models will note that this art form is appreciated by someone outside the field. One of the characters is a special hero, and he is a mere programmer! How many novels do you read where the hero is a computer nerd?

CREDITS

Special thanks must go to the following people: First, my dear wife Beth, for ideas and the original artwork. Special recognition goes to the following for their encouragement: Mrs. Sandra Zamenski, Mrs. Steven Matheson, Mrs. Lynn Gilzow, and Mrs. Whitney Parks. Important ideas as well as encouragement were given to me by Doctors J. Giuiliano, R. Schultz, and J. McGurn. To the many friends and professionals who helped with the design, assemblage, and proof reading, my thanks.

I appreciate the inspiration of the many gifted authors who have written about Biblical prophecy. They have provided clarity, hope, and inspiration. And of course the errors are due to my proofreaders, or perhaps the computer!

TABLE OF CONTENTS

PART I

TURMOIL

"His descendants settled in the area from Havilah to Shur, near the border of Egypt. And they lived in hostility toward all their brothers."   (Speaking of Ishmael)
The Holy Bible

Chapter 1: ISRAEL, THE NEW SUPERPOWER

****** **The Negev:**

Moise ben Fedeen began the last day of his life angry. He was angry at the hateful female officer who had assigned him to patrol the lower reaches of the Negev. He was angry at his wife, who had decided to take the children away again to her father's home in France. He was even angry at the Muslim terrorists who threatened to annihilate the Jewish race, and who, at this very moment were trying to smuggle dirty cobalt bombs into Tel Aviv-Jaffa.

Moise saw the telltale dust cloud long before the truck came into view. **It was just at that moment he felt something brush against his cheek, even as a sense of foreboding clouded his mind.** Moise dismissed it as emotional claptrap, left-over nausea from yesterday's argument with his wife.

He started his armored vehicle in preparation for maneuvering to intercept the approaching truck, while his partner, Peter Vermeer, dutifully reported the sighting and the imminent inspection to the operator at the Mer Dan station. The gully the truck was being driven down was a very poor choice of roads. They were undoubtedly up to no good. Probably smugglers. Moise placed his vehicle between two large boulders, making it impossible for the truck to go around them. He then stood on top of the vehicle, scanning the horizon with his field glasses. Nothing else was in sight. He focused on the approaching truck. The occupants appeared to be a farmer and his wife. Perhaps they were lost.

Moise held his position, while Peter signaled the slowly moving truck to stop. The truck slowed, but then sped up and turned abruptly, exposing the two Israeli guards to the rear of the truck and the withering fire of two Uzis. They didn't have time to raise their weapons. **A presence, sentience at another level, stirred, and seeing nothing to do, departed.**

***

The threat to Israel had never been greater. For thirty years, the divisions and jealousies among the most powerful Muslim leaders had resulted in little concerted effort against their eternal enemies. The emergence of the New Iranian Empire had changed all that. The Iraqi and Syrian leaders had been neatly assassinated at a most propitious time, just after the *New Brotherhood* was in place. The peoples of these nations were delivered to the *Great One* in the aftermath of the confusion and breakdown of the regimes, so neatly decapitated, so to speak. That was not the only important change in the always boiling Middle East. Israel had become, almost overnight, a great power, an economic super power. Two rather astounding developments had made this so.

First, there was the matter of solving the gridlock between the trading blocks, after GATT and later the WTO proved to be toothless. Four major trading blocks had emerged: The EEC, the newly expanded FTAA (a direct outgrowth of NAFTA and OAS), the TAIPAN Consortium (Japan, China, Indonesia, the *little tigers, and* Australia), and GRA, the Greater Russian Alliance.

Inevitably, impasse developed between them. Israel, with no allegiance to any of the blocks, had been able to secretly negotiate special treaties with all of the blocks and had become the middleman of the world. The Israelis were amassing wealth and influence at an amazing rate.

The other development was a chance breakthrough in the design of fusion power. Almost by accident, it seemed, a young engineer named Mervin Levy, studying at Tel-Aviv Institute for Advanced Physics, had performed an elaborate experiment, using a computer-controlled hot gas containment field. In a rush of insight well beyond his genius, he had felt compelled to write down this design floating around in his head. He worked for three days straight, stopping only to snack and nap briefly. The targeted application was a high-temperature gas fission reactor. But his sponsor and mentor, Dr. Shein Saito, of automatic control theory fame, recognized the much greater potential for plasma containment.

The day after a dramatic news conference held at the site of the world's first full scale operational fusion generator, the spot price of crude oil dropped by almost 30%. The price rebounded sharply over the next few days, as oil traders came to the realization that the logistics of the conversion processes would require at least forty years just to replace half of the existing power plants, world-wide.

Still, the threat to the livelihood of the OPEC nations was not well received. Only the intervention by the major petroleum user nations prevented the immediate invasion of Israel by her neighbors.

The ancient Semitic hatreds simmered, and the growing disparity of wealth between 900 million Muslims and 8 million Jews gave a facade of righteous moral outrage to the natural animosity and enmity between the cultures.

During the past month, unknown to the public, three cobalt bombs had been discovered near Tel Aviv-Jaffa and one at Haifa. The borders had been totally closed. Almost nothing moved along any of the highways without repeated inspections with sophisticated sensing devices or intensive manual examinations.

Avery Harrington, a former British subject, had become the Prime Minister of Israel, and it was under his gifted leadership that Israel had at last begun to achieve her full potential in the world. In the space of six years, Israel had become the premier energy supplier to the world and the indispensable go-between for all of the major trading blocks.

Internal government subsidies and *de facto* tariffs persisted, in spite of the lip service given to the popular political posture of free trade. But business was business, and where there was money to be made, and treaties stood in the way, the *special partner* was called in to expedite the trade.

The murder of the two guards did not make the evening news, nor did the subsequent capture of the Arab terrorists who killed them. Neither did the contents of their truck make the news. Especially the contents of their truck did not make the news.

The prime minister's security phone rang for the third time that day. "Yes, I understand, yes, thank you." was all his dinner guests heard. Another bomb. Surely one of them would get through someday. But not today. The Prime Minister strode back to the spacious living room, where he was entertaining several important political leaders from the Likud party this evening. "My friends, I want to propose a toast. Today we have concluded the largest agricultural agreement in history. It involves 10 countries and all of the blocks," Avery said, raising his wine glass with a flourish.

Abraham Schotz looked rather askance at the Minister. He had openly opposed Avery for several years, but Avery had worked tirelessly to win this man's approval and his support. Avery had infected him with his charm and his greater purpose. Early in their relationship, Abraham sensed a strange aura emanating from this man. He positively radiated energy and warmth.

Abraham stroked his beard with pride as Avery detailed the torturous machinations that had been required to close this latest and largest deal. Abraham was standing opposite the Prime Minister. He raised his glass, as if to propose another toast. "We almost lost it over that Korean rice issue, didn't we?" he said. "But you stepped in and saved the day," Avery responded, gesturing toward Schotz.

***

Avery Harrington was a striking figure. Now in his early sixties, he was average in height and build, a product of an English father and a Jewish mother. He had a dark complexion, sharp, handsome features, very dark deep-set

5

eyes, and black hair and mustache. Besides his penetrating eyes, the singular feature which often made people take an involuntary second look was the perfect symmetry of his face. His dark skin and hair and eyes contrasted sharply with his beautifully set teeth. His deep voice and striking good looks reinforced the natural charisma of his compelling personality. No one who met him was ever likely to forget him.

Early in his political career, he had championed the cause of mutual defense treaties for the Jews, and he developed strong allies for that purpose all over the western world and, of course, in Israel. In 1997 he had become a citizen of Israel, and quickly worked his way up into the higher echelons of the government, becoming the Israeli Ambassador to the United Nations. With the impasse between the two major political parties in Israel, the opportunity for a compromise candidate opened the door for Harrington. Once in power, he quickly cemented his relationships with all of the major power brokers in the country and became more of a force than any single political party.

****** **The White House:**
Able Larson was one of the good old boys whom the Williams' had brought to Washington with them. He had been faithful through trouble and triumph, and his loyalty got him the very influential job of the President's Appointment Secretary. Abe, as he was affectionately known, was quite parochial about the President's attentions and his time. No one, except Carrie, of course, could interfere with the schedule he kept for the benefit of the President.

Abe recognized the Director of the CIA immediately and rose to his feet in honest deference. "Abe, I must see the *Man* as soon as you can let me," the Director announced, trying to be diplomatic but intractable. Abe answered by pulling out his rather large black appointment calendar. "I will put you in next. How long will you need? If you can keep it within fifteen minutes, I can get him back on schedule without offending anyone," Abe added. The wiry, white-haired Director said "Sure, unless the *Man* wants to get involved with the problem I am about to present to him." Abe nodded, picked up his phone, and made it happen.

"Mr. President," the Director said to Grant, in his usual very serious attitude. "Bob," the President responded, not smiling. He knew he was about to get some bad news. He thought of this man as the *Grim Reaper* and even referred to him as that, in some of the Cabinet meetings. "I felt I should bring this to your attention," Bob said, handing Grant a one page bulletin outlining the particulars of the latest attempt to smuggle an atomic device into Israel. "How can one deal with such a world! Mass destruction in the hands of madmen," Grant philosophized, rather to himself. *It must not happen here*, he thought.

"Thank you, Bob. Does the agency have any recommendations at this time?" "No sir. We are intensifying our own surveillance in the region, and we have loaned them quite a bit of our latest detection equipment, but beyond that, we are just watching." "Good, keep me informed of **any** further developments," the President said, dismissing the Director.

When he told Carrie later that day, about this development, Grant was almost surprised that she did not know already. She had her own sources, and often knew things even before him.

****** **Jerusalem:**

After his guests left, the Prime Minister immediately called his security chief. "What about your New York contact?" he asked, "Have we gotten any response yet?" "No," the minister answered, matter-of-factly, "They have asked for a week to confer." After exchanging pleasantries with his old and trusted friend, the Prime Minister retired for the night.

Israeli military intelligence had warned of the possible attempt by the Muslims to smuggle bombs into Israel. This warning was acted upon with the full force of the government. Operation SIEVE was initiated, and operation MIDNIGHT MADNESS was moved into high gear.

SIEVE was the plan, long perfected and often trained for, to seal the borders and conduct intensive surveillance for just such devices. Stationary monitors were hidden in dozens of locations along the main roads and even strategic foot paths. Army guards were stationed at every intersection leading into the major population centers and, randomly, inside the cities. Undercover operatives roamed at will, checking any traffic which even had the potential of carrying bombs of any type.

MIDNIGHT MADNESS was simply the old cold war equivalent of *MAD*. ***The Israelis had bombs of their own!***

Chapter 2: THE NERD GOES to WASHINGTON

****** Holloman Air Force Base:

Jason Phillips looked the part of a young aerospace engineer, as he was, in a way. He blended in well with the busload of visitors on their way to Holloman AFB, White Sands, New Mexico. The bus driver sensed that he was someone special. Could he know that a meeting of strategic national interest was about to take place? Equally interested in his presence here was an older woman who operated the only remaining coffee shop on the base. She was a foreign agent, long ago placed here as eyes and ears for her government. Specific technical details were not necessary; knowing who came here, when and with whom, spoke volumes for those who cared to listen.

A third agent seemed more interested in watching the other agents as they observed Jason, than in Jason himself. This was the Deputy Base Commander. He wore the uniform of the U. S. Air Force but was more than what he appeared.

Holloman Air Force Base and its host, White Sands, had again just managed to survive the sweeping budget axe, for the sixth time in sixteen years of major defense cuts. Only super-sophisticated RPVs (remotely piloted vehicles) were tested here now. The heyday of the manned aircraft era had come and gone. Except for the Raptor, and the new B3, which kept everyone busy.

The bus finally ground to a stop in front of the squat little green security building, where all disembarked. The hot dust of another Southwestern day was just beginning to stir.

Jason asked for a Captain Martinez who, ostensibly, was to brief him on tests to be conducted later that month for his company, General Research. That was the cover. His real reason was to keep an important date with an old friend, a Colonel Steinman, soon to become Major General.

The dark-haired girl at the security counter served up his temporary badge and made the call to Captain Martinez. She showed more than the usual interest in this handsome visitor. Jason and at least two others wondered about this interest. But it was only because she liked his looks, and this was a very lonely post.

Captain Martinez was a heavy-set, dark-skinned man, with a quiet, business-like manner, but with a friendly smile. He let Jason open the Bronco door for himself. While they were still parked outside the security facility, Martinez identified Jason with a portable DNA testing device, one of only a dozen or so then in use. Jason knew immediately what it was; his only surprise was that such lengths were being taken to keep this encounter so secret.

The Bronco bounced along the road for about five miles before Martinez turned off onto a single-lane dirt path. He finally pulled up at a small turn-around, announcing that they had arrived! "There it is, Mr. Phillips," Martinez announced, pointing toward a small brick building about 20 yards away. As Jason entered the building, he could see the Bronco leaving. The room was empty of people but crowded with arrays of display and monitoring devices. On a central screen, he was greeted by the Colonel's secretary, Patty Winthrope, a woman he knew from his tour at Camp

Pendleton, "Hi, Jason," she enthused. "It has been a long time! The General will be right with you." Evidently the promotion had already come through. "Please have a seat. You are on camera, as you can see. This is a class three security comm link, so feel free to discuss any matters up to that level."

In the intervening moments, while Jason waited for his old friend and mentor, his mind began to register some of the many memories from his association with George Steinman.

***

After an accelerated track through Berkeley, Jason served a term in the Marines. He was stationed at Pendleton for his entire tour. This was just fine with him, because it was there, on the beaches south of Oceanside, that he met Jamie, whom he married after a whirlwind romance. The colonnade of raised swords at their wedding was the high point of his military career, although the organization did get a unit commendation for which he was mostly responsible.

Jason had shown an early aptitude for flying, for computer science, and for the special field of simulation called socio-economic modeling. It was that special combination of interest and talent which led to his recruitment by then Colonel Steinman, who had set up one of the most intriguing computer simulation projects ever done. Jason proved worthy of the task. Many of the major advances produced by this project had been largely the personal contribution of Jason Phillips. Steinman made sure that Jason knew he was appreciated. He cultivated his friendship, sponsored him in his technical growth, and counseled him in his personal affairs. George Steinman's gift was to recognize and to apply talented men and women in technically promising new applications.

***

"Hi, Jason, how are you?   I'm sorry I had to set this up like this, but logistics and security problems made it impossible to bring you here," intoned the man shown on the main monitor. "I'm fine, sir; I didn't mind. I am not sure I understand all the security, but I guess I'll find out," Jason responded.

Steinman didn't have time for personal chatter, even though it had been ten months since he had seen his young protégé. "Jason, I know you have served your turn for your country, but I need your help. I am putting together the most ambitious computer simulation project ever conceived, and it is of supreme national importance. I report directly to the President of the United States!" He paused to let the gravity of that statement sink in. "You must put your academic career aside for awhile. Your nation needs you. I need you. President Williams needs you."

"And besides that, it will be very exciting and rewarding," he concluded. "What do you say?" *What can I say,* thought Jason. Steinman was not one to give a person much of a choice when he really wanted something. "That sounds exciting, sir. Can we discuss some of the particulars?" Jason answered, catching his breath. *There goes my doctorate*, he thought.

The General proceeded to reel in his *catch of the day*. "By the way, the code name for the project is *ABACUS*, and even that is classified, Jason." He did not have to, but he promised Jason considerable administrative responsibility, heavy technical challenges, and a special government consultant's contract for five years, with a salary well into six figures. Jason asked for a couple of days, to be able to talk it over with Jamie and to see if he could gracefully sever his ties with the University. But he already knew he would do it. Academia could wait. Besides, how could you compare that kind of a salary with an Assistant Professorship?

Martinez was waiting outside when the conversation ended. It was not yet lunch time, and early enough for Jason to catch the afternoon hop back to Denver, and then home. The ride back to the security building passed without a word between Martinez and Phillips, and they were both comfortable with that silence. The *need to know* test obviously applied. "Good luck" and "Thanks" was their final exchange. The dark-haired security receptionist gave him that special treatment reserved for Washington VIPs. The resident international ears knew the routine. Other agents would know who was transmitting that morning. It was enough to know who. The *what* was elementary, given so many pieces.

****** **Saratoga, California:**
As Jason's flight made its descent through the high clouds covering the San Francisco peninsula, he stared out of his portside window, fascinated with the miniatures spread out below. The streetlights gave a golden glow over the lush mantle, which seemed to be floating on a sea of black ink.

13

The major freeways pulsed like arteries in something alive, and the whole scene was laced with rivers of light. Jason felt good to be alive, and young, and perhaps even important. San Francisco International was as busy as ever. Construction had been going on there for as long as he could remember.

Bright moonlight silhouetted the rolling hills as he turned into his driveway in the luxurious and tranquil community of Saratoga. He and Jamie had just purchased this little place, mostly on the strength of her father's personal loan. Things were just coming together; dreams were starting to come true. *How would she accept this*, Jason wondered, as he pulled into the garage.

***

Jason Phillips was a 24-year-old whiz kid. He came from a little ranch near Smith Valley, Nevada, but he wasn't just country. He was raised by his mother, a rancher and real estate dealer, one of the more important citizens of their little community.

Jason had been a skinny kid who never really filled out. He worked hard as a youngster, and he played basketball in high school. He had always looked a little emaciated. It was his metabolism; he always had more things to do than time allowed. He treasured life and seemed to be in a hurry to get everything in that was his to do.

Jason was into everything, including computers and mathematics. He won his pilot's license when he was only 16. He loved flying almost as much as riding the range. Jason had given up all this to study at Berkeley. His success there led him to George Steinman and Project SPAT (strategic planning and attack tool), and Jamie. After his stint in the military, he and Jamie had agreed to go back to Berkeley for his doctorate. That had been his life, so far.

***

Although Jamie greeted him with a warm embrace, Jason could feel the tension within her. "Hello, my beautiful bride! What's for dinner, or shall we just go to bed?" Jason teased. "I've got a headache!" Jamie said, grinning, and she was unable to restrain the laughter that line always invoked for them. "Can we talk about your meeting? Shall I run the water?" she said, half seriously. "After dinner, please, and, yes, there is a lot of security involved," he responded, suddenly feeling tired.

After dinner, they sat back on their sofa, with the TV turned onto the news. Jason's mind was already trying to unravel the mystery of the new project, and he wondered at the President's personal involvement in it. The TV blaring was a good security measure. He described his trip and the meeting, adding sufficient hyperbole to make what was a rather boring trip sound intriguing. Jamie read the expressions on Jason's face as he described, with unmasked excitement, the General's offer and the challenge of the project. She knew immediately that they would be moving soon, and that this might mean the end of his pursuit of his doctorate. But she loved this man and wanted always to share his adventure. Of course she would play it for as much as she could. "Well, what do you think?" Jason asked, as if they were deliberating about where to go shopping. Jamie didn't answer, but smiled her warm wonderful smile, and drew herself into his arms.

Unnoticed by either of them were four self-contained, miniature transmitters, placed in their modest home within hours of Jason's call to fly out to Holloman.

****** **The Pentagon:**

The trip from the White House lawn to Helicopter Pad 3 on the roof of the Pentagon took almost 7 minutes, including the careful, hovering descent in the strong evening breeze. It was dusk, and the smoky, busy, buzzing city by the Potomac became a jeweled fantasy from the air.

This city had always been a fantasy, as far as George Steinman was concerned. But here was the power, and he had at last tapped into it. Recently a mere Colonel, languishing as project head of an undertaking long past its glory, he had been snatched up suddenly, directly to the seat of power: Washington.

The General scrambled down the steps, casually waving to the President's pilot, who had brought him here. The army-green helicopter was already lifting off as he got to the door. Only a handful of people knew why this special new entrance to the Pentagon had been built. This door had no guard, not even a lock; but the foyer into which it entered was a maze of security devices being tended by a single young marine, in dress uniform. She snapped to attention as soon as the door opened and held her salute until the General returned it, although he was in civilian clothes. "Carry on," he said, mechanically, preoccupied with thoughts of the meeting he had just attended.

***

George Steinman was a career officer, a marine's marine. He had served with distinction in Viet Nam and, after a second hitch, had decided to make the career permanent. Although George had graduated from Caltech as an Electrical Engineer, he had found his niche in life as an administrator. He had gathered extraordinarily talented people around him, and it had paid off for him, handsomely.

While attending the Naval Post Graduate School in Monterey, he had become interested in socio-economic simulation and gaming theory. George pulled in all of his outstanding credits to land the job of Project Manager in the newly-formed group at Pendleton. He grew the project into one of the most important strategic planning tools ever devised by the military. In a way, Project *ABACUS* was a direct outgrowth of the work done at Pendleton.

One fateful day, while conducting a tour for visiting dignitaries, including several governors and senators, he was introduced to Carrie Williams, wife of the then Governor of Colorado. While the Colonel's adjutant gave the VIP spiel, George took the opportunity to apply his considerable charm to the Governor's wife. It was a mutual thing; Carrie sensed that this man was someone who could someday help her with her quest to promote her husband to higher office.

George Steinman was a large man, but his sharp, clean-cut features belied his bulk. His military style haircut added to the overall appearance of military authority and personal magnetism. Carrie put herself on a first name basis with him immediately, and George proceeded to peak her interest by describing how the system could actually be used to help control the economic and social behavior of any given group of people. For a few minutes, the usually overly-charming and vacuous wife of the Governor became a very interested interrogator, well prepared and insightful with her stream of pointed and penetrating questions. This meeting was to change the life of both her husband and this model of military mindset.

***

The General placed his hand over the glass face of the newest type of identification hardware. After about two seconds, the elevator door began to open. As the special express elevator plunged deep into the lower floors of this mammoth office building, George Steinman reviewed the events of the day in his mind.

The day had not begun well, and it had gotten progressively worse, up until his meeting with three selected members of the National Security Council and the President. The economy had been exhibiting a stubborn refusal to respond to governmental stimuli. In addition, the Middle Eastern nations were again railing at Israel and were demanding that the United States do something to control their surrogate.

When it was his turn to report to the Council, Steinman was able to provide encouraging news of Project *ABACUS*. He presented them with a set of analyses which offered several alternative strategies, formulated to solve both of these sticky and not totally unrelated problems. These strategies, as verified on the model, preserved the peace and jiggled the economy forward.   Although these were rather premature results from an analysis system not yet totally proven, Steinman opined that these strategies had a high assurance of being well accepted by the world community, and the people of the United States, in particular.   The group concurred, apparently.   The President himself escorted George out of the room and congratulated him on the timely results.

The elevator decelerated smoothly, stopping at the other end of its run.   Steinman walked down the glass-walled corridor to his office.   Almost all of the staff had gone for the day.   Only the second shift maintenance crew, consisting of three IBM and two MPS Research engineers, were on duty, along with Max McGurn, his brilliant Head System Software Architect, poring over reams of imponderable core dumps. There before him, and under his personal authority, was the greatest single gathering of computer power ever assembled. This computer was named STRETCH III, after a much earlier landmark computer system.   Except this one used thousands of wafers, rather than vacuum tubes.   Parallel in its architecture, each of its 64 nodes was capable of eighty thousand gigaflops. The project itself was affectionately dubbed *ABACUS*, by the First Lady.

Except for the master control panel lights, flickering in a kind of strobed rhythm, one might have thought that all of the blank monitors indicated a quiescent state for STRETCH III. However, during the second and third shifts, the monster was almost 100% occupied in learning.   Already expert in much of the world's history, culture, mathematics, physics, chemistry, and every other physical and political science, *ABACUS* was busy assimilating more, always more.

This gigantic model of the universe represented not only the known physical world and its surrounding space, but also over twenty thousand separate personality profiles and much of the complex interaction between them. For over a year now, this beast had been building its data base, its common knowledge, much as a human infant learns, by observing, acting, and interacting. By now, though, this silicon-based intellect had long surpassed the knowledge of any single person who had ever lived. Although schooled extensively in only a dozen languages, it possessed a vocabulary of over ten million words and was learning at the rate of 10,000 new words a day.

More importantly, *ABACUS* had been digesting the details of American and world history, from the earliest records, and was now current and on-line with every electronic news source. It had already digested the whole of the Google data base and had tucked it away in a small corner of its massive memory banks. Only during the day did the system design progress and the testing and analysis take place. This enormous socio-economic model was in a constant state of automatic self-improvement, as refinements were made to more correctly emulate historical fact. Applications analysts could barely keep up with the constant stream of improvements made by the system itself.

George knew what was going on. He had always known the potential mischief of which such a system was capable. But up to now, only good things had come from this massive cybernetics tool. World peace had been preserved, and the economy had been saved from what had appeared to be terminal depression. He had become one of the *first level* in the regime of Grant Williams and his charming wife, Carrie. They were going places and he was going with them. He was a military man, and he only wished to serve, at as high a level as he could, of course. Politics held little interest for him.

Grant Williams had inherited what seemed to be an impossible task: to break the economic morass which had mired the major global economies in a massive depression. He must somehow reverse the slide of the U. S. government down the slippery slopes of continued deficit spending, even as inflation exaggerated the burden of the debt service. Crime was out of control, public schools were an admitted failure, and the mood of the people was generally severe angst, with fits of rage.

George Steinman sat down at his rather oversized desk and pulled up his organization chart on the very large screen which filled one end of his office. The organization was almost complete now, with the acquisition of Jason Phillips and Brent Schultz. These men were the best of the best from project SPAT. Schultz had a talent for asking all the what-ifs, and, together with Max McGurn working the system software, and Jason working the application, they had made startling progress in a field which had not seen the progress that platform technology had enjoyed.

The network was already in place. President Williams had talked about this great data highway during the campaign. No one was quite sure how this was going to stimulate the economy, or fix the failed educational system, but George had explained the need for such an information conduit to Carrie, in one of their casual but not chance meetings, and she immediately understood. This part of the project had actually been funded under special Department of Education legislation. The rest of the project was wrapped in level 4 security and funded as an outgrowth of the *Star Wars* ongoing research. Actually, in the campaign, Grant Williams had not had a lot of good things to say about Star Wars, and so he completely disarmed the congressional Armed Forces committees with his request for expanded funding. He made sure that most of their pet projects were kept alive, but a significant portion of the funds paid for Project *ABACUS*.

George Steinman went out the regular entrance he had used many hours earlier this day, as he usually did. The special express elevator to the roof was used almost exclusively for trips to and from the White House. And again, as was his pattern, he had worked until a state of exhaustion had set in, and only then did he leave his work. On the drive home to his rather modest apartment in rural Virginia, he formulated his plans for the next day. In his sleep, George Steinman dreamed of new glories and new challenges, perhaps as SecNav, or at least CNO.

****** **Jerusalem:**

It was already the next day at the Institute for Strategic Analysis, in Jerusalem, where a special meeting was being held. A briefing by the newly created International Business Intelligence Agency (IBIA) was provided to a select trio of laboratory managers and to their government sponsor. Dr. Samuel Levanthol had very little patience with government functionaries, and it showed. The Minister of Commerce never enjoyed dealing with any of the several academic types who ran his project. The project fell under his authority administratively, as a part of the IBIA operation, but Levanthol regularly went directly to the Prime Minister to discuss the project, much to the Minister's consternation.

"Gentlemen, new information supplied by our operatives indicates that we are falling behind our 'sister'. (That is what they called *ABACUS*). It is imperative that we at least keep pace with them," the Minister said, taking delight in the dig. The Minister handed Dr. Levanthol three copies of the report his office had assembled, which showed rather directly what was happening within *ABACUS*. The operatives he spoke of were a contact very high in the White House, a deputy director of the CIA, and a certain deputy base commander. The work on Project TAT (trading analysis tool) would be accelerated.

ABACUS was not alone in the universe. Project TAT had begun four years earlier, not long after the team at Pendleton had achieved some of their early, spectacular, successes. Ironically, a major source of the early funding had come from the U.S. government, in the form of a grant to study advanced simulation techniques. All of the department managers had visited Pendleton, and although their visit was unclassified, they learned what they had come to learn.

Only a few of the staff members of both of these massive simulation tools knew the potential and the actualities for which they were used. Few Israelis knew of the existence of *ABACUS*.

Only two Americans knew, at this date, of the existence of TAT. **The President of the United States was not one of them!**

Chapter 3: THE HOLY MAN

The *Great One* and his entourage emerged from the large double doors leading to the main balcony. Upon seeing them, several lesser luminaries retreated hastily, doing obeisance, each in his peculiar way. The *Great One* acknowledged them with a wave of his arm, as if to sweep away the clutter in his path. He took the large central raised chair, and then waved the others in his party to their respective seats. Not a word was spoken during this enthronement.

The Great Square was seething with the devout. The mournful cries of dozens of young men flailing their bodies cast a despairing, yet fervent air on the assemblage. The midmorning prayers had been said, and now all eyes were upon the center balcony of this mosque, where the *Great One* was to speak this day.

The *Great One* leaned over and whispered to the gray-bearded and stooped cleric on his left. The aged Ayatollah Jeradine immediately got up and went to the front of the balcony. He raised his right hand over the mob below and the immediate silence was palpable. Even those faithful engaged in lashing themselves paused to listen, and to see.

The *Great One* very deliberately rose and stepped to the edge of the balcony. His face was stern, his eyes steel gray and piercing. He was of average height and slightly heavy, and he carried himself with the grace and strength of a younger man, and with authority.

(Talk of the emergence of a new Caliphate, in preparation for the Mahdi had been circulating for years.) He raised his hand over the crowd, as if in blessing. In their native Farsi, he said, "Men of this Holy Land, you are blessed for your faithfulness. Yours will be the truth! Yours will be the glory! Yours will be the victory! May Allah bless you and keep you. Amen." With that, he stepped back, and the mob below voiced its response, which sounded much like a roiled river, rushing down rocky banks.

The religious community in all of Iran had been shaken by the unexpected death of the beloved Ayatollah Mohammed Moshira. Death by murder, it was said, but nobody seemed to know. The great Ayatollah had been beloved around the Muslim world and had been a unifying force for the clergy. Under Moshira, the civilian government in Iran had a greater degree of autonomy than at any time since the late, unlamented Shah.

So this was their new Mullah, their godly leader of the faithful. Most, after getting over the initial shock of the news of Moshira's death, had speculated that the senior Ayatollah Jeradine, head cleric of Tehran, would succeed Moshira. The selection of Malik Al Shafei as Head Cleric of Iran was totally unexpected. Everyone knew him, as he had served as Moshira's chief of staff and occasional spokesman. But he had been considered by the people to be of definitely junior rank among the religious leaders of the country.

The *Great One*, Ayatollah Al Shafei, had consolidated his new power in a matter of days, rewarding the faithful and sweeping away any opposition with brutal asperity.

Fine private vehicles and government limousines were lined up at the palace of the *Great One*. A personal appearance was demanded of all of the major leaders in the government this very day. Change was in the wind, and the government officials dutifully arrived, but were stern faced and seemed annoyed. All but one. The President, one Mr. Shahela Bortek, did not appear.

The guests were unceremoniously ushered into the host's great room and seated in the casual setting which looked very much like Early Western comfort. As the *Great One* entered, all ten of the ministers rose. "Please be seated, gentlemen," he said. The ministers looked around to see who else was there. The absence of the President was of considerable concern.

"Gentlemen, you are all invited to participate in a new and wonderful era," the *Great One* said. "I believe Allah himself has spoken to me regarding our leadership in the whole Muslim world.*" 'Evidently he intends to use his religious authority to revive the Caliphate'*, was the inevitable inference. "The former President shall be replaced shortly," he said. Rumor was that the President had been hauled off during the previous night by agents of the Ayatollah to places unknown, probably never to be seen again. As the finality and the gravity of their situation became apparent to even the most slow-witted bureaucrat there, fear settled down upon them like a blanket of cold helplessness, gripping them in their common doom.

Mr. Justian Rochnam sat eating the evening meal. This night he had a special guest, whom he was entertaining, or who was entertaining him; he wasn't sure. Justian was an importer of heavy machinery and parts and was rapidly becoming wealthy, relative to the poverty and squalor of the average citizen. "Your new Ayatollah seems to be taking over," Justian said to his guest, as soon as they were left alone by his wife and a serving girl. "Why do you say 'Your' Ayatollah, my friend?" "Yes, *our* Ayatollah," Justian conceded. "But you know that I am not very religious. I take time for prayers, and I support your priesthood with regular gifts, but you know how busy I am with my business," he said.

Justian's guest was an old friend named Amel. They had grown up together on the back streets of Tehran. Amel had gone into the priesthood, and Justian had gone to France, to study engineering and business. "Justian, things are going to change rapidly in our country, and in the world. You must be a part of it. The Brotherhood needs you to participate in an active way," Amel said. Cold shivers ran down Justian's back. All his life he had seen the excesses of the infamous Ba'ath party. He wanted no part of their spying, rabble-rousing, and assassinations. He abhorred their campaign of fear. The new government had been clamping down on the old brotherhood, but now, apparently, it was to be revitalized under the new Ayatollah.

"I just don't have time to be involved in politics, Amel," he said, looking his old friend in the eye, showing as resolute a position as he could muster. "It is not the old party," Amel whispered. "Here is what you must do," he said.

Amel went on to explain to his friend the formation of a new secret society, selling it with the combined enthusiasm of a great patriot and a multi-level marketer. Amel enthused, "Just like you, Justian, countless others will be drawn into the new brotherhood. Our new ruling class shall consist of leaders in business, government, education, religion, the armed forces, the police, and even the farmers and nomads. The strength and fervor of our new leader, the most reverend Ayatollah Al Shafei will reach down into the lowest levels of the organization and give it life. We shall someday overthrow the old Ba'ath party," Amel said, in almost a whisper, glancing around to be sure no one overheard.

A warm embrace ended this fateful meeting between old friends. "Remember, Justian, call me if you need any kind of government help in your business."

***

A large shipment of irrigation pumps from Argentina could not be unloaded. Justian was on the phone to his shipping agent, who, through his government connections, always made sure traffic moved smoothly for the company. "What do you mean they can't unload them," Justian shouted. His agent was just as baffled as he. Had not the proper palms been greased? The excuse that the paperwork was not in order usually meant that someone had not been properly bribed. But this time, they refused to take his money.

After two days of futile telephone calls, visits to the local prefecture and the chief of the docks, and repeated appeals to all of his old political connections, Justian called his old friend. "Amel, this is Justian....yes, my family is fine...yes, thank you, Amel. Amel, the port authorities will not release a shipment of pumps I am importing from Argentina. Can you help me? Yes...you will? Thank you. Yes, we will talk later."

Within the hour, the pumps were delivered to Justian's warehouse, with all of the required paperwork. Justian sat sucking his hollow tooth, contemplating the new order of things. He correctly guessed that it was his old friend Amel who had put a stop on the unloading in the first place. *Well, this is the new way business must be done.*

***

The President hung by his wrists, suspended about a foot off the floor, fighting off waves of nausea and unconsciousness. He had lost track of the days, down in this dungeon where there were no windows, no fresh air, and no single element of human compassion. The air was heavy with the stench of fear and human waste. He had days earlier come to the end of his resistance and had told his torturers everything he knew about the leadership in the Ba'ath party, his political allies, and even his family. His last thoughts were a mixture of hellish torture and glorious bliss, as he contemplated the beauty and grace of his young daughter and thought of what these monsters would do to her, if it pleased them. His body was cut down and placed into an old army body bag, to be disposed of along with the garbage.

In another room in this same facility, several new recruits, including Justian, were being instructed in the virtue and glorious future of the new brotherhood. Just as Amel had predicted, there were individuals from all walks and persuasions. The common bond was unequivocal allegiance to the *Great One*. The holy month of Ramadan had just been celebrated in this sixteenth year of the new century. Appetites of all types were peaked, including that of the *Great One*. The time was ripe. Revolution had come peacefully in Algeria, the Emirates, Afghanistan, and Pakistan. Other governments were more intransigent.

***

****** **Damascus:**

The loud, insistent hammering on the front door woke everyone. A household servant answered; worried that they would actually break the door down if he did not. The President's personal guards, in their light blue uniforms, demanded the man of the house. The President's personal physician emerged from his bedroom suite, fully dressed, but looking sleepy. "What is it, Captain?" the doctor demanded of the taller guard. "The President needs you!" was all the guard would say, as he motioned the doctor out of his house and into the waiting army vehicle. Full sirens blared as the three-car entourage careened back to the President's palace.

The doctor was ushered directly to The President's bedchamber. The doctor went to work quickly, looking into the man's mouth, his ears, his nose, and his eyes. He extracted his instrument and measured the President's blood pressure. "He has gone into a coma, and his heart beat is very thready," the doctor announced to no one in particular. The President's skin was clammy and cold; death appeared near. "Get an ambulance here immediately," the doctor demanded of the Captain. "And alert the hospital to have an oxygen tent ready," he continued.

The rumor in the Muslim world was that the old party prevailed in Syria, but it had only been converted. Except for the maximum leader of the country. He had stubbornly refused to accept the leadership of the *Great One*.

A massive contingent of palace guards accompanied the convoy to the hospital, and two of his elite guards never left the President's side. The doctor carefully consulted three top staff physicians within easy hearing of the guards. Their common diagnosis was that the President had been poisoned. Probably through his food. Many of the President's household staff were even now being interrogated. Only the President's personal doctor knew the real source of the poison. Death was slow, but sure, in spite of their best efforts.

****** **Baghdad:**
At precisely midnight, Iraq's presidential palace was blown to kingdom come. Unfortunately for the President, he was sleeping there. Those who argued that IRAQ was not suitable for a democratic government seemed to be proven right again.

****** **Riyadh:**
A solitary assassin, disguised as a member of the palace guard, plunged his dagger into the kidney of the King as he slept. Uttering an anguished cry, the King slumped over instantly as life oozed out of his body. The escaping assassin was himself shot by one of the guards. The guard's assignment was just as important as the assassin's. Both tasks were ordered by the *Great One*.

****** **Cairo:**

The removal of the head of the government of Egypt was a much more difficult task. An open democracy and a free press made it almost impossible for a coup d'état. The takeover was done through legal succession. The vice president was picked personally by the Ayatollah Al Shafei, as were many of the country's legislators. A single agent working in the President's household had been able to administer arsenic poison over several months. The vice president had been installed only weeks before and was just now consolidating his power over the Executive.

Similar events took place simultaneously in Morocco, Tunisia, Ethiopia, the Emirates, and Yemen. By sunset of that day, each of these countries was directly or indirectly under the control of the new secret party controlled in turn by Ayatollah Al Shafei.

The simultaneous demise of so many Muslim leaders rocked the capitals of the Eastern and the Western worlds. The *Great One* had done this deliberately, partly to demonstrate to the Muslim world his great power and partly to reinforce the chaos that inevitably ensued. Each country had its full plate of problems and was unable to lend assistance to anyone else. The Ayatollah's men quickly rounded up their political rivals and moved in on the military and the media. Except for the demise of the old power structure, the coup was almost bloodless.

To those watching TCNN, the overthrow of so many governments simultaneously seemed more a concern of the West than of the affected countries. Ever since the Six Day

War, Western leaders had promoted a balance of power in the Middle East. Many analysts recognized that a balance of power was the reason for the early termination of the Alliance's war against Iraq under Bush I.

The prospect of a united Muslim world held great peril for the petroleum importers of the world and for those who pledged to support Israel.

****** **Tehran:**

The private jet of the President of Syria had just been cleared for landing. The sleek Learjet 740 swooped down like a bird and rolled gracefully to the first apron, its twin jets whining their shrill cry. A limousine began moving toward the appointed hangar, escorted by four armed vehicles. The person who emerged was the newly established head of the Syrian Republic, the Right Honorable Mohammed al Sherif, formerly Secretary of State and newly appointed Commander-in-Chief of the Armies of the Republic. More importantly, he was the appointed head of the Secret Society, and subordinate to the *Great One*. The President flushed slightly but made no comment about the absence of his host. He embraced his friend, the Secretary of State of Iran, and quickly entered the limousine.

***

A hush settled over the crowd as the President of Syria and the Secretary entered the large banquet hall in the city's finest hotel, the Sheraton Plaza. Everyone stood, expecting their host. When it was apparent he had not arrived, they all sat down, rather unceremoniously.

"I am sure he has been delayed for an urgent problem," President Sherif said to all those within earshot. Only his aide noticed his expression of irritation as he sat.

Twelve heads of state sat assembled at the lavishly prepared dinner table. Apparently the *Great One* had not met any of them at the airport. Security guards stood at attention in and around the room, as well as in the halls and on the grounds. It was clear that no one who was not supposed to be there would be. Noticeably absent were cameramen and reporters.

Only two months had passed since the night of the great revolution, and most of those present had not yet fully consolidated their power, but at the very least had established full control over the armies, the police forces, and the media in each of the countries. The party network would report any sign of resistance. Rebelliousness was immediately crushed. The people knew the routine; although some of the most hopeful wished somehow that a new enlightenment would be ushered in by the new regimes. But these hopes were soon dashed, as everyone could see that it was business as usual, with only the faces and titles changed. The rule of terror prevailed.

The assembled dignitaries were startled as a group of a dozen trumpeters blasted a flourish, announcing something. They soon saw that His Eminence was finally arriving, and without signal or prompting, they all rose as he entered. The *Great One* worked his way around the table, greeting each of the twelve heads of state formally and with great ceremony.

Only after he was seated did the applause fade away. Dinner was served. The King of the Kings was clearly in control.

***

The Ayatollah Al Shafei truly hated everything Jewish. It was not the lust for power that drove him; it was the hatred nurtured from his earliest memories. He had witnessed his mother and two sisters incinerated by Israeli bombs when he was only eight. All of his early life was filled with the violence of war, terrorism, and raw brutality. To exact revenge on his and his nation's mortal enemies gave purpose to his life and to his drive for power.

The weeks following the meeting of the surrogate rulers of the Muslim world had been spent consolidating the power of the *Society*. Under the *Great One*'s direction, steps were taken to broaden the society and to develop security networks to ferret out any hint of disloyalty. People disappeared, never to be heard from again. The word was spread that it would be the fate of anyone even questioning the wisdom or the dictates of the *Society*.

***

"Mr. secretary," Malik Al Shafei called, looking toward one of the many clerks he kept around during his working sessions. The cleric, really just a clerk, immediately moved obediently to the side of the *Great One*. "Yes, Your Holiness," the clerk responded, holding his tablet before him, ready to copy down the latest dictates.

"Address this note to my army commanders. Mark this *confidential* and put my seal on the letters." "Yes, Your Eminence," obediently responded the cleric clerk. "Screen the men under your command and send me profiles and pictures of all of the candidates who best meet the following requirements. I need men who are well practiced in demolition, communications, and close combat. I also need a few good pilots. Most importantly, they must all have strong reasons to hate the Jews, as I do. Send me these profiles as soon as possible, using trusted couriers," concluded the Maximum Leader.

Malik Al Shafei had been planning the annihilation of the hated Jews even before his plan to consolidate the bulk of the Muslim world under his new *Society*. In fact, that consolidation was a key element of this larger, more ominous, plan. It only remained to implement the details which had been forming in his mind these many years.

Chapter 4: THE PROJECT

****** The Pentagon:

Jason reached into his outside jacket pocket and came up with a handful of magnetic metro tickets. The first one he stuck into the turnstile assembly was short of the required credit, and he cursed under his breath, knowing he was late as usual. The 7:12 Metro to the Pentagon was about to pull out.

Jamie had finally found a home they both liked in a pleasant suburb in McLean, Virginia. It was only two blocks from the Metro station, near a park, and short driving distances to three shopping malls. It didn't take them long to adjust to their new budget.

Jason had been overwhelmed at the scope and size of the project. The platform was the single greatest agglomeration of raw computer power ever assembled, by a factor of 4. As the full ambitions of the program unfolded for him, he was awestruck. Cost seemed to be of no concern. To be a part of this, even in a position of some considerable authority, he would probably have worked free. He stifled that thought immediately.

Jason's title was *Chief Architect*. The other management personnel called him simply Chief, or Jason. Steinman had always insisted on an informal relationship within his management organization, which was unusual for the military.

Jason's job was to guide the design of the program to as near a perfect fidelity to the real world as was humanly, or rather, computer-assisted humanly possible. The system had begun where Project SPAT had concluded, and had met all of the expectations, and more, for its intended use. It had also exhausted its budget. Jason had come to understand that software development is an endeavor which can be an endless money sink.

Jason's counterpart, Brent Schultz, was the Director of Analysis and Testing. Brent's department, although equal in authority to Jason's design team, followed their lead and was technically subordinate to it.

Max McGurn worked the system. All of the industry representatives (IRs) were under his authority. His job was to provide the maximum throughput for the application, and system services, as they required. The three were a proven team and had a healthy respect for each other's special talents. They were George's *Boys*.

Supporting the project were fourteen think tanks, including the prestigious Potomac Institute and the staid Georgetown University Department of History and Science. These institutions, and the project staff itself, tapped into hundreds of universities around the world and had a standing priority access to all military and government intelligence agencies. In short, they had *carte blanche*.

Jason began with an analysis of the major expansion made to the initial SPAT framework. Besides the additional common knowledge data, the element size had been reduced by an order of magnitude from the resolution of the SPAT model.

Steinman had explained it to Carrie Williams once in these terms: "It is similar to the problem of simulating our worldwide atmosphere for the purpose of predicting the weather," he had told her. "Current technology limits the resolution of chunks of the atmosphere to volumes of about 20 cubic miles. If we had more powerful computers, we could refine the simulation to represent elements of one cubic mile, and the art of weather prediction would become more of an exact science. Except to simulate the economies, the social and political forces of any given population required simulating dozens of parameters, not just pressure, insolation, temperature, pressure gradients, and humidity," he told her. *And besides*, he thought, *we really don't understand all of the parameters involved yet.* But Carrie Williams understood well enough to lobby the President to provide the wherewithal.

This morning, Jason was having one of those special jam sessions with his colleague, Brent Schultz. They were examining the fine points of the price of gold, as it was influenced by central banking policies, production levels and plans, industrial demand, inflation rates and trends, consumer confidence, current short and long term interest rates, the yield curve, the current level of stock markets, relevant governmental policies, and a dozen other important parameters.

They had at their disposal all of the better models the leading economists had developed. Repeated tests against these models had taught them which parameters were primary forces, which were second or third order effects, and under which combination of circumstances these elements influenced that particular market.

Dozens of discussions like this occurred every week, between these men and their very qualified staff. The results of these discussions resulted regularly in major work re-direction for literally hundreds of researchers, in the associated institutions and their respective supporting sources. Always the ultimate test was whether or not the model refinement yielded better fidelity to the huge mountain of historical data. Sometimes, the dynamics between people and their institutions seemed to defy analysis. Humans, they always knew, were strange and unpredictable, and hardly ever logical. What made America *work* had to be included. Her morality, her dreams, her ambitions, and all of her ugly warts must be captured in the thousands of relational fractals, which defined, in a very dynamic way, the whole of the American model.

Jason often thought of the opening lines of Dickens' great novel: *These were the best of times; these were the worst of times...* Except these were the most critical of times. World conditions and the chaos developing in the American economy gave the team a sense of urgency. Long hours and superhuman efforts were the norm. *The tensions produced by the circumstances, the myriad complexities of the players themselves, in the context of a world rapidly accelerating into chaos, and economic upheaval brings out the best and the worst in many*, he thought.

The special pager worn by all of George's boys startled Jason. It was hardly ever used. Only once before had

Steinman called any of them, and that was not an emergency. Jason immediately left the lively conversation he was having with Max McGurn and two of his IRs (industry reps). "Excuse me," he said simply, and walked briskly over to his nearby office. Closing the door behind him as he entered, he lifted the phone and punched the special pre-set number in one fluid motion. "Jason," the General at the other end of the line said, "Straighten your tie, cancel your afternoon schedule, and get up here; we're going to the White House." Jason had never gone with General Steinman on his regular reports to the White House before. *Something really disastrous must be going down*, Jason thought.

****** The White House:

The huge OD helicopter settled comfortably on the President's special pad, just off the west wing of the White House. The two visitors were escorted into the security annex by the ever-present marine guards. Their badges were inspected, even though the men on duty recognized the General and addressed him by name.

As it turned out, they were not there to see the *Man*, at all, but rather, the First Lady. No one had ever addressed her as Co-President. But the powers in Washington were beginning to appreciate the real intellect in the Williams family.

Carrie Williams rose to greet them as they were shown into her spacious offices. "General Steinman," she enthused, holding out her hand for him. "And this must be your young genius," she continued, turning her full attention and

42

considerable charm on Jason. He blanched slightly, and then blushed. *Very becoming*, Carrie thought. She also collected talent, and she had more natural charm to work with, as far as men were concerned.

"George tells me that his project couldn't work right without you," she exaggerated. "Tell me, are things going well?" she addressed to George. What she really meant, and Steinman understood her to mean, was did they have a recommendation from the project to cope with the latest crisis? It seemed they had a potentially devastating international incident brewing in the Middle East. Israel had the temerity to answer in kind to the Arab threat of atomic annihilation. Apparently, Israel had placed bombs in many of their population centers, and even more egregious, in their oil shipping ports.

"This analysis has just been run, Mrs. Williams," the General responded, handing her a sealed briefcase. "I am sure that Grant will be pleased," she said, taking the case. "I shall take it to him as soon as the Israeli Ambassador leaves," she assured them. Turning to Jason again, she said: "Please tell your lovely wife, Jamie, that I am hoping she will come over for tea, this Friday. She should be getting her formal invitation by tomorrow morning." "Thank you, Madam President," Jason almost stammered, realizing immediately his *faux pas*. *Or was it*, Carrie wondered. Maybe this young man was more astute than she had imagined. "Well, thank you, George," she said, excusing them.

A few moments later, Carrie Williams, alone inside her inner office, deftly removed the seal on the briefcase, worked the special combination lock, and read the contents of the report. After making a copy of the summary page and slipping it into her oversized handbag, she re-sealed the briefcase and proceeded toward the President's office.

****** **McLean, Virginia:**

On the trip back to the Pentagon, the General had briefed Jason on the details of the latest international crisis and what the model had yielded, as a result of this input. The model, as usual, had been run well into the future, and for a matrix of parameters. The Muslim world would not invade Israel, nor would they fire their SCUD VII missiles, knowing the futility of such an attack and the certain retaliation by the Israelis. In the first place, the Muslim leaders would not make public the knowledge, or even suspicion, of the existence of these bombs. The model, in fact, over the whole range of nominal variables, showed that the tactic would almost certainly preserve the peace, tenuous though it would be.

Jason had learned a lot that day. He had suspected that the model was being used for political purposes on a regular basis and that at least some of the results were piped directly to the White House. Jason was beginning to understand.

The air was heavy with moisture, still and expectant that spring evening in Virginia. The ominous sky was fitting for Jason's mood; for he sensed that perhaps something was terribly wrong. After dinner, he and Jamie sat on their back porch, overlooking their spacious yard, and watched the gathering storm clouds. Jason described the events of the day, carefully leaving out all of the classified details the General had discussed with him.

The thunderstorm broke, and the first rainfall was lighted by the distant lightning. Soon the downpour, stirred by the swirling breezes, drove them inside. That night, Jason ruminated in his mind the events of the day. Lingering questions kept him half awake, half dreaming, for most of the night. Why was he brought to the center of power, there in Washington? Why had George handed over such sensitive material to the *wife* of the President? Had he sensed something of a special personal relationship between Mrs. Williams and the General? And what about all of this secrecy about the existence of the project?

****** **The Pentagon:**
The next morning, Jason found a copy of last month's The Journal of Economics on top of his desk. There was a large red **urgent** sticker on the cover, with a brief note from his friend and colleague, Brent Schultz, scrawled in pencil. A sticky-tab marked the featured article, written by one Professor Jaffa. Jason had already read it, or rather, had speed-read it. Interesting article, Jason recalled. But why was Schultz so excited about it? Jason had some priorities laid on him by the General, so he set the article aside for a later time.

Brent Schultz was another workaholic. He was athletic in build, and had an easy smile and a generous mouth, which matched his remarkable sense of humor. But when he got an idea in his head about something, he was like a bulldog. He would not put the thought away until it was thoroughly dead. He could not wait to tell Jason about some of the findings he had discovered over the past twenty-hour session with the model. Without even looking at Jason's secretary, he burst into Jason's office and demanded Jason's attention with his excitement. It was obvious that Brent had been working through the night. "Jason, you have got to hear this," Brent demanded. "O.K.," Jason agreed, as if he had a choice. "Have you read Jaffa's paper?" Brent said. He didn't wait for an answer: "I have tested his thesis on parts of the model; it works!" Brent paused, as if Jason would have completely understood and would respond.   "Wasn't it he who claimed that all political perspective derives from religion?" Jason remembered. "Yes, but it is considerably more complex than that," Brent insisted. "The basic idea he is promoting, which is not original with him, by the way, is that each person's perspective of every aspect of life is essentially shaped by his world view; but there are complicated translations, depending on his situational viewpoint," Brent explained. The expression *situational viewpoint* was project jargon, understood immediately by Jason.

Jason was beginning to be caught up in Brent's excitement. They had often wrestled with the values of the influence factors to be assigned to the effects of coupling religious values to political viewpoints. The General himself had written, referring to the nation, and the model of the nation as "her": "More than the political and economic dynamics must be included in the model; her moral fiber, her vision, her aspirations, and all of her dark inclinations must be captured. " Those words now seemed to resonate with what Jaffa had written, and with what Brent was telling him.

46

Jason interrupted his friend long enough to explain the urgency of the agenda required by the General. They both pitched into the effort, which was to re-run the previous day's simulation, with the added wrinkle of leaking the fact of the bombs to the Arab, Egyptian, and Iranian populations. They were to additionally examine the case where those governments did or did not deny it. Jaffa's thesis would have to be examined another day. Jason had Brent recheck the results three times. But why should they be surprised? The model said that if the sure knowledge of the Israeli bombs, planted in their cities and oil ports, was made known to the indigenous populations, there would be spontaneous, angry riots, worldwide. Nothing they tried with the model would placate the mobs. War would probably result.

Even as Jason rushed off to report these results to the General, he made a mental note of this political quirk. The rightness of the use of this model to help shape America's foreign policy again raised itself in Jason's mind. But these were perilous times; *any tool could be justified,* he thought, *if it could help avert WW III!*

****** **New York:**
Even at that moment, a clandestine meeting between the unofficial, but duly authenticated, representatives of the principals was beginning. "Mr. Ambassador," the dark-haired woman addressed her opposite. She used his formal title on this very delicate occasion. The high echelons of all of the governments involved knew how very close to war they might be. Everyone was walking on egg shells today. "Mrs. Harrington," the Ambassador responded. "I have been instructed to deliver this to your hands only," the lady said,

handing a large, plain business envelope to him. "Is that all?" the Ambassador asked, politely. "Yes, except, Mr. Ambassador, we are praying that we can all get through this crisis," she said. "If we can, we are prepared to provide our power station licensing to you all, at cost," she said, in a rather subdued but positive tone. "Thank you, Mrs. Harrington," the Iranian Ambassador said, turning to leave.

The sleek black limousine pulled out into the traffic and headed toward the airport. The Ambassador did not wait to deliver the envelope. He unceremoniously ripped open the envelope and read the official looking document. "Then, this may not be just a bluff," he thought. The document described where a special lead-lined chamber could be found. It was apparently a large container, meant to prove that size was not an obstacle for the Israeli smugglers. Inside, apparently, was a perfectly shaped hemisphere of Plutonium 239; 1/3 of a working atomic bomb!

The location of the partial bomb was meant to evoke the maximum shock effect on the Iranian hierarchy. According to the message, it would be found in the basement of the New Metropolitan Hotel, in downtown Tehran. Even now, the Ambassador's family and many of the high-level Iranian bureaucrats lived there. As the implications of this message gripped him, cold perspiration broke out on his forehead. The Ambassador felt nauseous. His first impulse, after he regained enough equanimity not to wretch, was to stop immediately and call his superior, the new leader of the whole Muslim world, the Most Reverend Ayatollah Malik Al Shafei, the founder of The New Brotherhood, the successor of the infamous Ba'ath party, Prime Minister of Iran, and soon to be

Caliph. But the Ambassador resisted that inclination, fearing that strict security in their communications could not be achieved. No, this was only a part of a bomb. Better to tell the Ayatollah personally.

The Israelis had indeed placed several large, conventional bombs in the oil port facilities of Iran, Iraq, and Saudi Arabia. But their stockpile of pure Plutonium 239 was too precious to be risked on such a dangerous gamble. The bombs had been placed years ago, and all thought of using them had been abandoned, what with the new energy source controlled by them. Avery Harrington had lived among the Muslims for many years, and he knew their mindset. He knew that in the game of high-stakes global diplomatic *chicken*, the perception was all important. The plutonium placed in the basement of their showplace hotel was real and would probably be incorporated into one of their bombs. It was a cost of doing business. It would have the desired effect.

****** **The Pentagon:**
The next day, Jason cleared his calendar in order to spend the day with Brent Schultz. In preparation, he had re-read Jaffa's paper and had browsed all of the many references Jaffa had cited. These included Gilder's *Wealth and Poverty,* Friedman's work, and the writings of Lewis, Schaeffer, and other noted philosophers and historians, such as the Durants. Even being a speed reader, he hadn't gotten much sleep.

The issue they were addressing was nothing less than:
What basic forces really drive individuals and society?
Conventional wisdom, official government dogma, and the politically correct thought was that we are all products of a

great random process and there really is no god. It further dictated that religious beliefs are left over vestiges of archaic superstitions and ignorance, and that the reality is now and what works in the present set of circumstances. All that we have is a limited set of remembered experiences, (including recorded history), hope for something better tomorrow, and the present moment.

This world view had prevailed throughout most of the major institutions of America for over sixty years. The exceptions were those churches which stubbornly held on to the *traditional* views. The new tax laws being written by the Williams administration would weaken these pathetic few to nothing but a noisy nuisance, with no political clout and very little public sympathy.

Jaffa's paper challenged all of that. What made it intriguing was the fact that Jaffa himself was an avowed atheist and an expert in socio-economic simulation. The thesis of his paper was that the religious beliefs held by individuals and societies were the paramount force behind the political and economic effectiveness of the entity. Whether there even is a god, or God, was clearly of no interest to him. But the efficacy of his new algorithms, based on this thesis, was startling. Most modelers simply dismissed his work as a bizarre attempt to regain the credibility Jaffa had lost over his discredited work in the last decade.

People like Brent Schultz were too truly open-minded to make judgments without thoroughly testing the hypotheses. The model, available only to the project staff, was the ultimate testbed. The results, preliminary though they might be, were astounding. Anomalous and ambiguous events in history yielded to this new algorithm set.

"Brent, I think you have stumbled onto something here," Jason said, smiling. They didn't keep score, but the rivalry between the three colleagues kept them honed and helped propel them onward. "Stumbled, my foot!" Brent parried, grinning impishly. "Brent, you know we have discussed this before. I am concerned about how this model is being used. It could do us all a lot of good, but it is being used in a very limited and somewhat selfish way." Jason was careful to pick his words, not knowing whether Brent shared his strong feelings on this subject. "Yes," Brent said, enthusiastically. "Let's talk." "Not here," Jason said. "Let's get out of here for lunch." It was already after one o'clock, but still not halfway through the regular work period to which both of them subscribed.

"Pick you up at your office," Brent said. Jason's office was nearer the front door, so it was logical for Jason to wait for him there. Brent shut down the experiment they were observing and carried an armload of documents and print-outs back to his office, where he unceremoniously dumped them on the large conference table next to his modest desk. "Suzie, I'm going out to lunch," Brent called over his shoulder, on the way out. "Back about three," he called from well down the hall.

The two found a quiet corner in one of the half dozen eateries within the confines of the giant building. They had purposely walked to one most distant from their wing of the building, hoping to not see anyone from the project. The late hour and the distance worked. They occupied themselves with small talk until they were satisfied that they had privacy. After a pregnant pause, Jason opened the subject they apparently both wanted to broach. "Brent, I am quite concerned about how our monster is being used." Jason paused, trying to read his friend and colleague. Had he touched a nerve; did Brent share this concern; or was he about to build a wall between them? In the many previous discussions they had on the subject, Brent had been rather non-committal. Whether he was playing his usual valuable role as advocate, or whether the misuse of such a tool bothered him, Jason was never sure. But now he needed to know. Brent started to speak, but then paused, as if to filter his communications. Jason had become a close friend and had always been a worthy colleague.

"Jason, this issue has been under my skin from the first day I walked into this project," Brent said, finally and decisively. "We are all aware of the potential mischief *ABACUS* could be used for," he continued. "I don't trust the President," he said, looking around to reassure himself that no one was listening. "And I especially don't trust his wife!" Brent said, rather casually, for the implications he was making. Jason shared his experience at the White House with the General and the First Lady.

The two shared specific information which, taken together, added up to a strong confirmation of their suspicions. They talked about how *ABACUS* could be further used for political advantage, and they purposed to be sensitive for signs of just such developments. But then they turned back to the vision which had motivated them both from the early days at

Pendleton. They had dreamed of a system like *ABACUS* which could help insure peace and prosperity for the nation, if not for all of mankind.

Brent and Jason discussed the potentially greater purpose this powerful model could serve. They agreed they should continue to perfect the model, not for the personal use of Grant Williams, or Carrie Williams, whoever was in charge over at the White House, but for the true advancement of the many sciences it served, for the preservation of peace, and the promotion of the understanding of man. The two men toasted their new understanding and their new commitment.

The next day, work on the new project would be re-directed to conduct exhaustive full-scale tests, using the modified algorithm set. These were glorious days. The world outside might be coming down around them, but the personnel of Project *ABACUS* were moving ahead, and with a little good fortune (and prayers), Jason thought, enjoying the irony, all of the worst possibilities of the *altogether otherwise* might yet be avoided.

Forces unknown to these relatively minor players were at work, orchestrating the plans of *the Cause*. But whether these men would be swept away, or would continue their purposeful work, was to be influenced by **powers greater even than those of the *Cause*.**

Chapter 5: A BETTER MOUSETRAP

It was time to show the boss. Brent and Jason had shared their work with their colleague, Max McGurn, even though the new algorithm set required very little system modification. Brent and Jason also shared their concerns over the *apparent* misuse of *ABACUS*, and their resolve to watch for further, more blatant abuses. The three were a true team; victories and defeats, hopes and anxieties were equally shared.

The new set was discussed only within the upper echelons of the applications staffs. It had taken only about six weeks to implement a complete alternate model. Then the testing began. The events of history, seen through the eyes of this other world view, made more sense and were rational and consistent.

The first meeting included only the General and his *boys*. George Steinman was rather an expert in this field himself, which made it a lot easier to explain. He was incredulous. He was very excited at the possibilities, but the political repercussions were always something he had to deal with. *These technical primadonnas could pontificate to their heart's desire, inside the project, but he carried the responsibility of selling it to a rather demanding and unforgiving sponsor, or rather pair of sponsors*, George thought.

The General scooped up the primary references upon which this new algorithm set was based and closeted himself in his private office, with instructions that he should not be disturbed.   The heavy reading he was embarking upon included all of the references Jason had devoured that first night, plus a few technical papers out of Bell labs and Colombia University.

George Steinman was particularly interested in the economic aspects associated with the new algorithm set.   The economy was not going well, and the current state of the model had not been able to provide any dramatic strategies. He was beginning to lose some credibility at the White House. He needed something dramatic to restore their faith in the system.   Or that might be the end of *ABACUS, and the General.*

The following week, at a larger meeting involving most of the top analysts, Jason and Brent made a presentation to the General regarding the efficacy of the new algorithms, as witnessed by the tests they had been conducting for over a month.

Whereas the standard model had an overall fidelity correlation of some 95%, this new set yielded an amazing 98.37% correlation.   The difference might seem small to some, but George was well versed in the theory of critical boundary effects, as it related to the different parts of the model, and knew that something akin to the *butterfly effect* obtained.   The alternate world view, upon which this set was based, was discussed only in the context of efficacy. Religious beliefs were of very little interest to most of the staff, and none as far as the General was concerned.   If this view, held by the masses, resulted in a more productive economy and greater wealth and well-being for all, so be it and hooray. It did not mean that George Steinman had to believe it, only to trust in the fact that it worked!

At the end of the briefing, Brent described the ongoing test plans which they were pursuing. The General blessed the plan, and thanked the whole group. He also requested continued briefings, to be held every two weeks. The General was anxious to gain a full understanding of the rationale for the new set, because he felt that he might just need something new, and soon.

**

The opportunity came sooner than George wanted. He was only beginning to digest all of the reference material his boys had laid on him and, so far, he had more questions than answers. They called it <u>Black Monday</u>. The stock market had the worst crash in history, including '29, '87, and '08. And nobody knew why. It seems that for a hundred different reasons, everyone wanted out at the same time. The usual explanations of profit-taking, or concern over the latest statistics, did not wash. George was at his desk when the red telephone rang. "George, are you aware of what is happening in the stock markets?" Carrie demanded. All pretenses about who really ran the government had been dropped by the top administrators and the congressional leadership. Mrs. Williams was the most liked and most feared woman in Washington. The people admired her to the extent that she had become the most popular First Lady since Eleanor Roosevelt. But every administrator above the rank of assistant secretary lived in fear of this awesome, charming, ruthless authority.

"No, I'm not, Carrie, what's wrong?" George responded. He was one of very few people in the administration or Congress who had the special relationship with the First Lady which allowed him to use her first name, but only in private, of course. "Then turn on FBN, and then get your little machine cranked up, and be up here with some answers by 9:00 o'clock tonight," she demanded. She did not wait for a reply, or any personal thoughts. This was a crisis. The congressional election campaigns were only about nine months away, and they must not let the economy slip back into a morass again, if they expected to hold on to the power she so desperately craved.

The General immediately called his *boys* into his office and watched FBN with them, until about an hour after the premature market close. "Well, there were about as many theories there as there were analysts," the General observed. "I'm glad I'm not in the market," Jason grinned. George was not amused. His cold response put a chill on the group.

"Gentlemen, we have a crisis on our hands. We must first analyze why this happened, and then we must make some sure-fire recommendations for the recovery and stabilization of these markets," the General paused for effect..."by 8:00 p.m. tonight!" His pronouncement was met with nervous laughter. "This project and all of our jobs are on the line." he said. "The economy is on the line," he said, shaking his head.

All staff members had been required to sign a contract prohibiting them from investing in any way in any stock or bond markets, or commodities or derivative markets. Further, they were pledged not to reveal any results produced by the model, regarding <u>anything</u>. So it was a surprise to Steinman when Jason revealed that he had been modeling the micro economics of the markets, for some time. He explained that he was using this narrow area of the economy as a special test case for the new algorithm set, because it was so wonderfully complex, and because there was so much detailed data against which to test.

"I have not used any data more recent than 6 years ago," Jason explained, anticipating their questions. "But I have that particular test program all set up to tap into whatever period might be of interest," he said.   They would, and he did. The results were astounding.   According to the new model, the crash was a bomb, waiting to explode.   Depending on what time frame was used to initialize the program, the crash occurred within two weeks of that day!   Explaining exactly why and what to do about it, were problems of a greater magnitude.   They had reached first base, but it was getting dark!

***

Now was the time.   George called the White House, at an extension which could probably reach Carrie.   After several rings, Mrs. Williams picked up the extension herself. "Hello?" she said, oozing charm and graciousness. *George could hear some acrimonious discussion going on in the background.*   Heaven help the bureaucrat on the other end of this telephone if this was not very important.   The polls had not been kind lately, and this disaster happening to the markets might just be the final blow.   Carrie was in a state of exasperation bordering on desperation.   "Mrs. Williams," George asked, knowing it was she, but not knowing who might be listening. "Yes!" she answered sternly, recognizing his voice. "Do we have a secure communication?" he insisted. "Who knows!" she almost shouted. "What the <u>bleep</u> is it?" The coarse language coming from America's *most charming* always shocked and irritated the General, although he had seen it all. George explained briefly the good news about the new algorithms, and the timely studies Jason had been doing. And then he insisted that they be given 48 hours to provide their results. "You have until 5:00 p.m. tomorrow," the First Lady said. George had hoped to have at least until 10:00 a.m. the next day, so he was delighted, but was careful not to show it in his voice. "We'll do our best," he promised. "I hope that is good enough," Carrie said, sounding very tired, and a little shaken. "For the sake of us all."

***

The Chairman of the Federal Reserve Board had gone on all the major networks at noon on that "Black Monday", to help calm the markets, and to confirm an unlimited credit line for the asking. She had seen it work in '08, and was sure that it would work now. Besides, there were all of the *Circuit Breakers* in place. One of them had just been invoked. The markets had been halted for the day when the market dropped over 5,000 points before noon. Perhaps it was the quaking in her voice that belied her calm. She was new to the job, having been appointed by the President (on Carrie's strong recommendation) just 3 months earlier. Her confirmation had been by a thin margin.

Every time the market re-opened that day, there were no buyers. Prices were set at whatever the specialists were willing to pay, and that was very little. The next day was declared a general market holiday. The whole market, actually the whole country, sensed the panic which was gripping the business community. Everyone was looking to Washington for a solution to the problem. And Washington was looking to Grant Williams. And Grant Williams was at a complete loss, except to look to George Steinman and his magic computer.

****** **Tehran:**

The Ambassador's plane was met by one of The *Great One's* massive bullet and bomb-proof limousines. An armed guard accompanied the vehicle. It would have been hard to tell, seeing the scene, whether the man getting off the plane was a dangerous criminal being taken into custody, or a VIP. Ambassador Wadii almost appreciated the irony, but the matters before them were too weighty, and the reaction of The *Great One* too uncertain.

The Ambassador had the presence to instruct one of the guards to stay behind to pick up his luggage and deliver it to his hotel. Used to not questioning anyone who seemed to be in authority, the guard dutifully saluted and withdrew immediately. The ride to the palace was long and loud. The driver insisted on keeping the lights and sirens going for the full length of the trip, up until they entered the royal compound.

The Ayatollah Al Shafei went berserk. Upon hearing the contents of the hand-carried special communiqué, and reading it himself, he tore his clothes and began screaming and wailing. Ambassador Wadii was seriously concerned that the traditional logic of killing the messenger who had the temerity to bring bad news would prevail, as it had with so many megalomaniacs throughout history.   The thought and the impulse crossed Malik Al Shafei's mind, but he was too rational, even in this fit of rage, for that.   After several minutes of this bombast, the Ayatollah gathered his wits and summoned his First Secretary.   He gave specific and detailed instructions for another summit meeting, the next morning, at 8:00 a.m. sharp.   It was of little concern to him that the surrogate heads of state would have to travel all night to reach Tehran by then.

The offer by the Israelis to help provide the new fusion power was very intriguing, and new, even more diabolical schemes were forming in his fertile mind.   The old arch enemy would be toppled yet, if not by one means, then by another.

****** The Pentagon:

The sum of it all, thought Jason.   That was it, he was convinced.   Like a supersaturated solution, ready to turn crystalline with even the slightest disturbance.   The markets had been building up to an almost unavoidable collapse, and it would have happened no matter what the trigger mechanism.

Jason reviewed in his mind the administration's policies and the policies of the previous two administrations, calculating in his head how the new model would digest and react to this stream of data.   The previous president had been elected on the strength of a split vote, the result of a third party candidate.   The previous president had promised lots of changes, and he had certainly made a lot of changes, few of them good. The *real* federal deficit had more than doubled in his four years. He hadn't even run for reelection. The debt service had climbed to a full 45% of the budget. A national VAT (value added tax) had been initiated to solve the deficit problem, but the Congress, in its wisdom, found new and ever more innovative ways to spend money. One New York writer had dubbed them the *Pork Barrel Express*. Nothing had changed. Except the young voters who had helped put that president in office had turned cynical again, even bitter.

Grant Williams' presidency was another product of a split vote. This time, however, he was the Independent, and rather than being a spoiler, proved to be the victor. His party, the New Independent Party, had run on the most populist, anti-government, anti-big business, anti-traditional values platform ever conceived. And the small number of voters who turned out to vote were in the mood for a radical change. So with the support of less than 16% of all eligible voters, Grant Williams became the most powerful government leader in the world. And no one really envied him his job.

For six months, the new administration had done almost nothing. They were reportedly analyzing the problem. "Doing nothing was the most helpful thing the politicians have done in many years," quipped many of the press pundits. When the new administration did begin to move their program forward, it appeared to most that it was the old *big government solution to everything* philosophy, simply re-packaged.

They called it the New Beginning. But it wasn't. Almost all of the old spending and tax programs were kept intact, even extended. Corporate tax was increased to 49%.

Individual tax rates climbed to a very progressive 75%, for the top bracket. If the promise of very cheap energy, and the reality of very low inventories, had not existed, the collapse of the markets might have occurred much earlier.

Jason and Brent had been doing all of the what-ifs for most of the night. After devising an accelerated testing/projecting plan, they had formulated a series of matrices, each of which represented the classic economic approaches. The best results they had obtained so far was a stabilization and gradual growth of the economy resulting from a conservative approach. For that trial, taxes were cut, investment incentives were initiated, and the rather massive government spending was actually cut. The problems with this solution were that the markets did not recover very well, and worst of all, the new administration did not get reelected! Jason knew enough to not even offer that plan as a viable alternative. Something dramatic, innovative, even revolutionary, was needed. *A long-harbored idea was beginning to come into focus in Jason's mind.*

Accountability and efficiency! Jason recalled those were two of the code words that the Williams campaign used constantly, criticizing the abuse of power of the Federal Government (to be read: previous administration). The message was well received. Everyone knows how inefficient and unaccountable bureaucrats are.

The trouble was, under the Williams administration, things got worse. They always got worse. Jason recalled the writings of Freidman, Gilder, and Walter Williams, who explained why this must naturally be. Government employees are no better or worse than those in private industry. Large numbers are dedicated public servants in the old sense of the word, he knew. Lincoln had said it 160 years earlier: "Government should not do for people what they can better do for themselves". These authors had all explained that without competition there was no efficiency, no real accountability.

Jason remembered that a man running for the Senate out of Nevada had claimed that deficit spending could be eliminated entirely, even as all government services continued, and at the same time taxes could be substantially reduced. The man lost, Jason remembered, not because he wasn't a viable candidate, nor because he wasn't convincing, but because he had refused the usual funding sources, preferring to be his own man, even if it cost him any chance of being elected.

Jason punched up the political data bank on people residing in Nevada. *If these people knew how much we know about them, they would be up in arms*, he thought. **Philip Roy**; that was his name. Jason burned a hard copy summary of the man's political profile, including the platform he ran on in his attempt at the Senate. Using the man's economic program in one massive experiment, Jason fed the proposed agenda into the test matrix, using the current state of the world as the start conditions. Jason's body ached, and his brain was becoming numb. He glanced at his watch; time was drawing short. It was well after midnight, and no solutions seemed to be forthcoming (no 'acceptable' solutions, he corrected himself).

Less than an hour later, a comprehensive summary of the results of the test simulation began scrolling up Jason's computer screen. *Could this possibly be*, he thought. A rush of excitement came upon Jason, as he began reading the results. Philip Roy's agenda seemed to work wonders for the economy, even as it triggered riots in many parts of the country, and overseas.

Philip Roy's program, as he had detailed it in his campaign for the Senate, included the most massive privatization ever undertaken by any standing government! It seems the gentleman was correct in his assertions. This was perhaps the miracle that the General, and the President, and the country were looking for. Before calling his colleague, Brent Schultz, over to verify his findings, Jason reviewed the projected outcome of the next presidential election. Williams in an easy landslide!

****** **Tehran:**
The assembled heads of states were there at the palace of the great Ayatollah Al Shafei, assembled and ready, promptly at 8:00 a.m. Tehran time. A little more than an hour later, the *Great One* himself strolled in, graciously going around the room, greeting each of his tetrarchs warmly, allowing them to kiss his hand and other acts of obeisance.

"Gentlemen," the Great One opened. The room was perfectly silent, and the retinue of puppets, and their seconds, sat attentively, hoping their great leader would somehow move them back away from the precipice to which he had led them so recently. "Gentlemen," he said in Arabic, "I have negotiated great concessions for us from those swine." The specter of an outside threat always united the forces; he remembered telling one of his sycophantic ministers the day before. "And I have a plan which will lead to their final destruction," he said. *We have heard that before*, thought most of the listeners.

The Ayatollah proceeded to explain to them the Israeli's offer, making it sound like a great victory that he had won for his people. The Great One paused in his presentation. "Clear the room," he commanded the chief of his Internal Security. The men sitting there did not know what to do for a moment. Seeing that only the guards were to leave, they settled down in their seats, riveting their attention on the imposing figure before them. The Ayatollah paused, for the dramatic effect, and then lowered his voice to almost a whisper. "For some time now, I have been working on a very secret plan to sabotage their fusion plants, but now, with this new treaty we will sign with them, we will have access to the information we need to finish the project. It will bankrupt them, and, when their wonderful plants prove to be dangerous, the oil will flow again. For a price, of course," he concluded.

The assembled heads of state were briefed by the Iranian Foreign Minister on the treaty to be presented to Israel, before they were packed off to the airport and back to their respective responsibilities. In their tidy world of shared power, they felt secure that Islam was in capable hands, and that they would share in a glorious empire, in the not too distant future.

****** **The Pentagon:**
Jason lifted the telephone to call the boss, while

maintaining eye contact with Schultz. The special bond between these men was growing, and they felt closer now, in the midst of this crisis. "General," Jason began, "Schultz and I have something to show you," he paused. "I'll be right down," George Steinman said, replacing his phone without waiting for more explanations. He was anxious for a solution.

Steinman had just about bought the new model, but the startling results he was shown by Schultz and Phillips gave him pause. He asked them to review for him the test program they had used to verify the fidelity of the new algorithm set. This took precious minutes, but the General was about to put his career on the line, and he wanted to be on solid ground. He then asked them to re-run the simulation, varying several new parameters. This would take them well into the day, right up to the time the General had his command appearance at the White House. He would call them at the last minute, just before his meeting with the President. Steinman then asked Jason to prepare a set of briefing charts for him, and to go over them with him, just as soon as they had the simulation underway.

After the General left to return to his office, Schultz said: "Now even the impossible is routine," he smiled at his friend. "Why don't you let me set this up, while you start preparing your little show and tell?" "Do you need any of my staff to help you whip it out?" he continued. "Yes, let me have your two best graphics people, and we can split this up," Jason accepted. "That is the only way," he agreed.

By 11:00 o'clock, the material had been delivered, and the General was briefed on the briefing. Jason had anticipated Steinman's every requirement, plus some additional graphics of his own. They had not worked together for six years for nothing. The General had a lunch brought in for himself and Jason. They went over dozens of scenarios over their several cups of coffee. Then the General, fresh from a shower and change of clothes, made his way to the elevator and on to the most important briefing he would ever give.

Steinman had considered taking Jason with him, but he abandoned the thought when he considered how intimate this meeting might be. The charts he had made for the briefing were sized down for just such a meeting. It was a good thing, he told himself, for even sized down to B size poster paper, the charts weighed a good 10 pounds, he estimated. The President would have to be impressed at least with the quality of the graphics produced over night.

****** **The White House:**
The General checked his watch as *Marine 1* (sans POTUS) settled on the lawn. He would just have time to go over the final results with Jason before his big audience. He stepped down from the vehicle almost immediately, hardly noticing the pilot this fateful sunny afternoon. After phoning Jason for the final results of the extended simulation runs, he paused at the only fountain he could find, hoping it would cure the dryness he felt in his throat. The results still looked good. The bottom line was still intact over almost all foreseeable possibilities. Still, George felt more than the usual adrenaline rush he always felt in the presence of the great power of this office.

The meeting place had been changed. The time had been moved up too, but George had not been informed. Nor was this an intimate meeting. The President had assembled his top-level staff of economic advisors, the Speaker of the House, the Right Honorable Sam Craven, Democrat, and the Senate President Pro Tem, S. Orrin Smyth, Republican. Carrie knew that if a major new program were going to be enacted, congressional leadership must be brought on board early in the process. Grant also brought with him three of his most trusted political advisors. They met in the smaller of the two cabinet meeting rooms used by the Williams administration. Altogether there were 14 people present, counting George and Mrs. Williams.

The General had been ushered in, but seemed to be hardly noticed as a high-pitched debate between the Secretary of the Treasury and the Chief of the Economic Council occupied everyone's attention. But then, the President interrupted them and settled them down. He nodded to George, and George nodded in return, indicating he was ready.

"Ladies and Gentlemen," Grant Williams intoned, sounding like he was about to launch into an extended political monologue, "Please hold those thoughts," he paused. "I believe and expect that General Steinman may have some new proposals for us to consider." He motioned to George to take center stage.

For the better part of an hour, George held their rapt attention. Several of those present had never met this man before. Rumor had built his image larger than life, and they all knew that both Grant and Carrie Williams held him in almost reverent regard.   But what he was telling them was totally foreign to most of their philosophical, political and economic senses.   Who was he anyway, and where did he get these strange ideas?   In quick succession, this civilian general proposed privatizing almost every branch of the federal government, imposition of a massive set of trade tariffs to be levied on China and Japan, strict budget freezes, and sizable tax cuts for both industry and individuals.   **And the Williams' were listening to him!** Senator Smyth seemed also to be in concurrence, nodding his head in frequent agreement.

When the General concluded abruptly, the assembled politicos were in such shock that there was a long period of silence, until they could regain their composure enough to begin asking rather benign and oblique questions.   This man spoke with the authority of someone who knew things would eventuate just as he proclaimed.

***

Grant Williams knew that with so many people at the meeting there would be massive leaks to the press.   The network news anchors all quoted "highly placed sources" for their banner stories of the major economic policy changes being contemplated by the Williams administration.   Grant had meant it to be just so.   He had always liked trial balloons. If the rumors were well received, he could proceed with confidence; if not, he would of course deny them and go on to another plan.   Congressional and Administration switchboards lit up all afternoon and evening and into the next morning.   To almost everyone's surprise, the rumors were well received by even some in the more liberal end of the political spectrum.   Things had gotten so bad that people were desperate for a solution. Major surgery was what the last two administrations were unwilling or unable to admit to, and the sickness had just gotten worse.

****** **The Far East:**

At police briefing rooms in and around Beijing, Nanking, Hong Kong, Tokyo, Osaka, and Yokohama, riot gear was handed out and plans coordinated to handle the riots which were expected within the day. It all seemed rather matter-of-fact. The government was actually encouraging them, with harsh rhetoric leveled at the Williams administration and the U.S. Congress. Schools were canceled, and specific areas were mapped as *demonstration zones*. Like clockwork, riots erupted in China and Japan, very early the next day. *Sources* had said that there would be a 100% tariff on all products from China and Japan, except critical medicines and a few categories of special machine tools. No conditions seemed to be attached to the policy. The policy, as stated, seemed intractable. Worldwide economic chaos seemed inevitable, if this absurd policy were adopted. China, Indonesia, The Philippines, and Japan would immediately retaliate, with a 200% tariff, their leaders were suggesting on their mid-day news programs.

Across the United States, government workers' leaders denounced the rumors as absurd and unworkable, even as they threatened massive political repercussions, in the event anyone was serious about these ideas.

In Kansas City, and Hoboken, and Fayetteville, and Lodi, and Woodland, and thousands of other towns and cities, and especially in the deep rural areas, Jack Smith and Luther

Johnson and Sam Gibbs were excited about what they were hearing over the network news. Phone lines everywhere were warm with use, and not a few of the calls found their destination at the offices of politicians and government agencies. In fact, they were swamped with calls, most supportive of whatever bold new plan the President was about to try. Desperation was driving hope that *something* would be done.

At the White House, the calls and letters were running three to one in favor of the massive surgery. The President had gotten their attention. He alerted the networks for a nationwide address, to be delivered the following Monday. That would be more than enough time to sense the political winds, he thought. And soon enough to seize the moment, if this were to be. **Not just the nation, but the world, awaited Grant Williams' "fireside chat".**

END OF PART I

PART II

THE ISRAELI CONNECTION

"Praise belongs to God, the Lord of all being,
    the All-merciful, the All-compassionate,
        the Master of the Day of Doom"
"when the sun shall be darkened,
            when the stars shall be thrown down,
        when the mountains shall be set moving,
      when the pregnant camels shall be neglected,
        when the savage beasts shall be mustered,
          when the seas shall be set boiling...
          when Hades shall be set blazing,
        when Paradise shall be brought nigh,
    Then shall a soul know what it has produced.
          On that day you shall be exposed,
        not one secret of yours concealed."

The Koran

Chapter 6: THE NEW WAY

****** **Washington D.C.:**

The mail room at the White House was particularly busy. The mail was carefully x-rayed. Those packages which were suspicious were handed over to the Capital Bomb Squad. Those letters considered as possibly threatening were handed over to the Treasury Department. The bulk of the mail was separated into bags by subject matter. The pro v. con tally was carefully updated and reported to the Chief of Staff, daily. The intensity of the prolifics and the threats increased to the point that the Treasury Department Agents assigned to the security of the First Family asked for and got permission to go on full alert status. The rumors associated with the President's new program threatened the food chain of a lot of people. Plans were being threatened. Empires were being interfered with; a lot of oxen were being gored.

The next day was Friday. The markets were still closed by order of The President. No one really knew if he had any such authority, but no one wanted to contest the action. There was, in fact, a collective sigh of relief from all quarters. The uncertainty of the wild rumors would undoubtedly have affected the markets adversely. Better to wait and see what the *Man* has up his sleeve.

At the project, everyone but George Steinman's top staff members and a few vital technicians were given the day off. They had certainly earned it. The facility would be maintained at level four physical security and would be host to a group of VIPs.

The press was told that the Williams' would be spending the long weekend at Camp David. *Marine One* did fly off toward the camp but it found its way around the outer beltway and settled in on the Pentagon. It was almost 1:00 p.m. and their guests had been shown the facility. They were all waiting in the executive briefing room for almost an hour, when The President and Mrs. Williams, escorted by Steinman, entered the room.

Most of the inner circle of economic and political advisors who attended the previous day's briefing by the General were there. The group had been given a security briefing by the General. They were shown just as much of the project as they needed to see, in order to convince them of the power and fidelity of the model. Even to this august group, it was presented as a research tool, employed by the Star-Wars and other military applications. That provided the assurance which was needed to validate the proposed new policies.

Many in the group saw immediately the potential power of the model, and each one was anxious to try out his (or her) pet economic policy. The Chairwoman of The President's Economic Advisors wanted to see the model deal with her favorite plan. Her plan called for more government regulation of the markets and a new transaction tax, to be levied on all market trades. The tax was to be only 0.1% of the gross trading price. Brent Schultz obligingly called up the program, which had been run in many variations already. He let the graphs speak for themselves. Economic morass ensued. The Chairwoman quietly settled down into her chair.

The Secretary of The Treasury had a lengthy set of various scenarios to try on the model. He was quite impressed to see how easily Brent worked with the model to put together all sixteen of the Secretary's cases. The most promising combination left the economy weak and struggling, according to *ABACUS*. Brent was careful not to include projections of subsequent elections; these people all knew the consequences for economic failure.

To their amazement, virtually everything they proposed had already been run on the model and Brent Schultz was able to almost instantly display the results on the massive screens which occupied most of the entire front wall of the theater. Nothing anyone suggested led to those happy results hoped for by all. After that, the group was shown how well the model duplicated actual historical data, given any well defined initial conditions.

With the First Family present, George was ready for the show they had all come to see. Rather than canned results, the system was employed to repeat a series of simulations, first run very early the previous morning. This time, however, the clock was set for one of the fastest time scales used in their research, namely, one day of simulation time per second of clock time. There were so many data spewing out of the model that no one could have possibly digested it, had not George interpreted the results for them. After a half dozen parametric variations, some of which were suggested by the officials, almost everyone seemed to be converted to the discipleship of George Steinman, his impressive crew, and the great brain behind the wall.

After a couple of hours of this, The First Family continued on to their original destination for the remainder of the weekend. The advisors stayed on, well into the evening, and requested innumerable additional test runs. They were to make their final recommendations to The President on Sunday morning, at Camp David. The onus was on them to prove to Grant and Carrie why they should not go ahead with the program.

Earlier, George had a private briefing for the First Family in his offices. He had shown them the strong evidence the project had gathered that the majority of Americans actually held to the so-called traditional values. The earlier set of algorithms had grudgingly accepted that possibility, but had never given credence to the fundamental behavioral effects of this world view. The Williams' immediately grasped the implications of this. During the campaign which put them into their high office, a few members of the press had the audacity to characterize Grant Williams as a weathervane. Carrie knew too well how true that had been, and largely at her insistence. She had perfected the art of populism and disguised demagoguery before this campaign was planned. She would not abandon the techniques which brought them this far. If *family values* and Bible believing was what would give them the majority support they needed for reelection, that was what they would have. She remembered the words of Karl Marx. *He should have been smart enough to use the fact, not try to change humanity*, she thought.

****** **Rome:**

The Swedish embassy in Rome was the site of the next meeting between Ambassador Wadii and Mrs. Harrington, the two emissaries representing almost the whole of the Middle East Muslim nations on the one hand, and the State of Israel, on the other. Mrs. Harrington had worn a wig, as agreed. A false mustache and plane lens eyeglasses were sufficient for the
Ambassador. Very few people outside of Iran would have recognized him, in any case.

The Ayatollah and his political advisors had explored all possible avenues of recourse. They considered demanding that the Israelis remove all of the bombs, but immediately saw the folly in that strategy. They considered making the whole issue public, in order to appeal to world opinion, but they couldn't do that either. In the end, they decided this was the best deal they could cut, consistent with the *Great One's* plans for the sabotage of the fusion plants around the world. They of course proceeded to search every space larger than a brief case in all of their public buildings, and the homes of the major officials. They would find nothing, except a lot of embarrassing contraband.

"Mr. Ambassador," the charming lady said, offering her hand in greeting. "Mrs. Harrington," the Ambassador replied, graciously supporting her hand for that brief moment, then bowing ever so slightly from his waist. "I think we can come to an accommodation," he said, not smiling. The lady's eyes lit up ever so slightly, and she gently and genuinely gave an audible sigh of relief. "Thank you," she said, simply. "Where do we go from here?" "I have brought a draft treaty which we want you to examine," he said. "If we can negotiate this treaty, it should solve our respective problems nicely," he continued. "We would expect to announce this jointly" he said, "with most of the provisions of the treaty to be made public. You will see when you have it analyzed," he finished, handing her a small, expensive looking briefcase.

For a part of a second she hesitated, remembering the casualties suffered by many of her countrymen during the past year from bombs, many of which had been carried in brief cases. She would put this in the bombproof trunk of her limousine as soon as possible, she thought to herself.

Ambassador Wadii held no such thoughts. He was a dedicated professional, and truly cared for his country, and longed for the day when he could raise his family in an atmosphere less poisoned by fear, hatred, and jealousy.

****** **The White House:**
The President's national address was scheduled for 9:00 p.m. Eastern Standard Time. Pollsters estimated he had an impressive 74% of the television audience.

The calls and letters and telegrams and faxes had continued to roll in, in ever increasing volume, as the various network analysts continued to speculate on the scope of the policy changes being proposed, according to *highly placed* sources. The favorable ratio had fallen to just under two to one, as media hyperbole injected a sense of unreal into the whole situation.

The White House communications crew was sparse, as media organizations go. Only two camera crews, one stage director, and a prompter technician were required inside the Oval Office. The network feeds located in the basement were monitored by two government, and five network engineers. Ms. Peggy Ketzke, the director, gave the President the agreed-to one minute, ten seconds, and two seconds prompts. The bright red lights over the two cameras told Grant Williams that he was on the air.

"Good evening, my fellow Americans," he started out, with confidence in his voice. "Over the past few days there has been a whole spectrum of rumors about the proposed new economic and trade policies which we have been considering." Grant continued, reading carefully from the prompter before him. Carrie had insisted that he read it slowly, and that he should not ad lib. "As you know, the recent collapse in our stock markets has focused our attention on our economy and the serious problems we have been facing, from the first day of our administration." He paused, taking a deep breath, and looked sternly, directly into the camera.

"For over a year now we have been studying the problem, using the most modern analytical tools available. These are very hard times and we must take drastic measures. The report of the results of our special task force has been accelerated in the light of the present crisis. I want to assure you all that their work has been thorough, professional, and tested," he said. It was his team, *if it all works*, he thought, but he was prepared to distance himself if it didn't work.

***

On Sunday, his economics and political experts had reported that they were unable to pose scenarios which would cause the program to fail. But they didn't endorse the program. The plan sounded like some cockamamie platform some wild candidate out in Nevada had conjured up someone said, and no one had ever heard from him again. The chief political advisors were not so ambivalent. They were willing to endorse almost any program which would perpetuate their man in office, provided a happy electorate, and produced a stable economy. The most compelling point was made by his Chief of Economic Advisors, Dr. Mary Moore. She pointed out to Grant and Carrie that none of the group had the credentials to verify the fidelity of the model.

Shortly after that, at a break in the discussion, Carrie Williams took her out to one of the gardens, ostensibly to show her some rare flowers, just blooming. Carrie took the opportunity to explain to her that the project itself employed twelve of the top twenty experts in this special science, including three of the top four experts in the world. The other one, Dr. Samuel Levanthol, happened to be working on a similar project of his own, in Jerusalem, Carrie explained. After their chat, Dr. Moore supported the program rather wholeheartedly.

***

"Beginning tomorrow, I expect to send to Congress an extensive plan to begin an orderly privatization of many of the functions of the Federal Government. Included in the plan will be provisions for the assurance of the employment of most of the present government employees.
"Within two weeks, I will call for a meeting of all of the

governors of our states and will propose a similar plan for their consideration. I will be proposing to the Congress that we reduce our overall corporate and individual tax rates and that we restore the 40% investment tax credit. Tomorrow, I will also sign an executive order establishing a blue ribbon panel to study the feasibility of re-establishing the gold standard for the dollar. And there is more," Grant paused.

The impact of his words was overwhelming, even to him, as he read them. Only Carrie's insistence had finally persuaded him to do this. The lights were uncomfortably warm, but the prompter was running and so must he. "My cabinet members will detail the plans for the public and for Congress, here at the White House, tomorrow morning starting at 10:00 o'clock," he said, (as if that would possibly satisfy anyone now). But he had other bombshells. "Regarding our continuing trade deficit with some of our trading partners, I will insist that Congress enact a 100% import tariff against all imports from those nations which have violated the Fair Trade Act, with but a few exceptions, for a period of one year. In the meanwhile, we will try once again to work with them to establish equitable and long lasting trade agreements. This act alone is projected to create over five million new jobs in this country."

Grant Williams paused, took a small sip of water, and then smiled, trying to sell his audience that he was in full control. The President went on to outline in only the most general terms how the privatization of government functions would cut the cost of the government operations dramatically and how the resultant tax reductions, made possible thereby, would lead to the rapid reduction in deficit spending. Carrie made sure that he did not get into any details. "That is what they hired experts for," she had reminded him. But enough of the new plan was revealed to expose it to the harsh light of public criticism, of which there would be an abundance. But all the experts together could not carry a single precinct, she insisted.

President Williams went on to close: "My fellow Americans, we can, and we will come out of this economic morass. There will be better days ahead. We will not let this nation fail. There must be hard work and sacrifices, for the good of us all. Please give me your patience, your prayers, and your support," he ended abruptly. "Good evening."

The address had taken just a little over seventeen minutes. The post-mortems and spin doctors continued until late into the night. The communications coming into every government agency down to the county dog catchers, and to every media agent known were jammed, even before the President finished his speech, and remained that way until about three in the morning, local time everywhere.

The approval ratio increased to two to one, even as those who perceived themselves to be the losers in this massive restructuring raised their protests to a deafening fever pitch. One astute commentator observed that only a third-party independent could possibly succeed in pulling this off, being free of all of the political baggage a Democrat or Republican standard bearer would suffer.

***

The next day, a full eight days after *Black Monday*, the markets were allowed to open again. Nervous managers soon relaxed a notch or two as the markets drove upward from the opening bells, recovering over half of the losses incurred that fateful day. Hope was rising and success became self-fulfilling, at least for the markets.

As advertised, extensive briefings were given to the press, and to the congressional leaders. The bottom line seemed to be that within the time of the President's current term, the deficit spending could be reduced to zero, more government service could be delivered, no major cuts in the so-called entitlement programs had to be suffered, and there would be tax cuts**!!** **It all seemed too good to be true.**

Chapter 7: SPY IN OUR MIDST

When the career government employees were reassured by The President that for persons with more than five years of service, their pensions would be considered vested, and that for most of them, their employment status would be guaranteed, the major source of the resistance to the new program subsided. Public opinion was not to be denied. Grant Williams' approval rating went up 30 points over the four weeks which followed his momentous speech, before leveling off at 82%.

Congress, ever mindful of the polls, jumped on the bandwagon, en masse. Their positions of power and, more importantly, their reelection, seemed assured. The government had simply found a more efficient way to operate, it seemed.

But the program, they were soon to discover, called for more than just a streamlining of the executive branch. Riding on the crest of popular reform, The President insisted that congressional staff budgets be cut in half. The rationale was simply that most of the oversight functions carried on by Congress were obviated by the massive privatization of the functions of government. With the elections just around the calendar, the Congress hardly whimpered. He asked for, and was given, a genuine line-item veto. For the fourth time, a balanced budget amendment was launched by Congress. The States would almost certainly concur.

****** The White House:
About a month into the era of the new Grant Williams

administration, dubbed by the press as *The New_Way*, George Steinman was called to the White House for a special briefing. But it was not conducted by either of the First Family.

The CIA had intercepted several messages between agents of the Israeli IBIA, and their headquarters in Jerusalem. These messages mentioned the General by name. The Assistant Director didn't know if the information he had obtained was of interest to the General or not. Further, he could not assess the value or risk this information might represent. He handed the General a sheaf of dispatches.

Almost involuntarily, George sank down into a nearby padded chair. He could see at a glance that he had a major security problem. Private and confidential directives which he had sent to his top staff members just a week ago had somehow gotten into the hands of the IBIA. There were only four copies; five, counting the copy sent by special security messenger to the White House. The existence of the project itself was the greatest secret. Knowing what it was used for and the potential for misuse was the most sensitive information within the Williams administration. The whole economic reform just launched would be in jeopardy if the public knew.

George played it straight. He knew this man from the military, years ago. He knew he was a true professional and could be trusted. He told him that this find was of enormous value and that they should pursue the matter with all diligence.

***

George Steinman would have bet his life on the trust he had come to place in his three lieutenants, his *boys*, as he had come to affectionately think of them. Even now, he could not bring himself to accept the possibility that one of them had broken that confidence. Nevertheless, he immediately brought in an outside group of military intelligence specialists. They were given free reign of the facilities and all of the personnel files. Only the actual contents of the project itself and its applications were kept from them.

After a month of investigations, wire taps, surveillance cameras, and shadowy interviews, the team found nothing. Their only recommendations were to tighten the existing procedures and to set up a series of planted messages. These messages were to be coded differently to various addressees, to see which of the departments might be responsible for the leaks.

****** **The Middle East:**
The new peace treaty had been ratified in record time. The agreement between Israel, Egypt, Syria, Jordan, Saudi Arabia, Iraq, Lebanon, and Iran, provided for the following:
1) Those specific States, and the League of Muslim Nations would recognize Israel's sovereign territory <u>as it was presently occupied</u>, together with a five mile buffer zone around the nation, to be occupied by United Nations Peacekeeper Forces and paid for equally by the adjoining States.
2) Free trade agreements were to be diligently pursued by all parties to the agreement, with an objective of full, free trade across all borders.
3) Israel would provide twenty 500-Megawatt fusion plants

for her neighbors, at no license fee, and on a cost basis. The plants were scheduled to be completed within ten years, with the first three plants to be operational within three years. The secret part of the agreement pledged all parties to non-aggression, particularly with respect to atomic weapons of any kind. All pledged to not initiate atomic warfare.

Amman, Jordan was to be the site of the first plant. Jordan was oil poor, and it was logistically easy for the supplier. The Ayatollah's agents were surreptitiously assigned almost every technical and managerial position available on the project for the user staff.

****** **Tokyo:**
After three weeks of posturing and government blessed rioting by the Japanese, a radical new trade agreement was proposed by them to the Williams administration. The pact called for an almost immediate equalizing of the trade balance, with explicitly defined and liberal quotas of Japanese imports to balance the proposed American imports. A commission was to monitor the flow of goods and capital, and was to report on a monthly basis. Within six days, the Chinese, Indonesians, and the Philippines nations responded almost identically.

The news was received with mixed reviews because the prospect of so many new domestic jobs had been stimulating the American economy ever since the tariffs had been announced. But the proposed agreement was considered a major victory for the Williams administration.

****** McLean, Virginia:

After three months of 60-hour weeks, Jason was ready for a vacation. The program had been well defined, even perfected by then, and only the implementation was left. And this was not the purview of Jason Phillips. It was Friday afternoon, and the General had just directed that he should stay away for three weeks. He could hardly wait to tell Jamie the wonderful news.

As he rode home on the Metro, Jason thought of Jamie, their life together, and their dreams and hopes. It had been months since he had time to think of anything except the project. He looked forward to getting back to Nevada to see his mother and the old ranch. He wanted to take Jamie hiking around nearby Lake Tahoe. Jamie was outside raking the first leaves of fall when Jason arrived home. He just said "Hi," and slipped his free arm around her slim waist and walked her up to their porch. "Guess what?" he said. Jamie already knew what. But she waited for him to tell her.

***

All their life together, Jamie had more to do with his decisions than he might ever know. She thought back on the day she met this man. Actually, Jamie met Jason not quite by accident, the way he always had been told. She had a roommate, Barbara, who worked with Jason at Camp Pendleton. When she saw his picture, she arranged to just happen to be at the same beach with Barbara, when they knew he would be there. Jason didn't have a chance. He thought he was sweeping her off her feet, but she was totally in control of the whole courtship. And she loved him, from that first meeting. The marriage had worked out well.

Jamie had a career teaching, but Jason became her much greater interest. She had succeeded nicely in school and had landed a position in the Vista School District, but the real world of recalcitrant third graders and an administration dedicated to onerous written reports, took the edge off of her initial enthusiasm. So when Jason asked her to marry him, she had already written out her resignation and had told several of her friends of her plans.

Jamie was a striking red-head, tall and thin, with a big, warm smile that made everyone around her feel comfortable. Her wide, deep-set eyes sparkled in the sunlight, and her athletic build did not deny her femininity. She had been born right there in Solano Beach and had gone through the education curriculum at UCSB.

***

For some months now, Jamie had been mentioning a desire to travel, especially to the Middle East and to Israel in particular. So it was no great surprise to Jason when she pulled out some travel brochures after dinner.

"With three weeks, let's do it all," Jason said, grinning at the thought of such a whirlwind vacation. Jamie reluctantly agreed, but they would have to fly now, instead of taking a cruise ship as she had hoped. Jason had a special appointment there in ten days, which he would only later know was an appointment. Jason wondered though, when Jamie pulled out special appointment slips to have their passports expedited. It helped to have friends in high places!

Like a master puppeteer, Carrie's strings reached around the world. **Who was to be manipulated now, and for what *cause*?**

****** The White House:**

Grant Williams was rather suddenly in great demand. For the month before the new era, congress persons running for reelection had been distancing themselves from the administration, calling him an amateur and an interloper, unfit for the high office he held. The common wisdom was that the vote had been so evenly split between the two major candidates, that Williams had gotten his office on a fluke. Now, with the markets up, the polls showing Grant and Carrie Williams as the most popular First Family ever, all that had reversed, and in the season before the off-year elections the Williams' were courted with all of the considerable urgency that incumbents can muster.

Carrie Williams was in her glory. Like a modern day Madam DeFarge, she kept detailed books on who did what to whom. Her network of allies, friends, and associates served her well in these important days. Where it suited her purposes, alliances were cemented. The opportunities to incur political credits were enormous, more than even she could satisfy.

***

As a child she had lived abroad mostly. As a young journalist she was well connected through her father, the former Ambassador to the Court of St James. She had met most of the leading political and social figures of the day. She had been making alliances of all kinds since she was a teenager. She had learned well from her father and had inherited from him good political sense. But her appetite for power was way beyond what she had learned from him. Carrie Witherington was an original and seemed destined for some great role. Avery Harrington recognized that twenty years earlier and had recruited her to his special *cause*. That had changed her life but not her intensity or her focus on getting and holding power.

Carrie Williams had been compared to Mary Todd Lincoln, even before the torturous election campaign. In an interview with Barbara Cranston of TINN, shortly after the New Independent Party convention, she had shared that it had been her plan since she was a teen that she would marry a successful politician and she would guide him to the presidency. The interview was very telling, but Grant Williams won the election even handicapped with the adverse publicity generated by that interview, and the scandal uncovered in the middle of the campaign regarding a former secretary.

Carrie Williams, the former Carrie Witherington, did not appear very bright. But she had the ear of the President, and that made her very powerful, indeed. It was through a strong attraction she had to military men that led to the circumstances which brought Grant Williams into the lives of George Steinman and then Jason Phillips.

****** **Amsterdam:**
The huge KLM 767 swooped down upon the main runway at Schiphol. Jason and Jamie had arrived in Amsterdam just as dawn was breaking over the Netherlands.

This was only the second time Jamie had ever been out of the country and it was a great adventure for them both. The trip was all the more exciting, given the context of the assignment that Carrie Williams herself had given this young housewife. Foreign intrigue and clandestine meetings were things she had only read about before. Not even her husband was to know the real purpose of this trip.

The two of them spent six glorious hours touring the canals and the harbor, visiting an old windmill and the obligatory wooden shoe factory. Jamie loved playing tourist and enjoyed the flowers and the quaint and colorful old shops. They returned to the airport early, so that they could check through customs, and then have dinner before their El Al flight to Tel Aviv-Jaffa. Jason had mixed emotions regarding all of the extra security precautions the Israeli airline took. On the one hand, he felt sure that no terrorists could possibly get on board their plane, but it reminded him of how much they had been the targets of terrorism for over fifty years.

****** Israel:

The old Boeing 747 touched down at Tel Aviv-Jaffa just after midnight, local time. Theirs being the last flight of the day, the lines through customs were easier than usual. What struck them both was the universal and almost casual show of arms by the airport guards and soldiers on the streets. Again, the ambivalence made them uneasy. The night life was still going strong in that bustling city, but it had been such a long day for them, and their body clocks sent strong messages that rest was called for. An old Fiat taxi took them to their hotel and within the ten minute drive they heard the driver's life story. Cabbies were the same the world over!

The next morning they were awakened by the maid, checking to see if their room was ready for changing. They were amazed to find they had slept for 10 hours. They had freelanced their vacation totally, so far. Each day they caucused over breakfast, deciding what adventure to enjoy. It had been one of the best vacations they ever had. Jason had shown Jamie many of his old haunts in and around Smith Valley and they had a whirlwind tour around Lake Tahoe. Jamie had never been there before and Jason enjoyed acting the professional and prideful tour guide, showing her Emerald Bay, hiking to Eagle Falls, and even showing her his favorite spot, the Upper Angora lakes. But this morning was different. Jamie insisted they go directly to Jerusalem, to the University. She had someone there that he must meet, but she wouldn't tell him any more. Jason went along with her, but wondered at the possibilities.

Even though he held his level four national security clearance, he had not been briefed on any security issues when he had his passport renewed for this trip. The process seemed all too easy compared to previous trips he had taken overseas.

****** **Amman, Jordan:**
Fifty-some miles east of Jerusalem, the agents of the Great One were dutifully analyzing the design of the new fusion power plant, looking for any vulnerable points or weak aspects which they could employ for sabotage purposes. Work had already begun on the facilities and the local staff was being trained for operating the plant. The unit itself and the critical PCS (plasma containment system) would not be delivered for another two years. Their Israeli instructors

carefully avoided discussions of important aspects of the design and even the operations.   But a little information let them know what other information they needed.   Documents from the two dozen plants operating worldwide were stolen, at great cost and risk of exposure.

There seemed to be two vulnerable parts of the PCS, the computer power supply, and the plasma motion sensor array.   But the frustrating thing for the agents was that the worst thing that would happen if you interrupted the PCS was that the boilers would be automatically switched over to the alternate fuel system, which would be a coal, oil, or gas-fired unit, depending on the plant.   And the world knew that.   That was part of the appeal of this new process.   There was nothing radioactive about the process, nor were there anything but innocuous by-products.   It was very hard to defeat!

The agents could certainly plant charges under the boilers, but the sabotage would be totally apparent from even a simple investigation of the physical site.   They had to develop a plausible case for unit self destruction.

The Ayatollah would not be pleased.   The man responsible for this operation was Justian Rochnam, a businessman and a full Colonel in the Secret Police.   He returned to Tehran by irregular and circumspect routes very dutifully every third week to report to The *Great One* himself. By the time he made his next report, he would either have to concoct a very good story, or he would fly directly to London and ask for political asylum.   The prospects made him shiver just to think of the consequences of disappointing his leader.

From the bus depot in Jerusalem, Jason and Jamie took a taxi, or rather, a taxi took them.   A military looking man in khaki seemed to pick them out and offer a bargain fare.   Of course he knew where the University was.   And yes, he had a cousin who lived in Chicago.   It all seemed coincidental.

At the University, they were met by a girl who said she was a student and was assigned as a guide to visitors.   And they looked like visitors!   Jamie reached into her purse and pulled out a card, handing it to the girl, and asked: "can you please show us to this gentleman's office?"   Jamie smiled at Jason and looked pleased with herself.   "Whom are we meeting?" Jason said, seeming only mildly interested.   "You will see," Jamie said, falling in step behind the guide.

Jason recognized the man behind the desk immediately.   Sam Levanthol had led the Israeli delegations which visited Project SPAT in Oceanside, years before.   At the time Jason had only dealt with him on a social basis.   He helped host the visitors during the off-hours.   The project had very carefully never been discussed off site.   But Jason had enjoyed showing this world renowned visitor around and had included his then current girl friend, Jamie, as co-host, showing the good doctor all of the usual tourist sites around San Diego, including the Zoo, Sea World, and a great restaurant, called Casa Di Baffi.   Sam had extended a cordial invitation to them if they ever got to Israel, but they had dismissed that as polite social nicety.

That evening they talked of Southern California and the good times they had in San Diego.   The next day Dr.

Levanthol and his wife Sarah showed Jason and Jamie the usual tourist sites, including the great Mosque, the Western Wall, the Arab market, Hezekiah's tunnel, and several other places of almost eternal historical significance. Jason had never been to Israel before, although he had traveled all around the area. Recalling the Bible stories of his youth, the land was magic to him.

The second evening, Sam asked Jason and Jamie if they would like to see his own project. Jason was stunned when he quickly became aware of the scope of their project. Its very existence had to be one of their best kept government secrets, just as *ABACUS* was truly one of the Williams administration's most closely guarded operations. Jamie jumped at the chance. Jason hardly ever talked about his work, except in the most vague terms. She wasn't sure at all what he did or what the real purpose of his work was. This was a chance to find out and she was so enthusiastic that Jason could hardly refuse.

The next day Dr. Levanthol led them through the elaborate security processes, not unlike the ones employed at the Pentagon. Jason had his guard up and had determined that he would not answer any questions about *ABACUS*. But none was asked, it seemed. What they saw was a rough equivalent of the massive parallel computer system used by *ABACUS*. Instead of the shiny tiled raised floor in his own lab, Jason saw unkempt cable runs which connected stacks of the Israeli version of the newest RISC computer systems, sold by INTEL and HP. But as Dr. Levanthol explained to Jamie the broader purpose of the system before them, Jason gleaned the scope of the project and guessed their obvious application. This system was critical for the operations the Israeli government performed as the *Special Partner*, the grand interface between all of the otherwise intractable trading blocks.

Jason was introduced to a Dr. Weston, a young Brit who was apparently in charge of the giant computer system. The two of them inevitably got into shop talk, both being careful not to allude to any applications. Dr. Levanthol excused himself, telling Jason he wanted to show Jamie some special displays in the next building. They were to meet later at the cafeteria in the middle of the campus. It was then that the reason Jason had been brought to the facility became apparent. Dr. Weston began talking about their pipelining algorithms, which made early MPP architecture work effectively. He was obviously fishing, Jason recognized. But it was of no use for them anyway. They had apparently made a bad error, if this *chance* encounter was what it seemed. Jason felt relieved to understand what they were about, and at the same time, a little used. But he took it with the good nature that was normally his. He explained to Dr. Weston that his area of expertise was in applications, and that he was not a systems specialist. Jason thought better of giving him Max McGurn's name and number. There would be enough explaining to do regarding why they were there visiting the competition, anyway.

As soon as Dr. Weston understood that Jason could not contribute any solutions to his major system problem, he lost all interest in this visitor. He took Jason to the cafeteria, thirty minutes early, excusing himself, and walking off briskly, apparently embarrassed for them all.

****** **The Pentagon:**

George Steinman kept up a steady contact with the Deputy Director of the CIA, whom he had met at the White House several weeks earlier. This morning he had heard from him again and the message was that he had some documents which the General might want to review.

Again, he was shocked and angry. The Deputy reported the discovery of another project document in the hands of the IBIA. And even more disconcerting, he showed him photographs of one of his top level staff in Jerusalem. Steinman's head was swimming. Of all of his staff, he trusted Jason the most. How could this be? He looked at the copy of the document again, closely. The intelligence staff assigned to the case had worked out a simple code to identify the individual copies of the sensitive documents he distributed to his top level staff, in an effort to identify the leak. They were even able to identify original copy versus good Xerox copies. George Steinman looked again at the code. He could not believe what he saw. Somehow someone had taken his own copy of the subject memo! He took out his appointment book he always carried and checked the date of Jason's vacation. Sure enough, the subject document had been circulated after Jason's departure. Still, what was he doing in Israel? He had told Steinman of his plans to visit his mother in Nevada, and to spend time in the Lake Tahoe area. He had never even hinted of any trip overseas. He made arrangements to send an urgent message to Jason. He would confront him directly, the only way he knew how to deal with tough issues.

George Steinman was not a patient man. He could not rest well until he unraveled the mystery of how his copy of the planted classified directive was apparently copied and the copy secreted out of the plant. He called his special intelligence operatives in to discuss it. They carefully went over the step-by-step procedure followed in the scheme they had hoped would pinpoint the leak. It seemed a dead end because the copy taken was clearly from the master copy and Steinman himself was the only one who could have taken it. The master copy was kept in Steinman's doubly secure safe, which itself was kept in an inner vault; probably the most secure space in the whole of the Pentagon. Any tampering with that system would have been detected. It remained a mystery.

George was extremely upset about having to report this to the First Family, and at the same time he was greatly relieved to know that his *boys* were apparently not the conduit. He phoned the White House for an appointment, but was put off until the following Tuesday. Which was fine with him, as it would give him more time to assess the damage and to talk with Jason, who was to report back the following Monday.

Gnawing quietly in the back of his mind, George wondered about the strange relationship between the President and the First Lady. Things seemed to be swirling around him. **Things he didn't understand; events over which he had no control.**

Chapter 8: ATOMIC EXPLOSIONS

****** **The White House:**

The President was awakened at 2:12 a.m. An AP report had been verified by the American Embassy in Japan. Nine people had been killed in a massive explosion on the western outskirts of Tokyo. The world's first full scale fusion power plant, purchased by Japan from the Israelis over four years before and completed a little over a year ago, had been flattened. A large part of Tokyo was without electricity.

Although several terrorist groups claimed to be responsible, the major speculation was that there had been a failure in the fusion reactor itself. Many Japanese had never really believed that the much-ballyhooed fusion process was not really radioactive. A large protest group marched on the Diet the next day, demanding the immediate shutdown of all (four) of the other fusion plants in the country. The Israeli Ministry of Energy had a crack investigative team on their way to Tokyo already. Two of the nine people killed were highly trained Israeli operations supervisors.

****** **Tel Aviv-Jaffa:**

Jamie had been rather distraught to hear that 1: The Israelis had apparently brought them there on false pretenses, ostensibly to pick Jason's mind, and 2: That they had blundered so badly, having mistaken Jason for their chief system expert, Max McGurn. Jamie was inclined at that moment to tell Jason all about the involvement of Carrie Williams; but she had promised the wife of the President of the United States that she would not do that specific thing.

Jamie had explained, quite truthfully, that she had been corresponding with Dr. and Mrs. Levanthol. She volunteered the opinion that the Levanthols had been used by their government, and that Jason should not be angry with either them or her. She began to regret that she had ever gotten involved.

They cut their vacation short by two days, flying home the next day on the first available flight. This gave them a long weekend at home, in McLean, before Jason had to report back to work. Jason had very interesting news to report to George Steinman. In retrospect, Jason realized that he had learned more from his visit to Jerusalem than the people who had somehow coaxed him there.

****** **The White House:**
One of the reasons George Steinman could not get an audience with the First Family with the ease he had almost come to expect was that they were both closeted with visitors from Israel. Mordicai Maroni, the Israeli Ambassador to the United Nations, accompanied the Israeli Minister of Trade, a Doctor Benjamin Gundermann. Dr. Gundermann was the second most powerful individual in the Israeli government for several reasons, primarily because of the importance of Israel's role as *Special Partner* to the four major trading alliances.

ABACUS had been limited in the analysis and policy development aspects of foreign trade. The secret arrangements could only be inferred at the most basic level. Quantitative data was impossible to predict. What they needed were the specifics of the myriad of agreements being formulated and executed by the Special Partner. Carrie

Williams had insisted that the President negotiate that from them, whatever the cost.

The cost, it turned out, was an exchange of data and technical help from the specialists of *ABACUS*. Gundermann proposed that there would be a complete pooling of information regarding foreign societies. Israel would not be required to divulge data on its demographics, and the United States would not be required to give them the corresponding information. Additionally, Israel would provide current information regarding their trading initiatives, and the United States would agree to share all system technology between the two massive simulation systems.

The existence of TAT (trading analysis tool) was no surprise to Carrie; she had known about the project long before its inception. Grant was told only as much about it as Carrie had decided he should know, at least for the time being, and until she unfolded the larger plan for him.

The proposal seemed agreeable to the First Family. Everyone was concerned that the complete operation be carried out with the utmost security. A formal treaty or agreement of any kind was out of the question. This was one of those *affairs of state* that was accomplished with a handshake and a knowing nod over a friendly drink. The meeting in the Oval Office was strictly *pro forma*. Carrie had explained to Grant just why the agreement was good for them and what it might lead to in terms of more successful trading policies.

The Israelis were happy with the agreement, because it would provide the technology and data base to put TAT on a par with *ABACUS*. Besides, they could delay fresh data defining their trading agreements, rendering the data relatively worthless, if it suited them.

Ever since the Israelis had become one of the major economic powers, speculation persisted regarding whether they had colonial ambitions, or even plans of empire. Grant wondered about this again, as he speculated about how the agreement would strengthen even further the Israeli hold on international trade. He made a mental note to have Steinman do an analysis regarding this possibility, as soon as possible.

****** **The Pentagon:**
"I think Mrs. Williams had something to do with this," Jason told George Steinman. "I don't know how, or why," he volunteered, "that is only a hunch." George Steinman was hearing for the first time of the existence of the Israeli's trading analysis tool (TAT). The CIA reports all made sense now. It was interesting that the one area the Israelis were not able to compete equitably with them was the system software. Dr. Max McGurn would appreciate that. Steinman was relieved to have his faith in his young protégé justified, but he was furious at the thought that Carrie had perhaps known of the existence of TAT and had not told him. At just that instant, something loose in his mind clicked into place. He remembered now that as an expediency, the latest stolen project directive was simply copied and sent to the White House. *That is it*, he thought. She or someone on the White House staff must be the leak. He would have to handle this matter very delicately.

****** **The White House:**

George Steinman arrived at the White House at shortly after 9:00 a.m. Tuesday morning. As was often the case, there was a meeting, then *the* meeting. Carrie received the General in her private office.

"George," she enthused," how good to see you." "Sit down, we have a lot to discuss," she said, thinking to herself that she had to do a little mending of their relationship, but confident that she could. She was pleased that her revelations would show this man, to a greater extent than ever before, just who was in charge. George didn't respond. He was resolved that Carrie should learn the extent of his displeasure about not being fully informed of TAT. He seated himself casually and turned to face her, showing his stern-faced military expression, as if to say, "O.K., this better be good." It was. Carrie admitted her previous knowledge of TAT and her involvement in the visit of Jason and Jamie to that project in Jerusalem. It was she who arranged to send the wrong man, she said. It sounded like a great coup. *Is she really that clever*, George found himself thinking. Carrie sold the idea that it was she, Carrie Witherington-Williams, who had found a way to extract that special information George needed for his model. And it was she who had negotiated a deal with the Israelis to have it handed over to *ABACUS*. Neither Grant nor George, or anyone else for that matter, knew of the regular extensive contact between Carrie and Avery Harrington. With a little luck, Carrie hoped, no one would.

Again, the *meeting* was rather a formality. The President introduced George to Dr. Gundermann.

Handshakes all around and the exchange of special telephone numbers ratified their understanding of the terms of the agreement and their mutual willingness to cooperate. Carrie observed it all with extreme satisfaction. *Puppets on strings, men are so easy to manipulate*, she thought.

****** New Delhi:

It was only 10 days after the power plant in Tokyo had blown up, or had been blown up; no one seemed to be sure. Except the members of the Israeli team of investigators, and of course they would be biased. That event had gotten the attention of the world, but the huge explosion at the New Delhi plant sent shock waves through all of the world's financial markets. Over two hundred people had been killed in the explosion. They were still pulling bodies out of the wreckage surrounding the plant. Much worse, the Indian government announced that there was massive residual radiation in and around the plant. It was rumored that the by-products of the process contained unstable Deuterium and Tritium.

The Israeli Ministry of Energy called a press meeting and presented several experts who explained that the fusion process did not produce any by-products of measurable radioactivity. But a poll taken shortly afterwards found that approximately 65% of the people in third world countries believed they were covering up the disaster. 52% seemed to believe that the plants represented a danger of some kind of atomic explosion. Justian Rochnam and his operatives had done their work well, it seemed. The *Great One* would be satisfied.

****** **The White House:**

What had started out to be a great month for Carrie and her cause began unraveling with the news of the New Delhi disaster. The promise of unlimited cheap power had fueled an economic expansion around the world and had helped lift the economy of the United States off the floor of eternal stagflation. The *New Way* had launched the economy into what appeared would be an increasing acceleration upward. But with the New Delhi disaster, the wisdom of this new power source came into question.

The Government Workers' Union had called for a massive march on the Capitol and the White House. They did not intend to be subtle. Everyone had watched with great interest the first processes of privatization. The administration had targeted the Postal Service and the Federal Prisons System as the first agencies to be opened to market forces. Financially it seemed to be a promising tax savings. The government employees, however, found that they would be taking pay cuts, losing job assurance, soft retirement cushions, and seniority. Worst of all, many in administration would be losing their positions, reduced to the common work force. Washington bureaucrats found themselves to be at arms length with the day-to-day operations. It was becoming uncomfortably obvious to all that the old political spoils system was being threatened. The network of the old guard dug their heels in and convinced large numbers of the working people to resist the administration's plans.

The difficulty, like so many of the administration's problems, was brought to the attention of *ABACUS*. The model provided several alternative solutions, but the most dramatic results (according to the model) could be obtained by requiring winning contractors to share a substantial amount of equity with the workers, through tax deferred retirement funds with short vesting requirements. This de-fused the movement and pitted the workers against the old government managers. And since there were so many more workers and managers who welcomed the opportunity to compete in a free market environment than those incompetent and complacent power brokers, the movement died from lack of support.

As the new model became more refined and sophisticated, and the use of it became routine, Jason and Brent and Max McGurn became more entrenched in the deeper meaning and significance of the philosophy upon which it was based. Together, they came to understand that the true success of the model, and therefore the country, would only come when there was a more widespread and intense belief in the value system upon which it was based. This point had apparently been lost on the General, but these three brilliant scientists resolved that they would get this point across, and urge the General to sell it to the President. **The future of the nation was at stake.**

The march on Washington had been avoided and the polls showed that the incumbents were doing well, although much of the support of the more liberal members of Congress had eroded, as loyalties were betrayed in favor of the President's new economic plan. The projections showed the Democrats would be in control of the House, with a slim margin of six seats. The Republicans would probably pick up another two seats in the Senate to give them a solid 60 member majority. A few independents were running under the mantle of the remains of the New Independent Party, but found virtually no support from the First Family. Like a black widow devouring her mate after the mating, Carrie had sabotaged the party after the final Electoral College tally. The Party had served its purpose; she harbored bigger ambitions.

Now, Carrie had turned her attention to how to best help her friend Avery Harrington. Almost daily calls kept her abreast of what was happening and how she could serve the *cause*. She had been assured that this latest terrorist campaign was about to be put to an end.

****** **The United Nations Headquarters:**
The distinguished Ambassador to the U.N., Mordicai Maroni, representing Israel, was about to speak. He had requested a special hearing on the recent disasters in Tokyo and New Delhi. Everyone expected a rehash of the recent technical arguments which purportedly proved that terrorism was indeed involved in the disasters. What they got instead made the top stories in the network newscasts the world over.

"Madam Secretary, Ladies and Gentlemen," Mordicai intoned. "My government and independent experts from six countries have been telling you that the explosions in the power plants in Tokyo and New Delhi had to be the work of terrorists. Today, I will show you the irrefutable proof." He paused, giving a hand signal to his assistants. The lights were dimmed and the main viewing screen came on with a still shot of one Justian Rochnam, Colonel in the Iranian Secret Police. "This man was responsible for the death of all of those innocent people and destruction of property," Mordicai said, emphasizing the word *responsible*. "Further, he has confessed this atrocity and is in our custody." A murmuring swept through the chambers. Some there knew he was telling the truth. Others would never believe it. "He will be turned over to the authorities in New Delhi and later be tried in Tokyo," Mordicai said, trying to be dispassionate. "He has named several of his agents, and some are even now being taken into custody. The others are being sought with all diligence," he continued. The Ambassador went on to explain how the radioactivity had been introduced in the New Delhi plant. Radioactive iodine had been encased around the main explosives, which had irradiated the general area before evaporating. Following that, he turned the presentation over to his technical people who again emphasized the cleanness and the reliability of the fusion process. They took the opportunity to announce the reopening of the other Japanese plants and the rebuilding of the plants which had been destroyed by the terrorist bombs.

****** **Washington, D.C.:**
With the issue of the fusion power plants somewhat put to rest, the primary elections would go as predicted and the administration went full force into the next phase of their program.

****** **The Pentagon:**
One of the nasty little secrets politicians guard in this age of computer technology and massive data files is the extent of the use of demographic (spell that political) data used in the continuous process of the reelection of all incumbents. From before the real year 1984, most congress persons have maintained extensive files on their constituents.

There are the donor files (the highest priority), files on all who ever correspond, files on all leaders (of all types) within the district and precinct files which detail the ethnic, religious, economic strata, voting registration, and public activities of almost everyone in the precinct.

National and State level incumbents go to no less effort to ensure satisfied constituents. The same level of detail per capita cannot normally be maintained, but the data banks are largely just as effective. Carrie Williams was quite proficient in the use of these data. Selective mailings were used, even during her husband's first campaign. They were subtle content-sensitive mailings, no contradictions or inconsistencies could ever be found. Extra pictures or alternate activity reports were substituted for those issues not particularly acceptable to a given ethnic, religious, or economic class or precinct. Some politicians had refined the process even more, down to the individual level. Early on, Carrie had learned of this powerful technique, and had become a true student of the art. This was one of the reasons she identified George Steinman and the project as vital to her larger plans, for both her husband, and more importantly, to *the cause.*

George Steinman convinced Carrie that the model could only be improved at this point by reducing the element size by an order of magnitude. That meant that the personal profile index would need to be expanded by a factor of ten. That would provide an almost unique index for every adult in the United States. This in turn meant that the model's predictions for voting results could be made to an accuracy of better than 98%! The General talked in terms of maintaining full economic control, but Carrie had always intended a more extensive exercise of governmental control than just over the economy.

Although only about a third of the system's storage capacity had been required for data, new units were added, to almost double the original capacity. The applications groups, under Brent and Jason, hardly questioned the move. It had always been their experience that there was never enough storage. Only Dr. McGurn questioned the need for the extra hardware. It was partly as a concern for the extra burden on his system software. But he also saw the potential for misuse of this powerful tool by the owners of the system. He quickly calculated that there was enough additional memory to store a full 10 page profile on every man, woman, and child in the United States. When he brought this up to the General, George blanched involuntarily. He wondered if Max had noticed. This use of the system was, George suspected, exactly what Carrie intended.

****** **Tehran, Iran:**
The Ayatollah was livid. The Israeli government had just declared the new trade agreement null and void. They had already pulled all of their personnel and equipment out of Amman, Jordan. Those Arab, Egyptian, and Iranian technicians training in Tel Aviv-Jaffa had been unceremoniously carted out of the country and told not to come back. There was very little to salvage from the situation. They had lost in the arena of world opinion. Applications for new power plants started pouring into Jerusalem once again. They were currently working on a 15 year backlog, with options carrying them out another 10 years.

This major setback only hardened the resolve of the *Great One*. This setback would not dissuade him.

Plan "C" was not to be shared with his political underlings. Only a select few in his Special Palace Guard, an elite group drawn from his trusted Secret Police, would be involved. He had set up a secure room in the basement of his palace, just for this project. The *Great One* lowered the lights from his control panel. The slide projector portrayed the two most recognizable icons for all of the Muslim faith; the Dome of the Rock in Jerusalem, and the Central Mosque in Mecca. "These are your targets, gentlemen," the Great One said. He watched his four specially chosen operatives for their response. No one reacted. Each had been chosen for his dedication to the Ayatollah. "This will only succeed, gentlemen, if we can hang it on our Jewish friends," he said. The four of them smiled at the delightful thought.

***

During the next six months his four operatives were in training, carrying out elaborate plots of terrorism with a new twist. A bus in Jordan was bombed and a Jewish tourist was successfully blamed for the attack. They said the man confessed before being stomped to death by the mob. An elaborate hoax was set up in Southern Lebanon to evoke an attack by Israeli aircraft on what turned out to be a children's day care center. This served to sharpen the group's skills, as well as to begin a buildup of even greater animosity toward the Jewish nation.

****** The White House:
In Washington, the Christmas season was being

celebrated with greater hope than people had in years. The people, encouraged by the new and unprecedented frugality of the government, felt hope for the first time in recent memory. The de-emphasis on government solutions for everything prompted people to help each other and themselves. It was almost like the country had returned to an earlier era, and it felt good.

It was Christmas Eve, and the softly drifting snow added to the sense of peace and serenity that people were feeling just now. The whole top echelon of *ABACUS* had been invited to Carrie's Christmas Party. As were dozens of others. This would normally be anything but a party. Carrie had worked the social calendar for many years. These social gatherings were normally workshops in political maneuvering. But this night was special. Carrie Williams was, for one of the few occasions in her life, totally relaxed and quite content to just be "The First Lady".

It was still relatively early in the evening and she had performed the amenities of her office, so she felt free to talk to whomever she might please. She pleased to talk to the attractive young couple off on the edge of the new much larger dining room. She worked her way over to the table of Senator S. Orrin Smyth. Seated with him were the Phillips, Jason and Jamie, and a gorgeous young blonde, announced as an aide to the Senator.

After chatting with the Senator for a few moments, she addressed Jamie: "My dear Jamie, could you come with me, I want to discuss your visit to Israel." She paused, making her next request sound like an afterthought: "And could you come too, Jason?" "Please excuse us Senator, and Miss. Langtree," she said, smiling graciously at the powerful Senate Majority Leader. Carrie Williams led them out of the dining room and down the main hall into a nearby complex of offices. The marine standing guard snapped to attention as they passed. Carrie hardly noticed. She knew that this particular complex had been electronically swept just the previous day, so that there was a minimum risk of having their conversation picked up. "Sit here please," she motioned toward two soft chairs. She seated herself in a like chair opposite them. "Tell me," she said, getting right to the point of her interest, "what is this new development in the model algorithms that George has been telling me about lately," she said. "According to the General, you came up with this innovation, and it has made the system work wonderfully," she addressed to Jason.

Jason and his two chief associates had been working on the General for months now, hoping he would raise this to the top level in government. And here he was, speaking to her. The graciousness that Carrie had always exhibited toward Jason allowed him to relax. Jason began with the Jaffe report, and gave Brent full credit for its discovery. He explained to her, in laymen's terms, the thesis of Jaffe's work and how those ideas had been incorporated into the model. Over the course of the next hour, Jason outlined for her the whole concept of how the traditional world view and the associated value system resulted in happier, more productive, and wealthier people, quoting Gilder, Freidman, and others.

After absorbing as much as she could, Carrie asked Jason to provide her with a copy of the documents they had used as reference material for this new algorithm set. Then she thanked them, and escorted them back to the dining room, where the after-dinner entertainment was still in full swing. It was a wonderful revelation for Jamie, who, for the first time ever, had a chance to understand exactly what it was that Jason did, and to understand how very important his work was considered by this lady who seemed to be in charge of everything.

That night, lying in bed, Carrie recalled for herself the events of the day. She had been amazed at the drama that had been unfolding. Her faith in the project had born fruit, and the dreams she harbored, which seemed rather uncertain only a short time before, seemed possible. The dramatic shift of policies in the Williams administration had precipitated a great political awakening in the country. People who felt disenfranchised suddenly were alive and ready to take up the cause, even as many of their old supporters felt betrayed and were angry and bitterly disappointed.

During the first campaign, the press had singled out the two of them; they were the darlings. The *New Way* was like a bucket of ice water down their collective back. But the press was committed and they were mightily swayed by the current success. Their support would continue conditionally. They would support the President and his charming wife, *win or tie.* As her mind slipped off into heavy sleep, Carrie decided it was time to embrace this alternate world view.

****** Tehran:
In his secret project room, the Ayatollah briefed his four special operatives on the latest exercise. This operation would be the last practice before the two master tasks. These

terrorist activities had been occupying almost half of the Ayatollah's time over the last six weeks, because he would not allow himself the luxury of involving anyone else, besides his four henchmen. The logistics required to support these intricate operations required his authority in any case, and the efficiency resulting from the arrangement gave him full control of the timing of the several operations they had performed to date.

Meanwhile, he had showered these four with considerable wealth and had alternately berated them to the point of breakdown. They were never allowed to think anything, except that they were very special warriors, selected to sacrifice their lives for their Ayatollah, and with their martyrdom, to gain immortality, and fame.

This last operation was actually easier than most of the ones they had performed before. They were to ignite the main shipping facility of the Saudi's. The Saudis had been the last major holdout in the Ayatollah's drive in the unification of the Arab world. This would add insult to injury. The Saudis were still shipping over 8 million barrels of oil a day, but with the price of crude down to only $48 per barrel, they were having to give up much of their rich lifestyle, to which they had become so exquisitely accustomed.

Of course the heart of the plan was to somehow make it look like the act was done by the Israelis. This was to be accomplished by planting the genuine remains of an Israeli bomber near the beach, to be torched at just the right moment. The Ayatollah had arranged for a special squadron of old F4 aircraft, painted with Israeli markings and equipped with genuine Israeli electronic components, to fly low over the complex. Another part of the plot was the planting of charges on board these special airplanes. One of his four henchmen would detonate the charges once the aircraft were well out over the gulf. It was not an oversight that they had failed to brief the pilots about this aspect of the plan. Backup plans were provided for almost every contingency. And yet only his *very special forces*, as he called them, would know of the plan in its totality. No one (it was hoped) would put all of the fragmented pieces of information together. Besides, all of the agents used in the operation belonged to the *Great One*, and most would never know how his part played into what would look like a heinous foreign operation.

It all came off like clockwork. On December 28th, headlines world wide screamed of the senseless and meaningless (apparently Israeli) attack. Of course the damage would easily be repaired. The port would hardly be shut down. In one month they would be back to full capacity. But to the world, especially the Muslim world, it was like adding salt to their earlier wounds.

****** **McLean, Virginia:**
The first Sunday of the new year found The First Family attending church with the Phillips' and their usual entourage of SS men at the Phillips' church, in McLean. The First Lady seemed especially attentive and reverent. After the service, Carrie invited the pastor to visit her at the White House. **Perhaps she had found religion.**

END OF PART II

PART III

THE AMENDMENT

ARTICLE V of THE CONSTITUTION OF THE UNITED STATES:

"The Congress, whenever two thirds of both Houses shall deem it necessary, shall propose Amendments to this Constitution, or, on the application of the legislatures of two thirds of the several states, shall call a Convention for proposing Amendments, which, in either case..."

Chapter 9: THE REVELATION

The news of the *Great Revelation* first broke on TCNN (The Christian News Network). What had been expected to be a rather adversarial interview, turned into the hottest news of the year in the area of religion.

****** **New York:**

The program logo faded with the sweet strains of the program's theme hymn, opening with a wide shot of the hostess and her guest. "Mrs. Williams, thank you for appearing today on our 'People Count' show," the gracious and charming hostess enthused, "It is such a distinct honor for us, and also a first, no pun intended," she mused. The full face shot of this important guest was selected for most of the rest of the interview. "It is a distinct pleasure and an honor to be asked," the First Lady responded.

"I was going to ask you about your involvement with the National Adoption Agency which you have so ably sponsored," the hostess said, "but I understand that you have something more important to tell us this morning," she paused. The picture switched to The First Lady. "Yes, I don't know quite where to begin." Carrie paused, her expression becoming somber, almost pained. "You know, I haven't attended church that much since I was a child, until just a few weeks ago," Carrie Williams said. "But my life has been changed, and I want to share that joy with everyone," she said, excitedly. She concluded with a pledge that the First Family was indeed going to return to the heritage that made America great, and that she, Carrie Witherington-Williams pledged to do every thing she could possibly do to further the cause.

The networks were caught unaware with this bombshell, and it was not until the evening news that this dramatic event was carried on all on the major networks. Although the network anchors were visibly shocked, none made any comment on the story, nor were there any analyses by the commentators. But all of their research teams were working feverishly on the issue, trying to understand just what had happened and what the implications might be. The First Lady, under great pressure from all of the media, reluctantly agreed to a full-blown news conference, to be held the following week. The reaction by the religious community was mixed. An unusual amount of skepticism was voiced by many leaders, and lay people in general. But everyone was interested in hearing more.

****** The Pentagon:

The original *Privacy Act* had been passed in 1967. The issue of privacy relative to the new threat of the *Information Age* had been widely heralded by civil libertarians, futurists, and just plain concerned citizens. When this first became an issue, the information gathered by various government and private agencies was considered privileged and private information, not to be shared beyond its legitimate and intended use. Gradually, obscured by esoteric rationale, government information began to be shared by other agencies. Sally Mae worked closely with the IRS. The NCIC data was shared with agencies only on the periphery of law enforcement. So it did not receive a great deal of attention when the Williams administration requested another seemingly mundane modification to the existing *Privacy Act* legislation. The provision for the full information sharing among government agencies for the purpose of *demographic research*, to be authorized on a limited basis by the President, was added to a standard debt refinancing bill. It was carried in both houses by voice vote. None of the *Hill Rats* had time to dig into the real purpose of this provision. They were all up to their armpits in the basic issues of survival. Incumbency had been dealt a body blow by the massive reduction in congressional staff funding. The First Family was after more than the reduction of deficit spending. The *New Way*, otherwise known as the Philip Roy Plan by *ABACUS* personnel, served them in many ways, some not intended.

It took only three weeks for the massive stream of personal data to begin flowing in from eleven major and dozens of minor data banks. The integration and conversion software had involved thirty programmers, working long hours, over a three month span. Included in the conversion were analyses which eliminated redundant data, flagged conflicts, and provided each citizen with two new numbers. One of the new codes was a person's political, economic, religious and educational profile. It was a coordinate system which placed each individual at a precise point in a multi-dimensional socio-economic space. In reality, it was a precise assessment of each person's political makeup, useful in predicting rather exactly how an individual would react to a range of government actions. The acronym for this interesting little piece of data was *SEX* (**S**ocio-**E**conomic Inde**X**).

The other number was a unique identification code which included the individual's Social Security Number, his name, and his SEX. This concise kernel of information had frightening implications, but nothing was done with this information *yet!*

****** **Tehran:**

The destruction of the Dome of the Rock was to be the Coup de Gras for the *Great One's* little band of very special forces. The destruction of the Central Mosque in Mecca would not be required, he was sure. The operation was risky because they had to deal with Israeli security and fairly massive amounts of explosives, but it was not the only aspect of risk for the Ayatollah and his regime. Two weeks prior to the event, large numbers of personal weapons were to be distributed to the peoples of Lebanon, Egypt, Jordan, and Syria, under the pretext of an imminent invasion by Israel. The risk, of course, was that the people would use the arms to free themselves of the puppet governments in each of these countries. The *Great One* counted on the natural animosity and the well planned propaganda campaign to direct the peoples' anger toward their ancient enemy.

The operation was to be executed on the first Friday in May, which would provide a very large number of casualties among the faithful. The explosives were moved to the local vicinity. Practice runs were made with the delivery vehicles and the false evidence of Israeli complicity was planted. A militant gang of Palestinians had been hired and trained for what they thought would be a takeover of Jerusalem, but was in actuality just the primary diversion to help ensure the real operation. The Ayatollah Malik Al Shafei contemplated the elaborate scheme he had personally devised with delight. In his daydreams, he imagined the violent reaction of the millions of faithful to the destruction of their sacred shrines.

His regular forces had been prepared with plans to move on Israel from all directions in a coordinated ground, air, and sea attack. The hated Israelis would not last six days. And the world would understand.

****** **Washington D.C.:**

The press conference agreed to by the First Lady was as big as the one following Grant Williams *New Way* pronouncement. The President himself was there on the stage, giving his wife all of the support his presence and the trappings of his high office could provide. But this was her show.

"Ladies and Gentlemen of the Press, Mrs. Williams will be taking your questions presently, but she would like to open with a prepared statement," announced Sheila Deana, Carrie's Press Secretary. "Copies of this statement will be available immediately after this press conference. Ladies and Gentlemen, Mrs. Carrie Witherington-Williams." People looked around to see if the Marine Band was there. Some would not have been surprised to hear them play *Hail to the Chief.* Carrie strode comfortably to the rostrum, notes in hand. Many who had known her for some time noticed a new and more subdued demeanor. The assembled mass sat in expectant silence, almost as if they were holding their breath. "Thank you, Sheila," the First Lady almost whispered. Everyone leaned forward, and strained to hear.

"As many of you have heard, I have experienced a supernatural revelation," she said, without smiling. It has changed my life, and is a source of great joy. I feel especially privileged to have received the *word.* I have shared the details of this revelation with only my husband. It is a very personal experience which I will always treasure. But I must act privately and publicly in response to the warnings which I believe are meant for all of us. I urge those of you who belong to a church or synagogue, but who haven't been serious about God, to begin going again, with a new sense of urgency. We will be hosting a special ecumenical council in Washington a week from Tuesday. We will be exploring how all of God's churches can be drawn into one powerful alliance to combat our drug situation, and pornography, and our gang violence. We must win our country back, we must return to our roots. We must remember who we are. I urge you all to pray for our nation, our President, and our church."

During the questioning, Carrie refused to reveal any details of her revelation, except a few of the warnings she had been given and which she had already outlined in her interview on TCNN. One intriguing question put to her evoked an interesting response. Barbara Cranston of TINN asked if she were starting a new church. "Absolutely not," she replied, "What we hope to do is to find that common high ground where we can all stand together and fight for what we all know is right." Some listeners felt that it sounded a bit practiced. The viewpoint that emerged from this interview was that Carrie was advocating the re-emphasis of family values. She railed against drugs, crime, abortion, and even the gays.

Almost overnight, the Williams' lost a large percentage of their former supporters, even as they gained substantial portions of the Christian Conservatives, and the so-called blue collar constituencies. Carrie's natural charm and becoming modesty converted millions of erstwhile enemies to instant disciples.   **No one was sure just what they were becoming disciples of, however.**

Chapter 10: THE WORLD AT WAR

****** United Nations Headquarters:

The Israeli Ambassador to the UN, together with his opposite numbers from Russia, the US, the UK, and France, demanded and got an emergency meeting of the UN Security Council. The press was especially alerted, and the security forces of most of the world powers were put on yellow alert. He had the attention of the world, and amazingly, there had been no leaks. The press had no idea what was about to be revealed.

The image of Mordicai Maroni appeared world-wide on most major networks. He appeared quite somber, and his message was dark. "Madam Secretary, Ladies and Gentlemen," he said quite deliberately. "It is my unfortunate task to apprise you of a crime so heinous and despicable, that you will at first have a great difficulty in believing. But bear with me," the Ambassador paused. "Agents of the Prime Minister of Iran, the Ayatollah Al Shafei, have been planning for some time now to desecrate the most cherished shrines of the Muslim faith, and to blame it on the nation of Israel."

Millions stopped whatever they might have been doing to give their full attention to this dreadful announcement. "First, let me assure you, that the Arabian government has been fully notified of the risk to the Central Mosque in Mecca, and our own forces have sealed off the sacred Mosque in Jerusalem. The four chief agents responsible for this planned atrocity have been arrested, and are under strict security. The proof we are about to show you was purchased with the lives of innocent people, and at the cost of our future intelligence.

But we felt compelled to prevent the destruction and death these terrorists were about to unleash." There was a pause while his media technicians began to display what at first appeared to be someone's home video.

The original sound was left undisturbed, but the video was supplemented with English, Spanish, and French text, translated as directly as possible. The first part of the tape was informal friendly banter, so the Ambassador felt no compunctions about speaking over the sound. "These tapes, Ladies and Gentlemen, were taken by a hidden camera placed in the Ayatollah's secret terrorist briefing room in the basement of his palace outside Tehran," he said. "They speak for themselves," he concluded, sitting back to listen and watch.

After only about five minutes of the tapes, the head representatives of all of the Ayatollah's puppet governments quietly slipped out of the chamber. They were mostly ashen faced. Some just seemed perplexed. None of them knew of this plot, but without exception, all of them knew that the *Great One* was fully capable of such a dastardly crime. The leaders were all on their telephones, demanding of their respective governments to know what was going on.

As the tape played on, there were gasps as the realization set in that the charges were almost certainly true. It was high drama, and the audience was riveted by the candid *home movies*. But these were men and women of action and were themselves a part of their respective governments. Their leaders would want to be speaking with them. After an hour, almost none of the members of the official delegations were present, but that absence was more than made up for by hundreds of radio and television stations which interrupted their regular schedule to broadcast these proceedings. Instant translations in dozens of languages were made, supplementing the original sound and the subscripted text.

In the empire of the Ayatollah, radio and television broadcasts were dutifully cut off as soon as the content was clear. The transmissions lasted just long enough to raise the question of some possible clandestine operation. Those with the wherewithal dialed into foreign short wave broadcasts, to hear the rest of the story. It was early afternoon in Tehran, and even earlier to the West. There was an unprecedented stirring all that afternoon, especially among the true Muslim clergy. Most of the foreign newspapers, blazing the story, were confiscated at the borders and at the airports. Enough got through, together with travelers returning from outside the countries, to confirm the story in the minds of most of the people. In the puppet states there had been a seething foment of discontent of being ruled by a foreign power, albeit a Muslim dictator. The Secret Police and the Secret Party were hated and feared as much as ever.

The next day the Israeli Ambassador dropped another bomb. In an afternoon interview, to follow up with the documentation of the evidence he had presented, he casually mentioned that their operatives, when they fled Iran, had just happened to take microfilm copies of the central personnel files of the Ayatollah's dreaded secret police, and the leading members of the new Secret Party. The names were all released as a *courtesy* to the Muslim world. Within hours these lists were posted in most of the larger cities of the

Muslim world. Within the week they were found in even the smallest of villages. The ayatollah's government virtually disappeared within a day or two. Many fled the country. Some committed suicide. Some were caught by the faithful and wished they had killed themselves.

The third day, martial law was declared in all of the Muslim countries formerly ruled by the puppet governments. Most of the tetrarchs had died at the hands of the people. The Ayatollah himself had disappeared. It was rumored that he had slipped out of the country in disguise. But the declaration of martial law could not confine the uprising of the people. With the millions of weapons just disbursed, the people were taking things into their own hands. These were moments to right old wrongs. Chaos abounded. The anarchy was so widespread, that most of the army units retreated to their armed compounds in a purely defensive posture.

The pictures broadcast by TINN were appalling. The whole Muslim world had gone mad it seemed. The secret agents were hunted down and beaten to death, or worse. Government icons were torn down or desecrated. The prisons were emptied; government warehouses were pillaged and sacked. Anything remotely connected with the hateful regime of the Ayatollah Al Shafei was put to the torch. The aftermath of this dramatic revelation by the Israeli government seemed to be an excuse for every ambitious gangster throughout all of the Near Eastern Muslim countries, from Algeria to and including Pakistan, to run amuck. It was estimated by the TINN staff reporters that over 12,000 people had been killed in the chaos, so far.

The fifth day after his explosive pronouncement, the Israeli Ambassador made the headlines again. During the special session called by the Secretary General to deal with the anarchy in Syria, Lebanon, Iraq, Iran, Saudi Arabia, and Jordan, the Ambassador committed his nation to funding a full 50% of the costs of bringing in United Nations Peacekeepers until order could be restored and provisional governments put in place. This act of overwhelming generosity was not altogether an act of philanthropy. The chaos threatened to spill over the borders into Israel, and no one was sure if one or more Arab leaders would not decide to blame all of this on Israel, somehow. The governments of all of the Muslim nations West of Israel, beginning with Egypt, had been able to contain the rioting, as were the governments of Pakistan, Afghanistan, Kazakhstan, and Tajikistan. Brazil, Mexico, India, China, and Japan sent large military contingents to Egypt for a few days of special training and outfitting. They were then assigned under UN command, as Peacekeepers.

The situation was mostly stabilized within four weeks. Very few of the Peacekeeper forces were lost and, under the able leadership of the Secretary General, provisional governments were set up with schedules certain for general elections. She declared the Peacekeepers would remain through those elections and the seating of democratically elected governments. It was the beginning of the emergence of the Peacekeepers as a strong arm of the United Nations which, for the first time in its existence, provided respect and admiration for this world body.

****** **Washington D.C.:**

The ecumenical council sponsored by the First Lady had met for a full day before the Muslim world burst into fitful chaos. This provided them a cause, a purpose, for a movement up to then based on the charisma of one woman. In the aftermath, the hurt and hunger would need to be addressed. Here was a chance for the Western (Christian) world to come together with the Eastern (Muslim) world. Carrie was delighted and she spent her considerable energies enlisting the cooperation of the many Protestant denominations, the Catholics, the Mormons, and all of the lesser churches, uniting them in this cause. She knew the *network* would work for her other purposes, but for now, it gave this new council, and her, the attention and high visibility she wanted.

The recipients were just as eager to be involved with this operation. Not only was there an enormous need for massive humanitarian aid, but by involving the Muslim clergy as brothers in this operation, the vehicle for the absolution of the clergy themselves was provided. And they needed absolution for they were silent partners of the *Great One*, sharing his power and glory, right up to the exposure of his heinous plot. No one raised any objections when the C-17s and aging C-5s were drafted to deliver all of the tonnage. "It helped when your husband was the Commander-In-Chief," Carrie had remarked to a confidant.

In a moment of reflection, Carrie thought of the fortuitous timing of the Muslim upheaval. *Does His influence extend that far,* she wondered.

Chapter 11: THE BROTHERHOOD

Another season had come and gone. Carrie was in great demand. She had become the favorite speaker at religious conferences. She very carefully avoided any detailed theology, stressing always, the Fatherhood of God and the Brotherhood of Men. "All men are brothers, children of God," she was fond of saying. Her favorite quotation was from the book of James, in the Holy Bible: "Religion that God our Father accepts as pure and faultless is this: to look after orphans and widows in their distress and to keep oneself from being polluted by the world." She supported all of the churches. In turn, her network grew. Their favorite causes became her favorite causes.

New legislation, lobbied for by the newly powerful religious community, enacted tough sanctions against crime, drug distribution, pornography, and child abuse of any kind. Churches and the clergy were given new tax advantages, and people were given special tax credits for charitable contributions, if given to those *qualified* institutions. Carrie herself monitored the qualifications and the validation of those institutions. Those institutions not in her network found it very difficult and frustrating to become qualified.

Over the year, Carrie sponsored other ecumenical councils. The theme of them all was the common brotherhood of men. She regularly referred to the *larger church of the brotherhood*. Carrie solicited funds from the faithful, being careful to ask for modest donations. Only nominal funds were raised, but her mail list was always growing. The money raised went for additional mailings.

****** **The Pentagon:**

At the Project, things were as busy as ever. It was no surprise to Jason or Brent that the inclusion of the massive personal data into the model only affected the fidelity in a very marginal way. Long before they had agreed that if the demographic profiles provided to the model were accurate, personal profiles were unnecessary. But of course, Carrie knew and accepted that as well. She had other things in mind for that aspect of the Project.

Brent and Jason were kept quite busy, constantly responding to the problems created by the *New Way* program. Privatization was theoretically an easy and straightforward process which invariably introduced market forces and accountability into any government agency. In reality, full free market forces were never allowed. Administrators always wanted to maintain the control they had always had, which control had usually led to the inefficiencies and cost and corruption which led to the need to privatize. The process was moving forward, however.

In the first year, the Postal Service, most of the functions of the Department of Agriculture, and various testbed educational systems were privatized successfully. Those savings would account for deficit spending reductions of 50 billion dollars annually. Importantly, hope had been restored to the people. The attitude that government had grown out of control had become widespread. Now the people began to participate in the process. The attitude toward government improved dramatically, as the deficit spending was cut by over $100 billion during the first year.

The effect of Carrie's *Great Revelation* also seemed to move the economy in a most beneficial way. People felt good about themselves and their country, and a return of the respectability of Biblical precepts seemed to revitalize the old Protestant work ethic. Productivity gains were substantial. Employee theft was significantly reduced. The highly litigious society was less so. As many of the HEW and HUD programs were cut back or eliminated, private charities, mostly churches, more than picked up the needs. The new tax credits and deductions for charitable giving were more than balanced by the reductions in entitlement program costs savings. On average, charitable redistribution was about four times as effective as the comparable government programs.

****** **The White House:**

It was in this framework that Grant and Carrie planned the campaign for his re-election. The question was not if he would be reelected; that was a given, considering the upswing in the economy, the new optimism, and the new constituency. The real issue was what vehicle they should use for reelection. Benign neglect had left the New Independent Party a mere shell, ready to collapse, unless they pumped it up again. Grant would be a shoo-in for the Republican nomination. For that matter, he just might pull off the nomination with the Democrats, although they had certainly alienated the liberal fringes. Threats to their lives had been received regularly since the New Way program and Carrie's announcement of her Great Revelation.

After a lot of behind the scenes negotiating, Carrie and Grant agreed to go with the Republicans, and at the same time, try to hold their following among the New Independents and conservative Democrats.

Grant announced his intentions at a well publicized press conference in November, a full year before the election. "Ladies and Gentlemen of the press," he announced, but his message was really for the rank and file and the leadership of the New Independents. "This has been a very gratifying past year and a half. We were slow getting off the ground, but we are now soaring, and have our sight on the clear air and warm sunlight above all of the dark clouds," he said. "Many things have changed over these past three years," he continued, "including Carrie and me." "We have learned that to affect a program, strong support in the Congress is required; having a mandate from the people is not enough." "We have found allies on both sides of the aisle and would not care to abandon any of our friends. The reality of politics is that we must join our forces if we are to achieve the high goals we have set for the nation."

He paused, looking around at the assembled press and his army of loyal sycophants, letting the suspense build. "After conferring with the leadership of the New Independent Party, Carrie and I have agreed with them to join our cause with that of the Republican Party." "I shall seek the Republican nomination for President of the United States of America. I appeal to our many supporters in the New Independent Party to join forces with us to help us carry forward the programs which you launched by thrusting us into this high office." No one in the room was surprised by the announcement, but Carrie and Grant had amazed the world so often over these past three years, that one could never be sure!

Mailings went out to all of their networks, including the lists from the New Independents, the Republican Party, the newly formed lists of the Church Of Brotherhood, and all of those peripheral semi-independent groups which had a propensity for support. Nothing would be left to chance. The Williams' campaign would even cooperate with their many sympathetic Democratic congressional candidates. And each group and sub-group would be sent specific pieces containing subtle nuances, by information content, implications, and by selective emphases. Carrie was concerned about their reelection, but an overwhelming electoral victory was only one of the objectives along the way to even greater ambitions.

****** **The Pentagon:**

Jason was planning another vacation. This time he would make it strictly domestic, and primarily to his old home, and his mother. Jamie, after the Jerusalem fiasco, would defer to his wishes. Jason had been wanting to confide with his mother just what was happening in Washington, as he understood it. He wanted her reaction to the morality of it all, and of his participation in the project. In preparation for his trip, he called for a hard copy dump of all the information available on her from all sources available through *ABACUS*. Jason, even though he well knew how they were connected to so many information bases, was surprised at the quantity and detail, and the sensitive nature of the dossier the system put together for him, on his mother.

****** **Points West:**

Jason and Jamie got an early start on their vacation, courtesy of the General. Mid-day Thursday, their flight left

Dulles for San Francisco. The 787 lifted off effortlessly, circled around toward the West, and proceeded to race the sun toward the Pacific Ocean. This would be a relaxing time for them; a time to get back to where they came from, in several ways. Jason would finally have time to take Jamie riding out across their old ranch in Smith Valley. They would be able to visit her parents in Solano Beach, and to let them get better acquainted with Jason. Jamie's dad was a Presbyterian minister and would want to know all about the First Lady's *great revelation* and her Church Of Brotherhood.

Jason didn't want to even think about his work, but he was quite interested in learning what people away from Washington and outside the government were thinking. They had just polished off the mini-meal described by the airline's literature as a gourmet dinner. Jason raised the arm rest between them and loosened his seat belt so that he could snuggle up to Jamie. He slipped his arm around her shoulder and gave her a quick little squeeze. "You know darling," he began. "This will be the first time since our honeymoon that we won't be returning to help solve some major crisis," he speculated. "Don't count on it," Jamie cautioned; "I'd feel more comfortable if the General didn't have our parents' phone numbers." "Well, the project is running smoothly, and Brent can handle any problems with the software as well as I," Jason said. Jason stopped himself from discussing anything about *ABACUS*, even in broad generalities; you could never know who might be listening.

They arrived at San Francisco in time to have a real dinner. Jason impressed his love by taking her to the Mark Hopkins hotel for dinner and then dancing. It was a wonderful beginning for what promised to be a true time of relaxing and re-creating.

The next morning, after sleeping late, they took the hop back to Reno, where Jason's mother, Mrs. Jack Phillips, had insisted on meeting them. That evening, after dinner, she asked for a full recap of everything that had been happening to them since their last visit, including their trip to Jerusalem. Neither of them mentioned their visit to the University, or about meeting Dr. Levanthol, or of the sister project they learned about. They described their visits to the Kibbutz and to all of the historical sites, and generally pronounced their trip a rousing success.

What his mother really wanted to find out about, they soon realized, was Carrie Witherington-Williams. Jamie described her visits to the White House and how the First Lady had befriended her, and how they had gone to church together, back in McLean. "Do you think she has really had a supernatural experience?" his mother asked. Jason and Jamie looked at one another for a moment, with a rather quizzical expression. They had discussed it, of course, but they had never really resolved it for themselves. Jason deferred to his wife. "We aren't really sure," Jamie said. "She seems to have changed in some way," Jamie continued. "There are coincidences which are hard to explain," interrupted Jason. "Things involving sensitive projects which I cannot talk about which make me believe that this may be just an act." "Well, you cannot fault the results of her conversion, if that is what she had," reasoned his mother. They went on to discuss the effect that Mrs. Carrie Witherington-Williams' revelation had on the nation. "I cannot understand what her motives might be, if this is just acting," his mother concluded. Jason paused a long moment, thinking about how Carrie's crusade had indeed helped facilitate the *New Way* program, and had enlarged the Williams' circle of admirers and supporters. And the nagging sense he had that someday the unprecedented accumulation of the massive personal data would be used in some nefarious political operation. "Well, I can think of some," Jason said, rather off-handedly, "but let's get on with what has been happening with you," Jason insisted.

***

Jason's younger sister Peggy had always worshipped Jamie and was even now finishing college with the objective of going into teaching, just as Jamie had done. Jason hated shopping, and when Jamie asked him, he happily volunteered his sister, which is what Jamie and Peggy wanted, anyway. It was the perfect opportunity for Jason to speak privately with his mother.

She had been his moral and spiritual mentor, and was wise, even beyond her years, about the world of politics. She had been active since before Jason could remember, serving briefly in the Nevada Assembly, as a legislator for her district. Her brother had been Governor of Nevada; she had served as his campaign manager. She had seriously considered running for the national congress, but gave it up in favor of providing a stable and comfortable home for Jason and his sister.

"Mom, I want to show you something," Jason said, as soon as he heard the girls drive away. He dug into his old briefcase and pulled out the dossier on his mother. It was 30 pages long. He handed it to her. "Look at this," he said.

140

She was amazed. She had seen classified reports on persons being screened for high security clearances, but this was more complete, and contained what was clearly very personal information. "How did you get this?" she said, showing her irritation at being investigated so thoroughly. "Is this a CIA report, or what?" she said. Jason sat down comfortably on the sofa opposite her. "Would you believe that the government has this much information on file about every citizen in the country?" he said. His mother looked perplexed. "Is this what you do?" she said, sounding disappointed.

Without telling her of the full nature of *ABACUS*, Jason explained how the recent legislation passed by the Congress had allowed the government to integrate all of the personal data bases both within and outside the government to produce a comprehensive dossier on every mother's child living or dead. He went on to explain the SEX code. He didn't need to spell out the implications. Her reaction was anger, mixed with disappointment that her son would be a part of such a scandalous activity. Jason explained that his responsibility had nothing to do with this massive new data base, and that his work had only to do with the development and operation of a massive socio-economic model.

Betty Phillips sat staring for many long moments. Jason waited patiently for her response. She was a handsome woman, even now, bronzed by the sun and hard work. She cared so much for so many. But mostly, she cared for Jason and Peggy, and now Jamie, and her country. Betty Phillips was fiercely patriotic. She had strong religious convictions and her feelings about God and Country were hard to separate. Finally, she turned toward Jason. Tears, which didn't come easily for this woman, had started to form, but remained in her eyes. "Jason, this is frightening," she said. "This looks absolutely Orwellian," she continued. "I'm sure you must understand the implications of this." "Who has been masterminding this?" she demanded.

"Would you believe Carrie Williams, herself?" Jason said. His mother was deeply shocked by this second revelation. She had supported Grant Williams in spite of his irreligious outlook. It had been with deep hope that she followed the *great revelation* and the apparent change of heart of both of the First Family. "When did she have all of this done?" she said, hoping somehow that this might have been done before her religious experience or "re-birth", as some described it. Jason understood the hope and the meaning behind the question. He paused, not wanting to devastate his mother further. But he knew the stuff she was made of and he knew she could handle the truth. This was why he had wanted to talk to her. She would know what to do. She had always known what to do, especially since the death of his father.

"This has been an on-going operation. Apparently it had been planned for some time, and even now is progressing on a high priority basis," he said. Another long silence. Thoughts and emotions were racing around in her mind. Had things gone too far, she asked herself. What possible reason would they have for doing this, she wondered. Grant William's reelection seemed assured, she knew they must know. "Jason, I am devastated, but I'm thankful you have told me about this," she said, finally. "Is there any way these files could be purged?" she said, smiling faintly.

"Watch them; keep me apprised of this, please," she said, deadly serious. "Can you arrange for a secure communication line for us?" she asked.

***

As an exercise in high-tech electronics, Jason had dabbled in experimental cryptographic techniques. He had set up his own unique scrambling device, used in conjunction with their home computer modem, and the portable unit he carried around with him at Berkeley. He had never bothered to pursue a patent on the process; things just got too busy. He was sure it still worked and he would dig out the old portable unit and take it back with him to McLean. He would add a new wrinkle, however. He had been tracking an intriguing project carried out by some graduate students at MIT, where they had successfully piggy-backed low volume graphics transmissions on TV bands over the relay satellites. This had the wonderful advantage that neither the sender nor the receiver could be located. He would tie a simple demodulator into the satellite dish, and into his mother's computer modem. Software would do the rest. Back at McLean, he would install a small transceiver dish in his attic, and they would be in business.

"Sure," Jason responded, knowing exactly how he could arrange it. The communication would be only one way, but phone connections could be made between public telephones available in nearby Reno, and Washington, respectively. Their phone conversations would sound rather innocuous, given the indirect references detailed over their secure link.

Before they left for the rest of their trip down to Southern California, Betty Phillips had another chance to discuss the matter with Jason. She advised him to watch for how the Williams' might use this tool against their political or personal enemies. She told him that she was going to surreptitiously begin a grassroots campaign to have the new law rescinded. Jason showed her his ingenious setup, explained it to her, and wrote out the procedures she needed to operate the device.

The time had evaporated so quickly, they didn't do half of the things they had expected and hoped to do on their vacation. But they enjoyed it all the more for being unstructured. Jamie grew closer to Jason's mother and sister, and understood better who Jason was, and why. The only surprises for her were pleasant ones. She would have to get back to them often, she resolved.

****** **The United Nations Headquarters:**
The Peacekeepers' operations were being successfully executed throughout the troubled spots of the world. Israel, rather than being the pariah they had been for so many years in the UN, had become the champion of the oppressed, the benefactor of most of the "third world" countries. The U.N. and the nation of Israel were giving hope to the hopeless, and were bringing peace to those constantly ravaged by war. The years of worldwide recession were ebbing now, and with new hope, commerce was flowing at an accelerating rate. The *New Age* was taking on a new meaning among the community

of nations, and Israel, and her charismatic Prime Minister, Avery Harrington, were at the focus of the activities.

Few knew that the current and most successful Secretary General, Mrs. Anteres Jandi, of India, was a close ally and former protégé of Mr. Harrington. As it had been developing over the past few years, many of his supporters and friends were becoming prominent and were being placed in positions of power throughout the world. Those he had recruited in earlier years had been faithful and deeply committed to Mr. Harrington and *the cause*. The great wheels of government and commerce were moving inexorably into position like so many planets spinning in their courses, destined for a final and cataclysmic event, known only to the mysterious Mr. Harrington.

****** **The White House:**
Pillow talk at the White House was like none heard anywhere else. Grant Williams had just kissed his wife and then turned over on his side to go to sleep. It had been a long day, and sex was very low on his list of priorities just now. Carrie wasn't interested either, but rather, wanted to plant an idea into Grant's mind. "Darling," she began, raising her voice at the end, telling him that this was a question, or more probably a rhetorical question. "Are you enjoying being President?" she said. "What kind of a question is that?" he responded, irritated that she would not let him go to sleep. She rolled over, next to him and pulled herself up to his back, and put her arm around his chest. "I am so proud of you," she said. "You know the programs we have launched have changed the course of history in such a positive way." "In another term, you will have this country back into full

prosperity," she said.   Grant just waited, knowing he would have to hear her out before he could finally doze off.   "But you could do more, if they would just give you time."   "Your rightful place in history is to lead this country into the United Federation of Nations, you know," she concluded.

She had said what she wanted.   She would tell him the rest of the plan when he was ready.   She would bide her time. Her dream had always been to be a major force in the formation of a true World Government.   For this cause she had changed her major studies in college; for this cause she had sought out and married this man; for this cause she would do whatever she had to do for the one man she truly loved. Meanwhile, the reelection campaign was moving into high gear.   Nothing had been left to chance, and with the opinion polls favoring Grant Williams by 70% to 30%, plans were unfolding quite on schedule.

The bigger battle, she was even now concerned with, was how to get her man reelected a second time (the Twenty Second Amendment, notwithstanding).   The repeal of this amendment would be a landmark achievement of her career. She would need powerful friends and powerful forces.   She was about ready to exercise one of her tools, the wonderful *ABACUS*, operated so successfully by one of her friends, down deep in the Pentagon.   There were a gaggle of Western Senators who were raising questions about the tinkering the administration had done with the Privacy Act amendments. She never had cause to dislike or target any of these four Senators involved with this issue, but politics allowed one to turn on friends if it was required, she always knew.   This was one of those times.   The next day she would order up a full dossier on each of these four Senators, and would dig as deeply as was required to find an *Achilles heel* of each of them. *ABACUS* could do that because if there were nothing visible in a person's files, the system could search the subject's complete personal network until some useful dark information surfaced. Carrie fell asleep delighting in the thoughts of the interesting challenge she had set out for herself for the next few days and weeks.

****** The Pentagon:

George Steinman himself was required to execute the special task Carrie Williams had for *ABACUS*. Senator Tom Crzynski of Arizona, a Democrat, was the first target. Long pages of personal information were provided by the initial direct inquiry. Nothing there, at least on the surface. His ties with the Phoenix Bank would warrant further research. Next, his immediate family was checked. A possible conflict of interest involving the Senator's work on the Armed Forces Committee, and a San Diego firm, partly owned by his brother, looked promising. The Senator's wife's uncle had once been indicted by a grand jury, but had been exonerated. He noted that for deeper research. Bingo! The Senator's senior female staffer had gone to Mexico for an abortion about six years ago. No word on the father. All a sympathetic press would need would be an innuendo. But the search continued, because Carrie wanted to really nail this man.

In her own mind, the Senator from Arizona wasn't really a threat. He could be recruited, actually, if she wanted to bother. But here was a perfect opportunity for her to test out some of her weapons. They weren't concerned about the coming election in the fall, but later battles would require all of the political muscle she could muster. This would be good practice. A chance to sharpen the technique, she told herself.

The sifting through the mass of personal data continued. George found a psychotic aunt and a suicidal brother-in-law. The systematic examination of every contributor to the Senator's campaign funds revealed several crime connections and unsavory characters connected to extremists of every stripe. The Senator's school, military, and business records were cross-checked, closely scrutinized, and painfully detailed. His political career was totally documented, including every public utterance on all subjects. Inconsistencies were carefully listed and each one was analyzed as to the potential political damage it might inflict. A special tax analysis program examined his returns from as long as twelve years earlier, looking for items outside the norm, possible unreported income, questionable deductions, and the use of dodges. In all, over 200 persons connected to the Senator were checked. Every major purchase made by the Senator's family, including trivia such as their choice of rental videos, was reported. The hard copy stacked almost a foot high. And this was before the manual investigations were compiled.

The best of the dirt was thoroughly documented and fed anonymously to the Senator's arch rival, the Republican nominee for his seat. The candidate would know what to do.

This was too much for even George Steinman to stomach. He confronted Carrie on the issue. He demanded to know what right anyone had to use *ABACUS* for such character assassination and negative campaigning. Carrie had anticipated this possibility and was prepared. She could either recruit him to *the cause* or have him assassinated, which action was reserved for only the most dire circumstances. Harrington himself would have to authorize such drastic action.

Carrie put him off until the next afternoon. She arranged for the Presidential yacht to be quietly brought to a public docking facility on the Potomac. Carrie told Grant she was going to be instructing George in last minute campaign work, and needed the security. Grant flushed slightly when she told him. He truly did care for this beautiful woman and was always a little jealous when she announced private meetings with single men. He made sure there was extra crew on duty.

The salt spray, and the lapping water, and the broad horizon seemed to focus any conversation. There, out on the open sea, where the landscape was simply the wind and waves, the rest of the world was something apart. "George, I have been waiting for the right opportunity to share something very special with you," she began, after they had been served lunch and drinks. (The crew was quite out of hearing.) "What I am about to share with you is known by only a handful of world leaders.

"Even the President, my own husband, does not know what I am about to tell you," she said. She paused, trying to read his face, and wondering if, in fact, it would cost this man his life. George only sat there, rather stone faced and cold. As he was still determined that she would know of his unhappiness over what she was apparently doing.

Carrie told him of her dream, the **cause** which she had dedicated her life to, and for which she had been working since before she graduated from college. With great passion and deep sincerity she laid out the great goals of *the cause*, and the leader, the great Mr. Avery Harrington. World peace and unprecedented prosperity were the goals for which they all were striving. And a true world democracy where people everywhere could live in at least a modicum of prosperity and without fear, and were free to develop their own highest potential. The Final World Order. Carrie outlined the steps the movement was now taking, and how the preparations had been carried out over the past 20 years. Many inexplicable and seemingly disconnected recent events were brought into focus for him, and explained in the context of *their* overall plans.

George Steinman was amazed. He thought he had known this strange and mysterious and beautiful woman. He had always been spellbound by her, not knowing why, but this revelation shook him to his core. Of course he wanted to be included.

As a proof of what and who they were, Carrie told George of the plan they were executing to control most of the world's food supply, and described a major resolution about to be brought before the United Nations, and supported by Israel and several third-world countries. It would be proposed and accepted that The United Nations would sponsor, oversee, market, and distribute certain basic crops throughout much of the third world.

***

During the following weeks, George Steinman followed the newscasts with special interest as he saw the events unfold exactly as Carrie described they would. It had been represented that this was a stopgap measure to help those countries toward self-sufficiency, when in reality it developed a strong dependency upon the U.N. The actuality of what was happening brought a cold shiver over his whole body. And all this, known to so few! He indeed felt highly privileged to be included. *The cause* would seldom ever be spoken of between them again, nor would he ever speak to anyone else of this. But his life was elevated to a new plane, he felt, and the excitement of being part of such great power drove him as no cause religious, or of nationalism, or even of the Corps had. George understood that his inclusion was due entirely to the power and utility of his project. And such wonderful ends would justify any means!

Having enlisted George Steinman to *the cause*, Carrie Williams felt relieved from the potential damage which could be suffered if the special operations being ordered by her at *ABACUS* were made known to the public. What she didn't know was that Jason had arranged with Max McGurn to regularly report all of the personal inquiries made of the system. Dr. McGurn set up a special high security code for Jason's exclusive use. It did not occur to the General that The System Manager operated on the very *highest* priority, and could monitor anything going on inside the system. Jason, in turn, passed on all of the relevant data to his operative in Nevada via his special secure link. What she would do with the data was a point of special concern to Jason, as it might give away the leak. Jason had pointed this out to her, although she was quite astute enough to recognize the risks. For now, she would wait to see what Carrie Williams full plans were, before acting overtly. *There must be some larger plan,* she thought.

The rescission of the Twenty Second Amendment to The Constitution of The United States of America would be the crowning achievement for Carrie Witherington-Williams, at least for this phase of her career. The larger goal was to lead the country gracefully into the Great Confederation of Sovereign States (the new name planned for The United Nations). But of course the sovereignty would soon give way to privileged membership, then to equality of all members, then to complete subordination. But this was another phase of the master plan of *the cause.* How to get her husband reelected was the problem to which she would devote most of her energy in the coming four years.

The Williams' were riding a high crest, what with the rebounding economy, the new feeling of patriotism, and the re-emergence of traditional values. Her network extended out into the state legislatures, most of the Governors, and many of the higher courts. It was entirely possible to ram through an amendment, in spite of the torturous procedures required. Carrie had been very careful not to let Grant endorse any of the term limitation legislation or initiatives, looking forward to the day when she would need to somehow extend Grant's term. This was not for her, she kept reminding herself, nor was it for Grant. It was for *the cause,* the sacred quest she had pledged her life to uphold and forward above all other objectives.

The network was established, the timing was somewhat propitious. The political credits were piling up, all due and payable. It was like money in the bank. What was missing was *the cause supreme*. Some imperative would be required. Some special reason to keep the present administration in power must be in place, if the rescission were to succeed. Some threat to the very existence of the United States of America, real or imagined, must be developed at just the right time. Carrie knew that something equivalent to a world war must provide the compelling rationale to change the rules of presidential terms.

Some political credits must be preserved for the election itself. They could not all be spent forcing the amendment through Congress and three quarters of the state legislatures. The *cause* itself could be the driving rationale, she knew, but the world was not ready for that yet, she thought. Carrie knew that she alone must provide the circumstances, perhaps with the help of her great patron and mentor. Grant would never know. He would be told what to do and how to respond to the crisis when it was manufactured. He knew that was his role. He had accepted it many years before. He had gotten pretty far letting Carrie call the major shots. Why change strategy when you are on a great winning parlay.

The planning and execution of this program gave Carrie the challenge she had been burning for. Manipulating Grant, and even the Congress of The United States, was not that much of a challenge, she had concluded. But the successful introduction and passage of a constitutional amendment was worthy of her best efforts.

One of the decisions she must make, relative to the amendment, was whether or not to use *ABACUS* to validate her plan. If she decided to do this, security would be a potential problem. She decided that she must risk it. She would depend on George to see to the security. It would be his first assignment for *the cause*, she would make him understand. And not being very trusting, she would review the procedures.

***

In a moment of reverie, Carrie sat back in one of her favorite easy chairs in her outer office. The office overlooked a part of the Rose Garden, and the view included a part of the Northwest quadrant of the city. She could just glimpse a sliver of the Potomac. She hated her inner office, which had no windows, but was equipped with some of the finest communications equipment available, and afforded the utmost security. A permanent part of the electronics was a supersensitive device which could even detect passive receivers!

Her afternoon calendar was clear. There was nothing pressing to be done until dinner and an evening planned for Lincoln Center. Carrie reviewed the events of the last five years.

***

The elections had been a miracle, of sorts. She had often wondered about the extent of the involvement by Avery. There had seemed to be a constant and almost orchestrated standoff between the candidates of the two major parties.

154

They rather ignored Grant Williams. In fact both of the other candidates had nice things to say about Grant until the polls alerted them to the fact that he was emerging as the front runner. Even then, they had held their fire, always wanting to somehow capture that independent vote which was credited to Grant Williams. So in the end, Grant won. Perhaps it was a fluke, but staying in power would not be, she reassured herself.

No one knew how high her ambitions were, or why. She had led a lonely life, albeit an exciting one. Three people had shaped her life, although no one would ever characterize her as malleable. Her mother had a strong influence on her personal values, and her religious beliefs. Her mother had been Jewish Orthodox, tending toward agnosticism. She had railed and militated against war from as early as Carrie could remember. Many of her mother's family were lost in World War II. They were either murdered outright, or sent to one of the many hellholes euphemistically called concentration camps. Carrie was made acutely aware of all of the atrocities, even at a tender age. Her mother considered it to be a vital part of her education. As a sub-teen, Carrie had decided she would be in politics and would somehow help eradicate war as an instrument of national policy.

Carrie's father was an outstanding career diplomat, achieving the highest office a career person could ever achieve, Ambassador to The Court of Saint James, otherwise known as The American Ambassador to Great Britain. Usually that assignment and most of the plum positions went to major contributors to the winning party. Of course the influence of Carrie's mother's family in Great Britain may have had a little to do with his appointment. Her mother's family included several of the wealthiest bankers in England.

Her father also strongly influenced her personal values and shaped her plans and dreams. The regular travels and the wide exposure to all strata of so many cultures gave Carrie an education no amount of library research or expository lectures could ever provide. An only child, Carrie was treated as an adult at a rather early age, and carried the responsibility well. She had accompanied her father to the White House, to #10 Downing Street, and a dozen other executive mansions around Europe and The Mediterranean. Her father was a-religious, if you had to categorize him. He often took Carrie to religious services, but she knew that it was only ceremony, associated with his job, and not a thing he would have done otherwise. He neither scorned nor praised the clergy in their private discussions. He just didn't seem to care.

The third person in her life had more influence on her values, her schooling, and her career than her parents had. She remembered their first meeting. All her life she had been remembering their first meeting. It was in 1998.

Carrie was 18, but she had the poise, the maturity, and the self-assurance of a successful career woman. She had won the right to take part in the Model United Nations, sponsored by the U.N. itself. She was the Delegation Chairwoman for England, even though she was an American. Her British colleagues thought that was a wonderful gesture of Anglo-American solidarity, and a careful check of the rules assured them it was perfectly legal. The Model U.N. was only open to seniors in *prep* schools.

She was seated on the plane, on the way to New York, when she met Avery Harrington. The whole delegation of students (eight) were very proud of the fact that their own Honorable Avery Harrington was to be the Principal Advisor for the whole conference. Shortly after the plane had leveled off to the cruise altitude, he came back from his first class accommodations to introduce himself to his country's delegates. The delegates had been chattering about the trip and their plans, and the excitement of it all. A silence had come upon the girls she had been talking with, so she naturally looked up to see what it was that had captured their attention so abruptly. He was looking directly at her, and he kept his gaze directly into her eyes. Carrie blushed, and her heart literally skipped a beat. He was indeed the most handsome man she had ever seen. "Miss Carrie Witherington." he said, not as a question, but a statement of fact. "Please allow me to introduce myself," he said, pausing, but not taking his gaze from her eyes. "I am Avery Harrington." She had no idea what he said after that. But she knew then that if it were possible, she wanted as much attention from this man as she could get. And as delegation chair, she would find ample opportunity to see the Senior Advisor on all kinds of matters, procedural, and otherwise.

She remembered that during the model session, she had never had the opportunity to be alone with this handsome, intriguing, and exciting man. But she knew that he was attracted to her. So it was with great excitement that she accepted a special invitation to be a house guest at the Aaronberg estate in upstate New York, after the convention. Mr. Aaronberg had been a political Ambassador to Italy, and was a long time friend of Carrie's family.   As chance would have it, they were also long time acquaintances of Mr. Avery Harrington.

Carrie felt especially close to Avery. There was, in her mind, an inevitable union of two spirits who melded in mind and soul. The two had spent almost their complete time together, even as they traveled to the estate.   Avery described his vision, and *the cause*. He intended to work toward a legitimate and lasting world government which would eliminate war, and poverty, if not jealousy and hatred. His dream was something she shared immediately, as it was also hers.   If the magnetic attraction had not been there, it would have been enough to join their common cause.   She often remembered the tenderness and the excitement, and the longing that the memory of their time together would generate over the years.

Carrie had communicated with him regularly since that time.   It was rather as a matter-of-fact that he mentioned his wife.   It was as though it didn't matter.   Carrie might never be his lover, but of course she would never <u>not</u> be, in her mind. What they shared transcended the comforts of domestic married life.   He was, in a very practical sense, her god. Over the years she had met many other followers of this great man and there was, quite surprisingly, very little jealousy between his followers.   **There seemed to be enough power in this man to charge everybody's batteries.**

Chapter 12: THE ASSASSINATION

****** **Smith Valley, Nevada:**

Betty Phillips enjoyed being back into politics. She would have preferred a strong, positive, and public role, instead of the clandestine, defensive role she had to play. She had carefully saved all of the many communiqués that Jason had sent. She had especially sorted out the huge volume of reports being generated relative to her old acquaintance, the senior senator from Arizona, Tom Crzynski. He hadn't been a particular ally in years past, nor did she much agree with him philosophically, but he was a decent sort. It seemed that the Williams administration had targeted him for political assassination. So his was a test case for two women, the one running the White House, and an anonymous lady in Nevada. The only advantage Betty Phillips had was her anonymity, and a certain highly qualified computer person in Washington.

The possibilities were many. One strategy was to simply pass this data to the Senator, perhaps anonymously, and let him defend himself. At least he could be warned that the attack was coming. Another possibility was the prospect of having Jason produce a comparable dossier on the senator's opposition, which the senator could then use as barter with his opponent, hoping for a truce, and an agreement by both not to use the material on each other. This involved some risk to Jason and exposure of her source, and besides, the material might just be leaked to the press directly. Underlying all of these considerations was the realization that the character assassination of the senator was only one possible skirmish; a larger battle might well be looming.

Betty Phillips remained ignorant of why Carrie Williams was after Tom Crzynski. One possibility she could infer from public press coverage was that Carrie was concerned about the threat he presented by his very public dissent regarding the modifications to *The Privacy Act*. Other possibilities were that he was an opportune target to use in order to sharpen her new assassination tool, or that there was some kind of personal animosity between them, or some combination of the above. She was nearer a completely correct analysis than she might have guessed. In the end, she decided to maintain her anonymity, to preserve the source of her inside information, and wait to see what Carrie Williams' larger plans were, if she could. Meanwhile, she urged Jason to be alert for that larger plan, and to maintain their security.

****** **Phoenix, Arizona:**

The *Phoenix Mail* was new in the state and was struggling. The common wisdom was that the city, even the State, was not big enough for another daily. But the editor, Sarah Browning, a young woman of immense talent and even greater ambition, would not give up easily. When a very large package was delivered personally by the campaign manager of the Senator's chief rival, she saw the makings of a major turn in her paper's future. The package was left for her perusal; she had their phone number.

The implications were as great as her imagination could stretch. Very little hard evidence, but a great abundance of innuendo. Sarah spread the documents out over her conference table, carefully grouping the piles into obvious categories. She called her publisher, to get official permission to do what she knew it was her choice to do anyway. Then she called her top level staff of editors and writers in to plan with her how to supervise the destruction of a political career.

The legal staff outlined the careful limits they must apply to the presentation of the material. The apparent underworld connections seemed the most lucrative possibility, so the Friday Evening edition opened with a full page spread, showing photos and excerpts from government documents. Two extra printings were required. New subscriptions tripled the usual rate over the next week.

The Senator denied it all. Adequate chance to defend himself was made available, of course. But the operative word was *defend*. The whole strategy of the campaign was changed, and with the natural advantage of a rather conservative constituency and the image of an anti-administration detractor, the incumbency factor was more than overcome. Carrie observed it all with the glee of a young girl watching two suitors fighting over her affections. In the process, she wrote notes for herself about what worked and what didn't. It was a wonderful laboratory.

****** **The United Nations Headquarters:**
The influence and popularity of the U.N. had been growing steadily since the successful peacekeeping operation which controlled the breakdown of order in the Middle East and the dramatic reduction in international drug trafficking, courtesy the U.N. Ocean Guard. Under U.N. auspices, Israel had begun to help developing countries through special trade and management arrangements whereby third world countries

were given, under supervision, the wherewithal to improve their industry and their agriculture. The U.N. managed the operations and Israel provided the resources and the markets for their products. The great thing for the Israelis was that they also turned a profit.

The budget requirements for the U.N. were growing with its size, but were largely carried by the client states. The United Nations, under the able leadership of Madam Secretary General Jandi, had successfully negotiated the former SSR satellites out of their atomic weapons stockpiles. While keeping the peace in the recent Middle East debacle, the U.N. forces had carefully seized all of the elements of atomic warfare in those countries, and had destroyed the research facilities which supported the development. In return, the U.N. had voluntarily committed to protect those nations, and to monitor and assist the development of their democratic institutions.

China, France, England, the United States, Russia, India, Pakistan, Iran, Indonesia, North Korea, and of course Israel, remained in the atomic club. Complete elimination of all atomic weapons was the stated goal of the Secretary-General, but that would take some doing, indeed. Meanwhile, special strike forces in the United States, India, England, and Israel, were put under U.N. command. It would now be possible for the U.N. to authorize actual combat operations, as part of the peacekeeping role which they were assuming from the U.S., and from NATO, which had become a mere shell.

Small dictators were not pleased with developments. The community of nations finally had some force behind their rhetoric. The time of the United Nations had finally arrived. Far from a debating society, the institute had become the viable political, economic, and military force many had hoped for from its inception. Behind all of these operations was the quiet, anonymous influence of *the cause*.

****** **Washington D.C.:**

The Republican National Convention was held in St. Louis, and was orchestrated as a love-in on behalf of Carrie and Grant Williams. The occasion was a swirling madcap party, with the only drama being provided by the question of whether the Williams' would keep old Harry Lipscombe on the ticket. Carrie's lack of fondness for him was broadly known. They had seriously considered bringing in the young moderate Governor of California, as a means of expanding their influence in the Democratic Party, but Carrie was afraid of upsetting the delicate balance of the strange coalition they had put together. Besides, good old Harry could be a formidable enemy, if not a very powerful ally.

Election night was another wild celebration. The economy was recovering strongly, even as the cost of government had been yielding to the major surgery that was privatization.
Never before had a single candidate garnered all of the electoral votes. Wisconsin and Massachusetts had been very close, but the final count gave it all to Grant Williams and Harry Lipscombe. The long coattails swept in additional Republican Senators, to give them an overpowering 72 to 28 majority. For the second time in 12 years, the Republicans even gained direct control of The House. Counting on supportive Democrats and Independents, Carrie counted a 68

vote majority. The network grew in the process, and through
it all, the Williams' continued to pile up political credits.
Even some of the Democrat leaders were neutralized by tacit
but well understood agreements to not bring them under the
withering fire of the Williams' machine, which had become a
modern juggernaut. The light at the end of the tunnel was
clearly a train; **but where was it going?**

Carrie had toyed with the idea of having Grant use the
occasion of his nomination acceptance speech to introduce
certain ideas regarding the transfer of at least part of the
atomic stockpile to the United Nations, but she wanted to first
stake out an absolute hold on the office of the presidency. So
she planted the seeds in his inaugural speech. There would be
greater press coverage and, of course, the great weight of
office to give the ideas more credibility.

****** **The Pentagon:**
An always difficult problem for even this model was
the accurate prediction of the acceptability of foreign policy,
especially when the sovereignty of the country was at stake.
Part of the plan of *the cause* was to build the United Nations
into the strongest military power in existence. The essential
first step was to be the establishment of a viable Peacekeeping
Force. The next step was to destroy all atomic weapons.
Major strides had been made in this direction. If the United
States could be coaxed into giving up its atomic arsenal, the
rest of the world would capitulate, it was thought. But The
U.S. would not do this, it was clear, unless there were a
simultaneous and well monitored disarmament by all of the
other club members.

One of the most elaborate set of simulations ever run on *ABACUS* helped to set the policy proposals the President was about to make in his inaugural address. The model had shown that if the process were done quite gradually, and with sufficient safeguards, the American public would not only accept the idea, but would largely embrace it as part of the *New Way* program. With only the Chinese as possible bogeymen, and the recent demonstrations of the effectiveness of the latest star-war gadgets, almost no one was in favor of a strong military anymore, or of the role of world policeman by the United States.

****** **The Steps of the Capitol:**

It was as good a day in Washington as the season could expect to deliver. The cold crisp morning had brought out the overcoats early, but most were shed by mid-day. In his mind Grant was comparing this, his second inaugural address, with Lincoln's second inaugural address. The war was over; they had won. Now was a time to reach out "with malice toward none," he thought. Carrie had no such imaginings. For her, the battle was just about to be joined. In the end, a little of what Grant insisted on was left in his speech. He could enhance his image as statesman, and then build on that.

The prayers had been said, the bands had played, and the Chief Justice of The Supreme Court of the United States had administered the oath. It was Grant's time. This would be a *defining time in history* for him and the country, Carrie had assured him. He felt up to the challenge, and was ready to deliver.

"Mr. Chief Justice, distinguished Members of Congress, distinguished Secretaries and Ambassadors, honored guests, my fellow Americans," Grant began. Carrie was pleased. Grant was in command and sounded strong for the task. She smiled reassuringly for him.

"An amazing set of circumstances has brought us to where we are today. The collapse of the Communist ideology was impossible to predict. The great world depression which began 8 years ago was unprecedented and largely unforeseen. Our recovery has been nothing short of miraculous (strong sustained applause)." Here Grant paused. At this point he could take a lot of personal credit, but he truly wanted to be magnanimous. Grant gestured broadly toward the large group of political leaders seated just below the speakers' platform, as he said: "Our recovery from the abyss of downwardly spiraling stagnation required the cooperation of all parties, leaders and workers from the Democrats, the Republicans, and Independents of all stripes (roaring applause and foot stamping)." "You have all been Americans!"

"The blight of economic paralysis is over; this occasion marks a new dawning." "God has truly blessed this country and the world, and we have given the government back to the people!" (Thunderous and sustained applause). "Today marks the beginning of a new era; the night is over, and we can live in the sunlight of true world peace and universal prosperity." "This is within our grasp; we must seize the moment." (Polite applause). Grant paused while he turned the pages of his notes before continuing: "Within just a few short years, if we are willing to dedicate ourselves, and to make the sacrifices and do the difficult work, poverty and war

166

can be fully and finally eliminated from this earth (heavy applause)."

"Only a handful of nations still carry atomic arsenals. These archaic vestiges of a cold war long forgotten should be systematically and in an orderly, well-monitored procedure, reduced to zero!" The raucous applause following this statement had been well orchestrated. Carrie had primed the elite members of her young *Brotherhood of Men*. She had them scattered throughout the assembly, in groups of no more than 20, and had instructed them to mute their responses until they heard the phrase "reduced to zero". So with this 'spontaneous' burst, and the crowd's natural propensity to reinforce any approval, it appeared to many that this phrase somehow had struck a particularly responsive chord. That crowd 'response' actually shaped much of the coverage of the speech and colored the attitude of many millions who heard it that day.

Grant continued after letting the demonstration run its course: "But while anyone anywhere is poor, we are poor; while anyone anywhere is oppressed, we are oppressed!" The applause that followed was a perfect echo of the previous demonstration, which was long enough that the network commentators felt obliged to fill the space with mindless observations, emphasizing the obvious.

"It is truly the time for a new world order, where all men are brothers, and all men are free." (Applause). "I shall propose to the new Congress that the last four of our carriers be taken out of moth balls and consigned to the United Nations Ocean Guard. Our standing conventional forces should be reduced by 50% over the next four years. Our nuclear forces should stand down indefinitely pending the final atomic treaty (FAT) ratification by all of the remaining atomic powers." "These savings, taken together, will reduce our lingering national debt by $400 billion over the next four years!" (Strong applause) "I shall propose and I shall insist on a comprehensive balanced budget amendment!" (Applause) "And, after considerable analysis and consultation, I may propose that the American dollar again be backed by gold!" (Strong applause).

Grant paused for a sip of water and again shuffled his notes. He was carefully following her detailed coaching, Carrie was pleased to see. Grant continued: "On our domestic agenda, we shall continue to privatize every function of government which is amenable to the process, and we shall continue to try to foster greater productivity and innovation through tax incentives and government grants. Fusion plants should be providing over half of our growing energy needs within the term of this administration." (Polite applause). "The continued redevelopment of our transportation systems is a high priority. Productivity gains suggest that this is one of the best investments we can make."

***

Grant Williams went on for too long, as politicians are wont to do. Eventually he ended, going back to the high points of his speech: "And finally, my fellow Americans, we must all dedicate ourselves to this proposition, that all men everywhere should be free, and the work so nobly begun shall not fail". The obvious allusion to the Lincolnesque style was his master stroke, as far as he was concerned. Carrie had been annoyed when he insisted on using that ending, but the important seeds had been planted, and **she would see that these seeds were well watered and cultivated.**

END OF PART III

PART IV
THE WORLD AT RISK

"I heard, but I did not understand.   So I asked, 'My Lord, what will the outcome of all this be?'   "He replied, 'Go your way, Daniel, because the words are closed up and sealed until the **time of the end**. Many will be purified, made spotless and refined, but the wicked will continue to be wicked. None of the wicked will understand, but those who are wise will understand."
The Holy Bible

Chapter 13: THE BATTLE JOINED

****** **The White House:**

The *cause célèbre* was to be the achievement of FAT (final atomic treaty). If things played out as Carrie wanted them orchestrated, the carrot of world cleansing from atomic weapons was to be just out of reach. It was to appear to be beyond grasp within the second Williams administration. That would be the compelling rationale behind extending the administration into a third term. Carrie sat in her inner private office, contemplating the possibilities. She believed in it herself, and if there was ever going to be an occasion to overcome this term limitation thing, she had the golden opportunity. She would carefully avoid any overt action in this matter. It must be obvious to all and spontaneously forwarded by others.

To see that it would eventuate as she wished, she would enlist the sympathies of the religious portion of her greater network. She must somehow lead the religious leaders in the country to demand Grant Williams' continuation in office for the high cause of atomic-free peace and prosperity.

To do this, Carrie invested most of her waking hours during the first six months of this second term dealing personally with the leadership of the whole spectrum of the American clergy. A typical operation would find a highly placed Catholic, an Episcopalian, a Lutheran, a Baptist, and one or two representatives from fringe groups visiting the White House. After the full V.I.P. tour, including a visit to the Oval Office and Lunch, she would bombard her charmed visitors with pleas to urge their congregations to support, yea demand that Grant Williams be allowed to bring this great plan for world peace to full fruition. She knew that if the timing were right, this would obviously require that third term. The people would demand it.

At the risk of overheating the economy, Carrie insisted that her friends on the Federal Reserve Board keep the money supply up, and interest rates down. Things were falling into place. Without her knowledge or encouragement, but with her great blessings, the *Washington Post* featured an article about FAT and noted the time schedule projected by the administration. They brought out the idea of the rescission of the Twenty-Second Amendment. She would note very carefully the response to the suggestion.

****** **Smith Valley, Nevada:**
Betty Phillips had been in awe of the Williams', as they demonstrated a *tour de force* as they ran a textbook campaign, winning the unprecedented unanimous vote in the Electoral College. But she sensed that the development of their mighty political machine was designed for more than the reelection of Grant Williams. Hearing the inaugural speech provided her with the insight as to what this greater cause must be. It was hard to be against such a noble cause as world peace and the high goal of the FAT, but she was. The gradual erosion of the sovereignty of the United States in favor of the United Nations and the several trade pacts had been concerning her for years. The puzzlement for her was whether the Williams' had empire on their agenda or were they, as she suspected, **part of a larger conspiracy.**

****** **The Pentagon:**

Jason checked the *ABACUS* Special Status File for the third time that day. There was nothing unusual. He was becoming almost paranoid about being discovered spying on the First Family. He was especially concerned about his boss, George Steinman, because the evidence was indicating that he was a willing accomplice.

"Mr. Phillips," interrupted his secretary. "Call on line 3," she said, without waiting for an answer. The voice on the other end of the line was his mother. She had never before called him at his office, so he was sensitive about some possible emergency. "Jason, I need to come and visit you and Jamie; it's about your Aunt Jane. She has an important business proposition about the ranch. You need to hear about it. She and I will be flying out on the *red eye* tonight; Flight 272 arriving at Dulles at 7:40 tomorrow morning. Hope this isn't too inconvenient for you," she concluded.

"Great, Mom," Jason enthused. He had many times reminded her that all of the calls to and from *ABACUS* were routinely recorded and/or monitored. *This must be important*, he kept thinking. "No problem; we'll both be there to pick you up. It will be great to see you." Jason's mind was working at turbo speed. She would probably want to see the latest intelligence on Carrie's operations. "I will have the latest issue of *Baron's* for you, so you can feel right at home," Jason concluded. She would know what he really meant, of course. There was no Aunt Jane, and yes, he would have the latest intelligence on the First Family to show her tomorrow. Nothing had given cause for Jason to worry, but his own natural instincts, his military training, and their experience regarding the Israeli fiasco all served to cause him to take the extra precautions.

****** Dulles International Airport:

It frustrated Jason that the metal detector at the entrance to the airport gates detected the metal in his shoes. After emptying his pockets and removing his belt, the buzzer again sounded. This prompted the guard using the detector wand to pass over his person especially carefully. It annoyed Jason, but didn't really delay them. His only concern was the paperwork he had in his brief case. Jamie spotted Betty Phillips coming out of the loading chute. It had always reminded Jason of herding cattle, back in Nevada. "Mom, how are you," Jamie greeted Jason's mother with genuine enthusiasm, giving her a warm embrace. Jason had never fully shared with Jamie regarding his concern for how *ABACUS* was being used unethically by Grant and Carrie Williams. It was not that he did not trust her discretion nor that he did not value her opinions, but only that he did not want to put her at risk in this potentially dangerous game of spying on the First Family. Neither Jason nor his mother said anything about Aunt Jane. Jason had simply told Jamie that Betty was just coming out on a lark and that she would probably only stay for a few days.

It was not until they arrived at their home in McLean that Betty Phillips had a chance to talk privately with Jason. "Can I show you our new garden?" Jason asked, knowing that they would want to go outside to avoid being monitored. Jamie thought it was a bit strange because Jason seemed to have little interest in gardening and it was, after all, *her* garden. But she realized they wanted to talk alone, and she did not object or interfere. "I'll have some coffee for us in about ten minutes," she announced.

In the quiet of Jamie's garden, Betty told Jason what had alarmed her so much that she flew across the country to tell him. She had pieced together the evidence which Jason had been providing regularly and had become convinced that Carrie's plans included:
1. An all out campaign to have the 22nd Amendment to the Constitution rescinded in order to get a third term for her husband.
2. The complete dismantling of the United States nuclear arsenal.
And 3. The transfer of much of the foreign policy of the United States to the U.N..

She was still unsure of what grand designs the Williams' had, or whether they were doing this for purely altruistic motives. One thing she seemed certain about was that anyone willing to violate the public trust as blatantly as the Williams' were doing with the abuse of the information provided by *ABACUS*, was capable of dangerous things. She felt that the country was in grave danger and that they must be stopped.

Jason mostly listened, but did tell her that he had shared their concerns with Doctors Schultz and McGurn. He had made the decision to include them for two very practical reasons. First, he explained, he needed their cooperation to pull off the fix he had in mind for the project. Secondly, he felt he needed them to ratify his decision to act against the government. That was a step he could not take lightly, and the assurance by his two long time friends had given him the courage and the resolve to do it. He had suspected the things his mother just told him, but he was waiting for her to independently arrive at the same conclusions. His mother left the next day. She was relieved that Jason had come to the same conclusions as she, and was gratified that his colleagues shared their concerns.

****** **United Nation Headquarters:**
Funding for developing nations was not the full extent of the Israeli support for the U.N. A rather large computer system was donated to the U.N. by Israel, along with a small staff of experts to install the system, develop the required software, and train the regular employees of the U.N. This system was intended to be a superset of the Interpol net, the NCIC, and the NCCR data bases. It quickly exceeded expectations and became instrumental in breaking up several major drug cartels and traffic in stolen radioactive material.

The system worked so well that the owners of the individual contributors felt that it was only natural to turn control of the complete interface to the U.N. Before anyone could object, the U.N. became, in actuality, the ultimate crime information center. Only incidentally had it become the controller of vast resources upon which these individual agencies came to depend. Of course *the cause* was primarily responsible for the success of the massive coordination undertaking. And so, as planned, the United Nations Organization began moving toward becoming the true World Government.

****** **New Delhi:**

The normally staid Madam Secretary General Anteres Jandi was giving a party. All week the world press had honored her as the greatest leader to have graced the office of Secretary General. Her own Prime Minister, The Honorable Dwight Solomon Nehru, who resented living in her shadow, had heaped accolades upon her publicly in abundance this special week. After 6 years in that prestigious office, she was retiring. Mr. Nehru was gratified to hear that she was not interested in local politics.

The question of her successor had been on the minds of political pundits and practitioners even before there had been any talk of her retirement. She would be a hard act to follow, and the growth in scope of the office and the organization would require a truly charismatic leader to keep the massive alliance together.

It was no surprise that The Honorable Avery Harrington was there. There were several prime ministers, kings, presidents, assorted secretaries of state, and most of the important ambassadors to the United Nations in attendance.

At the height of the evening, after a sumptuous meal and gift presentations to her staff, Mrs. Jandi arranged for a special announcement to be made in the adjoining banquet hall, adjacent to the Grand Ballroom of the New Hilton, where she was hosting the affair. The press corps was there on cue, complete with television cameras and satellite feeds. The guests seated themselves around the two dozen or so large dining tables, fully loaded with finger food, champagne, and light wine. Mrs. Jandi stood talking with a group of

177

dignitaries at the most prominent table. When she mounted the raised platform and approached a speakers' dais, an expectant hush fell on the party.

"Ladies and Gentlemen, I have an important announcement I want to make," she began, rather forthrightly. "As most of you within the United Nations Organization know, I have been working with the heads of all of our member state delegations to try to find someone who can carry on the work we have begun, and who can unite all of us in the common cause of world peace. If it were possible, we wanted a proven world leader of some preeminence, someone who can fill the rather large office the Secretariat has become. The office has certainly outgrown my own poor abilities. The office has become the most important executive position within the community of the nations of the world. Ladies and Gentlemen, we have found that person!"

Mrs. Jandi motioned to Avery Harrington in the hushed pause that followed. There were instant conversations all over the floor, and as soon as the implications were understood, people began standing, and polite applause grew to a thunderous ovation. The two of them stood on the platform together for a full two minutes as wave after wave of hand clapping and shouted approval were exhibited.

Finally, after Mrs. Jandi motioned for the audience to be seated and quiet, she was allowed to continue. "I have been authorized by The General Assembly and The Security Council to announce the results of an informal preliminary vote concerning the nomination of my successor." "The indication in the General Assembly shows overwhelming (she didn't say unanimous) support for The Right Honorable Mr. Avery Harrington." Again, thunderous applause broke out, dozens of cameras flashed, and all of the conversations began again, often with all parties to each group talking simultaneously. "The indication in the Security Council is unanimity," she said, after again gaining their attention and a semblance of quiet. "Prime Minister Harrington has consented graciously to his resignation from all offices within the government of Israel, and to accept, if elected, the office of The Secretary General of the United Nations. Ladies and Gentlemen, I give you a great statesman, a visionary who lives for world peace, and a true citizen of the world, Mr. Avery Harrington."

Another demonstration followed, all favorable. Mrs. Jandi withdrew from the stage, signaling the time for his response. After about half a minute more the crowd allowed their new hero to speak. "Madam Secretary, Ladies and Gentlemen, I can only say that I am honored and that I will, if elected, devote my full energies to the work so nobly advanced by the organization during the last several years under the able leadership of your present Secretary General." "Thank you." Upon leaving the stage, he was immediately surrounded by reporters and cameramen. He patiently answered their questions and comments as he worked his way to the front lobby and an entourage which escorted him and his party to a quieter gathering of associates and friends.

This had been an extraordinary procedure, and might have been resented, but for the massive orchestration behind his nomination. The public announcement was a pure formality, as would be his official nomination and election.

****** **Dugway Proving Grounds:**

"Panel one green," shouted the First Lieutenant at the second console of the massive control center. "Panel two green," echoed a civilian to her right. And so on through the complement of glowing screens and special displays. "It is a **go**. All stations proceed!" said the Test Director, into a microphone and the radio network attached to it.

Fourteen missiles were launched within seconds of his pronouncement. Missiles were flying in their direction from Canada, Australia, Russia, China, Africa, and South America. A few would arrive in only minutes. Most of the rest would converge in about twenty minutes. But they were ready. The origin of the firings and the countermeasures they might present were unknown to the crew, identified as *Defense One* for this occasion. All they knew was that this was the most comprehensive and difficult test that would ever be required to show the effectiveness of the defensive network dubbed IDN, which stood for *International Defense Network*. Ground, Air, and Satellite-based tracking and destroying components would be utilized in this all-out demonstration of the highly advanced version of what was originally called *Star Wars*.

The test was a complete success. All incoming missiles were destroyed even before reentry into the atmosphere. The next day it was publicized world-wide. The purpose of the test was to convince the last holdouts in the Atomic Club that the MAD concept was obsolete, ineffectual, and unnecessary. The FAT (final atomic treaty) could (hopefully) at last be finalized!

****** **Jerusalem:**

The VIP limousine pulled up to the Prime Minister's rather modest home on a hillside overlooking the city. This would be the first *official* visit by the Vice President of the United States, the Honorable Harry Lipscombe. The trip had not been arranged by Carrie Williams. Rather, it had been Grant Williams' idea, or so he believed. Vice President Lipscombe was here to be briefed on the new government being organized in Israel as a result of the Prime Minister's resignation. Avery Harrington was still the Prime Minister. His resignation was effective in sixty days, which would closely coincide with his election to the office of Secretary General of the United Nations.

The Vice President was met almost immediately by the Prime Minister. The two greeted each other as long standing acquaintances, not the stiff formalistic acknowledgment of diplomatic protocol. "Harrison, thank you for coming." "Mr. Prime Minister, Avery," the VEEP corrected himself. "It is good to be official," Harrison said, grinning. "That is one of the things I wanted to discuss with you," Avery said, returning his smile, as he led him into his home office.

****** **The Pentagon:**

"Doctor McGurn," Jason greeted his old friend, as he entered his office. "Jamie says that you and Eva must come over for dinner next Friday, if you can." Max ignored the statement for the time being. Max simply said, "Let's talk," in a rather stern, foreboding voice. Jason lifted a finger, pointing to the ceiling, or the light fixture, Max knew not. "Let's include Brent, shall we. I need to talk to you both about a business opportunity I have, a kind of investment. I

181

need you both to hear it," Jason said. "How about *Hot Dog Heaven,*" Jason asked, turning to go, as a signal to Max that he didn't want to continue any serious conversation in the office. "Great," responded Max, rather casually. "About 11:30?" "Right," Jason called, from well out the door.

***

'Hot Dog Heaven' was Jason's preferred meeting place with his close associates on the project, Max McGurn and Brent Schultz. In the setting of an occasional lunch out of the office, they could walk some considerable distance from the Pentagon, across several large open spaces, and enjoy the outdoors, and the assurance of not being overheard by *office electronics*, as they called the many surveillance systems used throughout government offices. Of course they were acutely aware of the many remote devices and took practical precautions, such as meeting besides the fountain in the adjacent park, and covering their mouths when they were discussing the project.

Max was the first to speak. "Guys, she is trying to set up Elbow Head to be King," he said. "How can she do that?" questioned Brent. Everyone knew who Max was talking about. They had pet names or acronyms for most of the major players in the drama. Max paused, just long enough for Jason to answer for him. "Rescission of the 22nd Amendment," Jason blurted. Max looked rather startled, and he turned to face Jason. "How did you figure that out?" Max demanded. "The question is; are we going to let it happen?" Jason responded.

After comparing notes and explaining their inferences to Brent, the three of them got quickly to the point of decision which they had known for some time now that their journey would take them. They had many meetings on the subject. In the earlier ones, they had philosophized at some length on the morality, the practicality, the futility, even the rationality of what they were about to do. None of the three had ever voiced his conclusion regarding those very aspects; it was an on-going discussion. Now was the time for decision. "I'm with you Jason," Max said, simply. "Yes," joined Brent, "it must be done, and who if not us, and when, if not now," paraphrased Brent, deadly serious.

So the die was cast. Events beyond their control had forced them into a fateful decision. Jason suggested they only discuss their plan and the operation required to support the plan, away from the office and only two at a time. The social life they shared quite naturally was a perfect vehicle for their planning sessions. There would be a lot of barbeques at the McGurns' and Phillips' homes this summer.

The basic idea of Jason's scheme was to simply cripple Carrie Williams' great tool by telling the model of the *great unwashed*, in America and across the world, that *they were being modeled!* The resentment would *theoretically* render the Williams' administration politically sterile. The fact of their knowing could not be an overt data entry; it must be imbedded in the very foundational *kernel* of the model dynamics. Interestingly, only the three of them fully understood that particular coding. Without their help it would probably be impossible for any outside experts to understand this particular inference algorithm, much less any imbedded anomalies.   The three had agreed that this should be the extent of their endeavor.   **It was their hope and expectation that this would be enough.**

Chapter 14: THE ULTIMATE VIRUS

Jason went home from work early this day; that is to say, he left at the *normal* time, which for him was early. He had kept Jamie out of his clandestine operation until now, for security reasons, and to avoid worrying her needlessly. Now he must tell her. He reasoned that it would actually enhance the security of the operation if she knew what *not* to say. His real reasons though, were to alert her to the danger they might all be in, and to go through the argument which had compelled them to take the action they were about to take. He needed her assurance. He had the assurance of his peers and his most trusted advisor, his mother, but Jamie's approval would make it unanimous.

***

After dinner the two of them sat out on their back porch, as was their habit, to talk over the events of the day, to reminisce, to dream, and plan, and simply share. Jason was amazed to find out that even Jamie, who was only very peripherally aware of what *ABACUS* was used for, and who only spoke to Carrie Williams very occasionally, seemed to somehow piece together what was taking place in Washington. She totally approved of what he and his colleagues were about to do, whatever it was. The details of the plan would be of no interest or particular understanding for her, but she was amused to think of the model as some sort of *real* entity, and would react very much as the American public would, if people knew they were being manipulated.

On Friday, as was a somewhat regular habit, Jamie and Jason had Brent and his girlfriend, Sasha, over for dinner. It turned out to be too cold for an outdoor affair, so they sent out for Pizza and Root Beer. Soon after dinner Brent and Jason closeted themselves in Jason's study, and began their detailed planning in earnest. Jason had developed his own security zone in his study. No device, active or passive would go undetected in his special private enclave. Brent almost immediately saw the elegance of Jason's program modification, and predicted dramatic success. Most of their attention was spent on how to avoid being detected. Even though they were civilians under contract, they feared more than financial reprisals. They were particularly concerned for their families. They had come to understand the ruthlessness of the First Lady.

The two of them went over all of the 'what ifs' until late into the night. They determined to test their security by first installing a virtual placebo, then observing the results. No overt test program could be undertaken; it all had to work right the first time.

****** The White House:
"This can't be right, George!" the First Lady shrieked. "We have them in our pocket. Of course they will buy it." George Steinman had lost some of his initial enthusiasm for *the cause*, but he was committed, and he was loyal, if nothing. "I had some of our best staff on this and I checked the input myself," George countered, defensively.

One of the unknowns in the Rescission Plan was the reaction of the press, and what role Carrie should let them play in the process. For almost three years she held the loyalty of most of the press. Carrie was counting on them to lead the nation into the inevitable conclusion of the course of events. It should be the press who would prompt the populace of the need to do away with the prohibition, not too unlike an earlier prohibition. To be sure, however, she insisted that every major move was first verified by *ABACUS*.

Her current issue was how to neutralize the U.S. Military Establishment, regarding the total disarmament of the United States nuclear arsenal. Their strenuous opposition could raise doubts as to the wisdom of the administration's program, and by extension, the need for the amendment. Her idea was to use the media branch of her network to initiate a coordinated campaign for the disarmament, and against the military position. She was sure it could be done, done effectively, and willingly. Except now this high-powered computer jockey was telling her it could not happen, and it wouldn't work!

She toyed with the thought of going ahead with the move, just to bring this conceited brass hat down to earth. But the track record of *ABACUS* had been too good up to now to risk her campaign on some nuance of policy which could be corrected *before* she launched it. It was very comforting indeed to have a crystal ball!

"George, something is wrong. Go back and find out why this projection says what you say. Then get back with me." She offered him her hand, as his cue for dismissal, and to tell him that everything was still all right between them. Her charm was one of the reasons for her immense success, as she was aware, and it cost nothing.

****** **The Pentagon:**

The General was between the proverbial rock and hard place. He could not share his problem with his staff, but without them, he might not be able to solve it. George Steinman had personally checked on the input case profile and had monitored the execution of the test case, the variation of parameters to prove the linearity of the solution in the vicinity of the input set, and had even had his staff go through the exercise of running the CRC (cyclical redundancy checks) to verify program integrity. **The results remained the same!** It was impossible.

Ever since that afternoon on the Potomac with Carrie, George had distanced himself from his *boys*. He was not at liberty to take anyone into his confidence regarding *the cause*. Jason and Brent and Max had noticed it immediately; it had been the trigger for them to start observing more closely what *ABACUS* was being used for. If anything was too clandestine to be beyond their trust, it must be nefarious, indeed. At least that was the natural reaction by these men who had been privy to the whole spectrum of domestic and international policy studies before. *But now was not the time to lay out the whole scenario for them*, thought George Steinman.

"This thing has gone haywire," George told Jason, as he handed him a clipboard listing special file cases. "Please run these cases, using archive data," he said to Jason, rather stiffly. "If there is *any* deviation from the original results, I want to know the particulars; no detail is too unimportant," he concluded. George turned to go, but paused. "Give that top priority." He did not wait for an answer.

Jason knew what the results would be, having just ran several of these same critical cases the last few days. He had run them to reassure himself and his colleagues that earlier results would not be altered by his program *fix*. The totally predictable results were on the General's desk before Jason went home that day. The Placebo worked quite well *so far*.

The three knew that George could either bring them into his confidence, or bring in an outside specialist. They were mixed about which they would have preferred.

****** Jerusalem:

The soon-to-be Secretary General had a regular stream of visitors calling on him at his residence. None of them was more important this particular day than Dr. Samuel Levanthol. "Sam, find out what is going on with their model, and with this General Steinman. If you see any sign of an error in their program, don't tell them; talk to me first. Go to our embassy there and see Ambassador Maroni; he is one of us. Tell him you need a code "C" communications line. He'll put you through to me personally, wherever I am, whatever the time." Avery Harrington looked at his old friend with compassion. They had come a long way together and things were taking shape dramatically for their *cause*. "Sam, be alert for resistance within the project. Good luck; give Sarah my love." He embraced the old man, and sent him on his way. Avery noticed a new stoop to the old man's posture, and made a mental note to bring in a younger person as soon as he could to head up Project TAT. It was only fair to let Dr. Levanthol retire. Just as soon as he had completed this last critical mission.

****** **The Pentagon:**

"George, I haven't heard from you, what's going on?" Carrie demanded from the other end of the line. "I just don't know; we have tested this thing, torn it apart and reconstructed it, and although it has been able to re-create all past results, it seems to be in serious default, at least in this one area," George reported, with clinical efficiency.

"Dr. Sam Levanthol will be calling on you tomorrow; show him every courtesy. He can find the problem if anyone can," Carrie told him. He wondered, but hesitated to ask how Dr. Levanthol might fit into the larger scheme of things. In the absence of knowing these things, George would treat him gingerly, and assume he might pose a security threat. He could only hope that Carrie knew what she was doing.

He had never discussed the possibility of bringing his *boys*, or at least Jason, into *the cause*. He wondered now if this might not be a prudent thing to do. He would have to discuss this matter under the best possible security conditions. Which meant that he could not bring it up now. "If you think that is best," George responded. "I do. Call me when he leaves." This last statement had numerous implications, and George would ponder the meaning of it over the next day.

Jason was not surprised at George's decision, but the choice of the outside expert somewhat puzzled Jason. Regardless, he was glad to renew his acquaintance. And yet there was reason for concern. **If anyone might be able to detect his subtle modification, it would be Dr. Levanthol.**

It was the time for renewal. The earth, in its eternal cycle, had come to that balance in nature called the Vernal Equinox. The warmth of the sun had its wonderful effect on the climate, and the plants, and even people. Even so, Sam Levanthol felt old and tired. He would not live to see the dream he had been sharing with his friend and benefactor, Avery Harrington. But he could see things taking shape, and he had no small part in moving the plan forward. He had long ago pledged his life to *the cause,* and he felt privileged to be a major player for Israel.

****** **The Pentagon:**

"Dr. Levanthol, how good to see you," Jason said, being careful to not add *again.* Any reference to his visit to Jerusalem would not be initiated by him. Jason had discussed his visit with his colleagues, Brent and Max, but in only a casual way. His own sense had been that *ABACUS* was way ahead of TAT, and would remain so.

"Jamie insists that you have dinner with us as soon as your schedule permits," Jason announced, greeting his old acquaintance with a warm smile and firm handshake. "Thank you, Jason, that would be splendid," Sam responded. He was thinking such an invitation might be forthcoming and he was sure it would be an opportunity to learn about the internal politics of *ABACUS*, as Avery had instructed him to do.

"Your General Steinman has asked us to provide an outside analysis of the problem you are having. I would hope you would do the same for us, someday," Sam said to Jason, putting the situation as graciously as he could. "Thank you,

191

Doctor," Jason responded. Sam wondered how much this brilliant young man might know about the *cause* and Carrie Williams' complicity, and whether he was involved with some kind of purposeful sabotage of the system. At the same moment, Jason was wondering if Sam might be a part of some larger conspiracy which somehow included the President, or at least the President's wife. Complicating all of this was a genuine affection each felt for the other. Loyalties might get to be complicated for them both.

****** **United Nations Headquarters:**

"Yes, Avery, that's correct. Two abstentions. It would cost more than it is worth in my opinion, yes," said The Secretary General. Anteres Jandi had been orchestrating the formal election of her designated successor. In spite of Avery Harrington's personal support for each of the Muslim leaders elevated to heads of state following the aborted regime of Ayatollah Al Shafei, two of them refused to publicly support him for the position of Secretary General of the United Nations.

At the other end of the line, the Honorable Prime Minister doodled in his personnel directory, marking two other names in his lists, each near the name of the reluctant leaders now holding office. Avery Harrington always had alternate plans. An avid chess player, he had learned early on that the winner was usually the one who was able to see further ahead in the game.

"That's fine, Terry," he enthused. "You would have to be a Jew or an Arab to understand how hard it is to give up the old animosities. It is visceral, even hereditary," Avery mused,

192

for her benefit. "Things are going well almost everywhere," he added, being careful to speak only in generalities. *Everywhere except in the White House*, he thought but did not say.

On the master planning board in his head, Avery would regularly scan the state of developments. The movements toward a true world body and the concomitant nuclear disarmament were progressing pretty much on schedule. The question of American policy remained the most troublesome aspect for him and *the cause*. He had often wondered about the wisdom of operating through *the spouse* of a head of state, rather than directly. So far, Carrie seemed to be able to move things along for them, but Avery had grave concerns regarding her dependence on *ABACUS*, and the externals which he could manipulate for her. The one major misstep she had made up to now was the recruitment of her General Steinman. She had done this without his prior approval, and this was a breach of discipline he could never tolerate again. In his book there were a half dozen names near Carrie's. All the others were men.

****** **McLean, Virginia:**

It had been a long two days, actually three packed into two. Sam Levanthol was ready for a little relaxation and the comfort of friends. Jason had driven his car this second day of Sam's visit and was able to pick him up at his hotel early enough to make it home for the 7:00 o'clock dinner Jamie had specially prepared for Sam.

"Hello Doctor Levanthol and welcome!" Jamie greeted him. "Sarah would have loved to come with me, Jamie," Sam

193

said. "She thinks the world of you, and she sends her love." Jamie had prepared a devastating rack of lamb with all of the supporting cast. Fine California wine enhanced the dinner and relaxed both hosts and guest.

After dinner they sat around and talked, reminiscing about the good times they had in San Diego, then in Jerusalem. Sam told them stories of when he was a boy, in Nazi Germany, and of the close escapes he had. At one point, tears came to his eyes as he related how he found out that his whole family had been shipped off to the "work camps".

The conversation eventually got around to local politics, and Sam listened for what he could infer from Jason's attitude toward the administration. Jason and Jamie both enthused over Carrie and the President. They had discussed it the previous evening, and Jason instructed his wife to not disparage anything about the administration or of his work on *ABACUS*. Sam soon realized that this was a dead end. Except he sensed they were being less than candid, and this bothered him. He knew them well enough to know they were not naive about either politics, or of the use of *ABACUS*. He quickly turned the conversation to world politics and the role of the United Nations. From the discussion, he could only conclude that Carrie had neither taken them into the *cause,* nor had she influenced them greatly with her politics.

On the ride back to his hotel, Sam pursued Jason a little further regarding his feelings about the use of *ABACUS*. Jason would not rise to the bait, but rather, expounded on the potential good uses of *ABACUS*. As Sam got out of Jason's car at his hotel, he said "Jason, I was studying your core algorithms today. Very interesting. I'd like to talk to you about them soon." Jason blanched ever so slightly, but enough for Sam to notice, since he was looking for whatever reaction Jason might display. "I have an early flight out of here tomorrow, but I'd like to have a private video-phone meeting with you later," Sam said. Jason was visibly relieved. "Please tell General Steinman I will fax my report to him Friday, from my office," Sam concluded. "Give my thanks again to Jamie," Sam said, holding out his hand to Jason. "You are a lucky fellow, Jason!" Sam turned and hurried into his hotel lobby, without looking back.

During the drive back to McLean, Jason recounted all of the subtle bits of conversation with Sam. Why he had come and what he had learned, or suspected, remained unanswered, as far as Jason could determine. One thing he was rather uneasy about, however, was that Sam seemed to know that someone had altered the core inference algorithms, and that Jason knew he knew. The next day or two he would find an opportunity to discuss these developments with his two co-conspirators.

****** **Jerusalem:**
The third taxi within the hour pulled to a stop in front of Avery Harrington's modest home. The Prime Minister greeted his old friend with open arms. "Sam, you haven't even been home yet!" Avery observed. This would mean there was important news for him, probably bad. "Yes, Avery, we have a problem," Sam confirmed, looking grave. Avery led him silently into his private office. This would be information for his ears only.

****** The Pentagon:

Jason could not wait for their usual meetings over Friday evening meals. Hot Dog Heaven it would have to be. "Gentlemen," Jason began, as soon as their situation seemed secure, "Sam may be on to us!" Max and Brent stared at him in stunned silence for long moments. "How do you know?" Max said, simply. "I don't, for sure. He just said 'I found your core inference algorithms rather interesting' to me, in a rather pointed way. I may be just paranoid," Jason responded.

The three of them discussed as many of the possibilities and options as they could imagine. They discarded the option of permanently disabling *ABACUS* on the basis that if they went public, it didn't matter. Finally, they decided to go ahead, as if nothing had been discovered. They had already taken as much heat as Steinman could deliver, over the strange results yielded by their fix. Max would install the final part of the fix, during the late shift. He would also cover all possible audit trails and adjust all of the CRC tests, so the fix would be undetectable.

****** The White House:

Things were not going well for The President. Carrie had gone ahead with her campaign to discredit the Military Establishment through the media. She assumed that the strange results from *ABACUS* were some kind of a computer glitch which would hopefully get fixed.

****** Atlanta:

It was only a little leak. Jerry Gilletson of TINN found a strange four page memo in his mail only two days before Carrie launched her rather clandestine operation. The notes seemed to be some internal White House memo which directed some sort of research into the loyalties of a large number of media personalities. His name was on the list. The inevitable inference was that he and his colleagues were about to be used. A quick call to two other names on the list verified that they too had received the anonymous note.

****** **The White House:**

When Carrie's Press Secretary called with the feed which was rather identical to the script laid out in the memo, it gave a great deal of credence to the authenticity of the memo. Carrie was amazed to learn that her prompting seemed to fall on deaf ears. Her first thought was: *so maybe the computer was right.* Self doubts and fear began to creep into her consciousness. The inexplicable drop in Grant's approval rating in the latest TINN/New York Times Poll did not allay her concerns.

***

Grant Williams dove into the pool, throwing the overly-chlorinated water across the narrow decks and onto the walls. He quickly surfaced and leisurely swam the length of the pool and back before stopping to rest. In an unusual show of willfulness and unconcern for the business of the nation, he had canceled his whole afternoon agenda, and had given himself the rest of the day off. He needed to think. Carrie had usually given him space during most of his career, as he had given her, but lately she had been smothering him, and he was in urgent need to declare himself a man. Or at least a person. He had determined that what he really wanted to do was to have some time to himself, have an early dinner, and then proceed to get rousing drunk.

****** **The Pentagon:**

"Yes Carrie, I understand, yes; I'll be there." The General hung up the receiver, glanced at his afternoon schedule, and scooping up his ever-present brief case, strode out of his office. "Patty, cancel the rest of my appointments for today and get Charlie on the pad ASAP," George commanded, in a firm but friendly tone. She knew where he would be going, or rather thought she knew. George Steinman had been visiting the White House a lot lately. His personal secretary had seen the joy go out of the relationships he had with his *boys* and the rest of the staff.

****** **On the Potomac:**

Carrie Witherington-Williams wore a light summer dress, even though it was only spring. As George approached the Presidential Yacht he could not help admiring her figure and grace. This was only his second visit on board this vessel, and the thought of it flooded his mind with the vivid and exciting memories of his first visit, many months ago.

"George," she pronounced, offering him her hand. George was tempted for a second to sweep her into his arms. "Mrs. Williams," he said. Crew was all around, trying to be unobtrusive, but they were there nevertheless. Carrie meant to be all business, but just now she felt vulnerable, and a little helpless, and she held his hand for several lingering moments.

The crew served sandwiches and soft drinks, and then left them as alone as they could, on the lower observation deck, as they headed toward the open sea. "George, I think your computer was right on this media thing," Carrie said, resignedly. "The hateful thing seems to always have been right!" she added. "Right now, we are at a critical juncture. We must have another good projection from *ABACUS*. All we have done up to now has really been prologue; the next five years will see us succeed gloriously, or fail miserably," she said, focusing all of her energy toward George. He started to say something, but paused.

"This is our preliminary plan," she said, handing him a heavy, sealed envelope. "I do not need to tell you how very sensitive this information is. If you need to clear your lab, or do this at night or on the weekend, then please do it. But do it soon. We need to know if this plan will succeed," Carrie said, without smiling.

"Go ahead and open it. I want you to make sure you understand it. We can discuss it now," she said. As George opened the envelope and proceeded to digest the elaborate plan, Carrie climbed up to the upper deck and enjoyed the smell of the salt air and the rush of the wind in her face. She was determined that *the cause* would succeed, her air-head of a husband notwithstanding. Grant clearly did not want to serve more than his allotted terms. He would have been satisfied with one ride on the wheel, if she would have allowed it. She could not understand his reluctance to achieve greatness.

****** McLean, Virginia:

It was that time of day Jamie loved the most. They had finished their dinner, and had moved out to their porch. She had come to understand the allure of the old-time porches, and the porch swings. She did not have children to watch, but it

199

was that precious time when she shared her life with Jason, in a special way. He was her sounding board, and she his. All of the private thoughts they could not share with others, they could now speak and know the thoughts would be weighed and sifted, and only the good part would be kept.

"Jamie, it will soon be over, one way or another," Jason said, looking into her eyes, and sounding rather sad. "It has been an exciting four years here, but we need to be making plans." Jason had taken the precaution, just as Max and Brent had done, to leave sealed documents with friends and relatives, together with the appropriate instructions....just in case. One of his regrets was to place Jamie at risk. She was innocent. But he knew she would not have him do anything differently. He had even put his sister and his mother at some risk, as well, but again, he knew they would also have agreed with what he had to do.

"I have. Been thinking about it, I mean," Jamie said, smiling. "We have some savings, and your car. You could resume your studies at Cal," she said. Jason stared off into the sky. "Or, I would love being a rancher's wife," she added. "I know your mother and sister would like to have you back home." "Tomorrow or the next day, things should start breaking down. The very next policy planning operation should trigger events," Jason said, ignoring Jamie's reference to school or home. "I am a little worried they might do something," he said. He was more than a little worried. There was no rational plan he could come up with, however, to give them even a modicum of protection. His hope was in the successful disguise of the virus.

Surely, if Sam Levanthol knew that they were involved, he would not do anything to endanger them. Surely.

****** **The Pentagon:**

It was into the 20th hour of the same day. After George's afternoon tea with the *Duchess*, he had gone home for a short rest and returned to his office after the day shift had left. He had carefully formulated the Master Plan Carrie had given him as input data, and had run the model over a simulated five years, as the plan called for.

He did not believe the preliminary results. Nor did he believe the detailed results. Nor did he believe the model even after he had checked and re-checked his input files. By three in the morning, he had run the model for 8 full five-year executions. He had also run every diagnostic he could find, as well as all of the classic test cases on file. Nothing! The model declared itself well, even healthy. All of the test cases repeated earlier results *exactly!* George was beginning to become ill. Without leaving a memo for Patty or any of his staff, he simply erased the plan file and drove home.

If Sam Levanthol, nor any of his own hot-shot computer geniuses could not find anything wrong with *ABACUS* it must be all right. Any reasonable variation he had made from the basic plan showed the American people rejecting the program, and the President, as well. **He too, felt a strong urge to be alone and to drug himself free from his immediate problems.**

Chapter 15: TROUBLE IN CAMELOT

****** **A Washington Suburb:**

After the third series of rings on his bedside telephone later that same morning, George Steinman had switched the painful device off. This bought him another hour of sleep.

"All right, all right!" George almost shouted at the unknown intruder incessantly ringing his front doorbell. He fought off the heavy fog and by sheer willpower forced himself to his feet. The room was pretty wobbly, but he managed to gain his balance and stumble over to his closet where he kept his house robe. He draped it around him as he moved toward his front door, navigating strictly from memory.

George squinted through the one-way pane beside the door to see some young marine officer in dress uniform continuing to ring the bell. "What do you want?" George barked through the door. The marine on his porch drew himself to attention and announced: "I am from The White House." As if that answered everything.

George suppressed a strong impulse to tell the young man to simply go away. "Don't just stand there, step inside," the General insisted, as he swung the door open for him. "I am to deliver this message to you personally, sir. I am to report back immediately on your whereabouts, as well." "Who sent you?" George demanded. "The President, sir."

"Okay, the phone is in there; go ahead and make your call; I am going to hit the shower. Let yourself out." "I was ordered to drive you to The White House as soon as possible, sir." George paused, thoughtfully. He didn't have to wonder what this was all about. He knew. The President and Carrie had come to be almost totally dependent upon *ABACUS* for all of their major decisions. And now he had to stand on the carpet and tell them that their paragon of all truth and knowledge had failed them.

George took a long stinging shower and dressed in his best civilian suit. He would not disgrace the uniform with this dastardly deed he must do.

****** **The Pentagon:**
Everything was business as usual, except certain high members of the staff knew that it never would be again. The General's absence told them what must have happened. The three of them made extraordinary efforts this day to make things appear ordinary; until they would be told by their superior that it was not.

Jason kept himself occupied with his current task, which was to help formulate candidate plans for the privatization of the Department of Interior. Even that non-controversial, low risk program, he knew, would now not meet with approval by the public. A week ago, it would have. Even as he worked, his thoughts were with Jamie and the several attractive options before them after this project was officially declared dead.

Jason and his two colleagues had often discussed how *ABACUS* could be applied to so many serious problems. They all believed that *ABACUS* could more than pay for itself, working out the economic and social problems of the nation. What they had often wished for was the strong light of day to be cast upon the system, and to have it put under broad public oversight, so that everyone would *know* for what, exactly, it was being used.

The day wore on, through lunch and beyond, late into the afternoon. Still there was no word from the General. Jason and Max and Brent were more than anxious to share their feelings with each other, but this day, especially, they avoided each other.

****** **The White House:**

George had rarely been in the Oval Office, for many practical reasons, but he was there now, closeted, so to speak, with the First Family. "George, tell me again how the model reacted to our plan," said the President. Grant was somewhat ambivalent about this startling turn of events. He really did not want to take on a third term as President; not even as figurehead, which he knew he was. In fact he was almost delighted. Maybe now, someone would listen to him, instead of this pompous computer genius.

"Sir, something may have gone wrong with the system, or perhaps there has been sabotage, or just *perhaps*, it is giving us correct projections. In any case, *ABACUS* projects 82 per cent disapproval for the whole plan. It appears that even with the rescission of the term limitation amendment, we would lose the next election, against almost any opposition candidate." "Well then, that's it!" declared the President, turning to Carrie. "We'll just have to formulate other plans." *Like leaving a winner,* Grant thought.

It was Carrie's turn to want to be alone, and to find some escape from this disastrous turn. "This is the second and last failure of that monstrosity of yours, General!" Carrie announced. Turning to Grant, she said "We cannot count on this source any longer. It doesn't matter why it doesn't work. It just doesn't," Carrie concluded. Carrie abruptly excused herself. For once, Grant was in command, and he cherished it. "We will find something for you to do with your giant brain," Grant said to the General. "You must excuse me now, George; I think I will take a short vacation!" George did not respond, but rather, lowering his eyes, quietly withdrew. At that moment, he knew this was the end of the line for him with this man. Carrie, however, was another issue. A flood of questions overwhelmed him. The idea of a vacation sounded very appealing. He would call Patty tomorrow morning and announce his absence for an unspecified duration.

"Abe, get in here," Grant sang into his intercom. It took Mr. Able Larson less than seven seconds to arrive, notebook in hand, pen at the ready. "Yes, Mr. President?" "Abe, cancel all of my appointments for the next week. After that, who knows? I'm going to take up Prime Minister Henry's kind invitation to vacation with him up at Banff. Please see to the arrangements. I will be at Andrews about 9:00 tomorrow morning. And, oh yes, I think I will pick up my good friend Pickering, at Boston, on the way." "Yes, Mr. President. Is Mrs. Williams traveling with you?" The President paused, then started to say something, then paused again. "Hmm, I don't care, ask her!" "Yes sir!" said a startled Able Larson, making as quick an exit as possible.

Carrie made her way back to her own spacious offices and immediately closeted herself inside her inner office, notifying the secretary on duty that she was not to be disturbed under any circumstances!

Carrie was a little girl again, just for a moment, or perhaps she wished she were. She could have brought her broken toys, or hurt, or shattered dreams to Papa and he would make it right. Now there was only one man to whom she could take her broken toys, such expensive toys that she had accumulated.

***

"Hello Avery, this is Carrie. Oh, Avery, everything is coming apart. I need some reassurance from you just now," Carrie almost cried into the special scrambler phone. She detailed the problem as she understood it. She offered no solutions. She had become so dependent on *ABACUS* that she was paralyzed with its failure. What she had never been able to bring to Avery was Grant's reluctance to be a part of her master plan. Avery had of course found this out through other channels.

Avery Harrington knew he had a problem of major proportions on his hands, and knew how important it was to restore Carrie's equanimity, and her confidence. He spent the better part of an hour reassuring her that things would work out for the cause they shared, and no matter what, their final objectives would be met. They talked of the better days ahead, when mankind would be free of fear from want, and war, and disease. Avery painted once again the vision that had driven so many of his powerful followers these many years. It was what Carrie needed and she came down off the ceiling and, at least for the moment, felt calm and secure.

Avery suggested a few days rest for her and a personal meeting with him a week or two hence, for the purpose of developing alternate plans. He would have other solutions, he assured her.

****** **Boston International Airport:**
"Yes, that's right, the President," a frustrated James McLaughlin said into his telephone. "Again, six complete dinners from Anthony's. Lobster, with all of the trimmings. Yes, it must be here by Noon. Make sure everything is properly iced." he said, breaking the connection with his thumb as soon as the order was properly acknowledged. It was late, but James was used to long days, uncertain hours, and a regular stream of special requirements. Supplying Air Force One was just another assignment, as far as he was concerned. He did his job well, and with pride. The fare ordered up directly from the White House would be there and waiting. They would not be disappointed.

Across town however, the next morning, a dark-skinned wiry man was preparing a special surprise which would also be loaded on the plane, and it would be *very disappointing*. This man would be just another driver for the delivery service used by the local restaurants. Nothing would appear untoward, although the service would be just slightly delayed. Added to the supplies from Anthony's would be an extra container, presumably full of rocky road, the President's favorite ice cream. But instead of ice cream, it would contain seven pounds of plastique and a sophisticated detonation device which would trigger the bomb if the container were opened, or at precisely 13.8 PSI ambient, whichever came first.

The agent carefully packed the stainless steel container with paper insulation, dry ice, more insulation, the explosive charge with the detonator imbedded, and finally more paper, dry ice, and a last layer of insulation. The container would feel cold to the touch, as would any steel vessel, containing ice cream. Small vents around the container, just below the lid allowed for escaping carbon dioxide, and the equalization of the ambient pressure.

Finally, the agent came to the risky part of the assembly. He attached the multi-sensor device to the steel lid, using an extremely fast-hardening epoxy glue. After attaching the wires from the detonator, he carefully depressed the mechanical lever and set the switch. As often as he had done this, cold sweat still formed all over his body at this critical part of the assembly. He carefully placed the lid onto the container, starting at the lever position. He had been careful to bend and score the container, so that the lid would have to be forced open. A rubber mallet to seat the lid was the last part of his ordeal. Delivering the goods was the easiest part of the assignment. Then he would be on the next plane out of the country, wearing a disguise and carrying professionally forged papers.

****** **Andrews Air Force Base:**
The *United States of America* was checked and ready. All flights in and out had been canceled until further notice. It was 10:00 a.m., and no sign or word of the President and his

party. The crew waited. The tower waited. The Military Police escort service waited. Finally, at almost half past the hour, one of the big black presidential limousines rounded the flight operations building, and headed toward the waiting 747.

****** **Boston International Airport:**

Frank Caughlin had drawn on-board security duty this day. He would stay with Air Force One until it returned to Washington. He looked forward to seeing Lake Louise again, and the clean Canadian air.

His only duty was to check the cargo and any new items loaded on board here. He moved toward the cargo doors, which were just now being opened by the crew. The President often ordered food from some of his favorite restaurants around the country. The delivery service seemed to be late. Usually, they were there waiting when the plane arrived. Finally, after almost everyone, including the President's friends from Boston were on board, the delivery truck made its appearance.

"Sorry guys, it took me 30 minutes to get through security." said the slight, dark-skinned driver. His coveralls had an embroidered name *Harold* above the company logo. No one spoke to Harold; they hardly noticed him. But the crew brought the contents of the truck over for Frank to examine. Caughlin first looked over the papers which came with the delivery. He looked over the truck, and the driver. Then he systematically began to open and examine each of the steel containers, which had the distinctive *Anthony's* emblem stamped on the lids and covers. Everything was iced, and the stainless steel almost burned his fingers.

"Captain says close it up," announced the nearest crewman. Frank seemed to not be in any hurry. But he skipped one of the Lobster Dinner containers, and proceeded to examine the next to last container. The crew started the motors which were closing the cargo hatch. James lifted the last container, smiling at the designation of its contents. It weighed right, and it was even colder than the others. "O.K," he said, hoisting up the last one to the crew assigned to secure the cargo for flight. He just slightly resented the fact that he, along with the rest of the crew, would have to subsist on cold sandwiches.

The tower gave the President's big plane special clearance, and the 747 thundered down runway 270, straight out to sea. Soon, while still climbing, the pilot steered the aircraft westward, toward the heartlands, and *doom*.

The President was holding forth in the forward lounge, entertaining his friend Frank Pickering, and a couple of young ladies Frank had brought with him for this gala occasion. Carrie had excused herself, saying she did not feel well. She remained in the President's compartment, alone. She really did not feel well, although she had gotten over her state of depression after talking to Avery. But there was in her mind a sense of foreboding. She was trying to recall exactly what Avery had said to her.

At precisely 1:12:07 p.m., EST, at an altitude of about 28,000 feet, the end came. Within less than a second the massive craft was torn apart, enveloped in flames, and hurtling earthward. **There would be no survivors.**

210

Chapter 16: THE AFTERMATH

****** **The Pentagon:**

Patty Winthrope was the first to know of the tragedy. "Oh **no**! Oh no, no!" was all she could say at first. Because *ABACUS* was tied into every news source, the project personnel learned all there was to know the moment anything was reported. Most left early; a few stayed late, scanning the bulletins for a glimmer of meaning to it all.

Jason called Jamie as soon as he heard, and could speak evenly. His mind imagined all kinds of alarming possibilities. It did not help that the General was still missing, and had only been rumored to have been seen at the White House. "Jamie, are you all right?" Jason said, expectantly. "Yes, of course, why shouldn't I be?" "Air Force One is down; it does not look good. The President has probably been killed; perhaps assassinated." There was shock and disbelief on the other end of the telephone. Unspoken concerns over the troubling events of the last few days were shared by them. As soon as he could close all of the current files he was working on, Jason told his secretary he was going home, and that she too could take the next day or two off.

****** **The White House:**

Vice President Harrison Lipscombe placed the military on high alert and began fielding inquiries from governments around the world. As the evening wore on, the inevitable conclusion emerged, confirming everyone's worst fears. The President, his wife, and all other parties on board Air Force One had been destroyed, somewhere west of Concord, Massachusetts.

At 10:00 p.m. EST, the Vice President went on the air to try to calm the nation. He outlined the military security measures he had initiated, detailed the steps being taken to investigate the tragedy, and finally, announced that if the news were totally verified, and the President had indeed died, that he, Harrison Lipscombe would be sworn in as the President of the United States, in the Oval Office at 10:00 a.m. the next day.

****** Jerusalem:

The Prime Minister of Israel put the country and his operatives on full alert. Starting at 5:00 a.m. Jerusalem time, he too spent several hours speaking to world leaders, important friends in the United States, and made plans to attend the funeral services, whenever that might be. New plans, indeed, would have to be formulated. But *the cause* was still there and the objectives just as urgent.

****** Heathrow Airport:

A thin, dark-skinned man navigated through the customs maze efficiently and quietly before melting into the city. He was noticed by no one; and if he was, he was soon forgotten.

****** Paris:

In a small back room in a modest two story house in the Muslim quarter, a meeting was being held. Six young men and a woman were listening intently to the speaker. Maps indicated missile silos, and air fields, and other targeted areas. The silos and the fields were all within a 400 mile radius of Jerusalem. The middle-aged man directing the group bore an unmistakable resemblance to the man who was recently the head of the whole Muslim world.

****** A Washington Suburb:

"Miss Patricia Winthrope?" the police detective standing on her porch asked. "Yes, what is it?" Patty had faced all of the tragedy she could handle this day. Apparently there was more. "Are you an acquaintance or relative of General George Steinman?" the detective continued. Patty gulped; *not him too,* she thought. *Had he been on Air Force One also,* she wondered. "May we come in?" Patty responded by stepping back and opening the door wide.

The two policemen stepped inside and stood in the middle of her living room, looking awkward. "How do you know General Steinman?" the second detective inquired. "He is the Director of an important classified project at the Pentagon. I am his executive secretary," Patty said, casually. "Could we sit down?" the first detective said, seating himself. "The General was found this afternoon in his home. He was either murdered, or he committed suicide, we don't know which."

Patty felt nauseated. Panic over a world gone mad. She had known and respected George Steinman for eight years now and he had *always* treated her like a lady. He had become the most important man in her life, even though there had never been a hint of romantic involvement by either of them. "You are listed as his next of kin or one to be notified in case of an emergency," the first detective explained. Patty was numb, and could only stare at the officer. "Can you come downtown tomorrow and identify the body?" Patty frowned at this tasteless, tactless directness. She shook her head no, then feebly said "maybe tomorrow." The two detectives rose and started toward the door. "I'll send a car around for you tomorrow afternoon," the first detective said as they left, closing the door behind them. Patty fell over onto the couch and sobbed long sobs, trying to close out the world which had just collapsed around her. She could only rely now on her faith in God, and she said a prayer for herself, George, the President, and the country.

***

****** **Smith Valley, Nevada:**

A large red-tailed hawk circled silently overhead, searching for his breakfast. Jason felt livened by the chill of the morning air and the solitude of this place. He had settled down for some quiet moments of serious fishing at a favorite spot of his on the Walker River. His line was in and he had gotten as comfortable as he could, half way up the bank. He hoped he wouldn't get much action this morning. He was still unwinding from the catastrophic events of only three weeks before. The clear Nevada air always helped him see things in a better perspective. The tragic news still haunted him. A strong feeling of guilt had settled to the bottom of his consciousness like a heavy meal. He repeatedly rationalized that what he and his associates had done with *ABACUS* was a separate issue from the assassination of the President, but gnawing quietly on his inner thoughts was the suspicion that it might have been somehow related.

On the positive side, the President and his lady had died heroes. Already funds were being gathered for a foundation, and some in the Congress were proposing that his likeness be impressed on the Nickel.   It would never be necessary, Jason hoped beyond hope, to have the misuse of *ABACUS* brought to public attention.

Jason reviewed the options he had with Jamie. Fortunately for him, Jamie had squirreled away a large part of the budget he had given her, which was almost all of his regular pay. This would get them back into a nice home near Berkeley, or would get them started in a local business, perhaps ranching, in conjunction with his mother.   The tragedy brought relief to Betty Phillips. She mourned as much as most ordinary citizens who had never met Grant and Carrie Williams, but she knew perhaps even better than Jason what they were about, and she was relieved that her part too was ended.

****** Jerusalem:
Harrison Lipscombe was on the line of the special red phone in Avery Harrington's home office. "Yes Mr. President, thank you." Avery was flattered and a little surprised at Harrison's continued fierce loyalty and the fact that he made a point to discuss world matters and the *cause* with Avery almost daily. Some world leaders, whom Avery had helped gain offices of authority and influence, felt compelled to exert their independence from Avery and the *cause*, once ensconced in their position. Almost no one abandoned him, but some assumed a different priority in their affairs, and put their more parochial issues ahead of world peace and prosperity. "Yes, Mr. President, I think that would be well. I will see what I can do to help, behind the scenes, of course." "Thank you." "Good morning Harrison; thanks again. With your help we may yet achieve our common goals." ...."Yes, good evening."

Avery gently rolled the receiver over into its cradle, as if putting the phone to bed. He had been in thoughtful contemplation this evening, planning the next bold move. It had been such a tragedy about Carrie. He had strong feelings for her. But she of all people would want their common dream to be forwarded and eventually achieved.

Plans were slightly delayed regarding the installation of Avery as the new Secretary General in deference to the tragedy. But the work was moving ahead, as deliberately as ever. The United Nations continued to grow into its role as peacekeeper of the world, and as the clearinghouse for international police intelligence, and as the champion of all of the underdeveloped nations. The reluctance of the United States to agree to its full atomic disarmament remained a major obstacle for the *cause*, but with Harrison Lipscombe in the White House, things just might eventuate as Avery had long ago scripted the plan.

Harrison, and Avery, and Dr. Sam Levanthol had gotten together quietly only days after the President's funeral, to discuss *ABACUS*, specifically. Harrison was briefed on what Sam had pieced together about the sabotage. At issue was what to do about *ABACUS*. They could probably just let it quietly die, but it had proved such a powerful tool for Grant Williams that they were reluctant to do that. A major question was whether the other (remaining) principals were willing to just let it quietly fade away. Given the robust and growing economy, Harrison could work his will in the Congress and stand for election on his own. But *ABACUS* might provide the insurance which would almost certainly guarantee success.

****** Smith Valley, Nevada:

The sudden pull on his line interrupted Jason's reverie and brought him to his feet, ready to do what he supposedly came there for this morning. As he swept his catch into his net, with a grunt of satisfaction, he heard someone shouting his name.

Climbing up on the bank, he saw Jamie running toward him, waving and calling his name. He knew she saw him so he just waited silently. He could tell from her demeanor that nothing was very seriously wrong, so he did not need to hurry. In fact, he had been deliberately not in a hurry this whole time. It was a time to regroup and contemplate their future. It was time for quiet re-creation.

Jamie was so out of breath when she finally got to Jason that she couldn't talk. She gestured, and made incomprehensible sounds, but couldn't quite articulate what it was she was so excited about. "Calm down sweetheart, it is O.K.," Jason reassured her, holding her from falling down the bank. After a few deep breathes, Jamie got her voice back, and told him excitedly about a phone call he had gotten about thirty minutes earlier. "President Lipscombe himself!" Jamie assured him.

***

"Yes, I am returning his call," Jason said. On the way back to the house he had thought about the range of possible reasons the President of The United States could be calling him about. Two possibilities seemed probable. First, with General Steinman gone and the project in deep trouble, there were probably a lot of questions. Second, if the new president wanted to continue to use *ABACUS*, he would certainly need someone like Jason to help resurrect it. He wished he had time to talk to Max and Brent before he talked to Harrison Lipscombe. But the call was urgent and, after all, he was The President. "Yes sir, Mr. President. Yes, well, I'd like to explain that, yes." Certainly, tomorrow? Yes. I see. All right, Mr. President. I'll be there. Yes, good-bye." He *knew* about it all.

The President had disavowed his support of the use that Carrie Williams had put the project to, and seemed anxious to add safeguards into the system before it was restored. But he wanted it restored, and he wanted Jason to be the new Director of the project, with his associates, Doctors McGurn and Schultz as his Deputy Directors. He was to be at the White House tomorrow. A thousand questions flooded his mind. Jason tried desperately to get ahold of Max and Brent, but they were both declared to be on extended vacation, and unavailable.

Unknown to either Jason, or Harrison Lipscombe, their conversation was recorded, and dispatched hastily out of the country. There seemed to be a lot of tourists of late, just to see the beauty of Smith Valley! **Over all this, an agent of a higher power observed, and stood watch over this special man, destined to play a future important role.**

END OF PART IV

PART V

NEW LEADERS

"You will hear of wars and rumors of wars, but see to it that you are not alarmed. Such things must happen, but the end is still to come…"
The Holy Bible

Chapter 17: NEW KINGS FOR THE *CAUSE*

****** Jerusalem:

The Prime Minister's driver met him at the gate at Tel Aviv National Airport, and helped him with his luggage, even though Avery Harrington always traveled light. Storm clouds greeted him on his arrival back to Israel. The swirling dark clouds brought much needed rain, and that was always considered a blessing on the land. The smell of the purifying ozone refreshed him, and made coming home a wonderful event, especially after a successful trip.

Avery Harrington had just finished a whirlwind expedition around the world. He had visited Jakarta, Islamabad, London, New Delhi, Baghdad, and Washington D.C. "Sharon, please set up phone calls to this list of names I have. Check on their local times, and make the appointments at least 30 minutes apart," he said. "I am exhausted, and I am going to go crash for now. I will be back here at 9 a.m. tomorrow," he concluded.

***

Avery Harrington orchestrated a succession of top government officials in Indonesia, Iran, and Syria by calling on members of his extensive network within the *cause*, by support of the world-wide press, and cash infusions where appropriate. The *quid pro quo* was, of course, that each of these leaders would support Avery in his nomination to become the Secretary General of the United Nations. The follow-up calls he made to these gentlemen confirmed the arrangement, with more support for their own power bases, promised or implied. His last call was to his friend, Madam

Anteres Jandi. It would soon be time to formally elect him to that high office. He could have won the seat before now, but these new players promised a unanimous backing, which Avery felt would insure that their plans could be enacted in an expeditious manner.

Prior to the special session, called for the election of the new U.N. Secretary General, Avery Harrington exercised his powerful network, to place various operators in strategic positions in the governments of those few countries who were reluctant to endorse him before. Specifically, Mohammed Ali Sharlavani was installed as the Foreign Secretary for the old Persian Kingdom. The previous Secretary resigned after massive evidence, implicating him in the theft of significant oil shipments, surfaced.

The Deputy Vice President of Indonesia, General Susilo Indrawali, was promoted to be the Ambassador to the U.N. when the previous Ambassador was nominated to the top court in the country. Avery Harrington's special ally in Syria was Doctor Agha Khurbet SaadAllah, a very influential leader in Damascus circles, who prevailed on the President of Syria to instruct his Ambassador to the U.N. to back Avery Harrington. Thus it was that even in the Muslim countries, there was widespread support of Avery Harrington through his loyal network of men and women who believed in the *cause*, and shared his dream of peace and prosperity for all.

****** **Washington D.C.:**
Jason Phillips looked rumpled, which is what most people look like when they arrive in Washington after taking the red-eye from Nevada. There was no time given him to

come a day early and properly dress himself for the President of the United States.

Jason's level 4 security papers, and an alert to the security office at the White House by Able Larson, the appointment secretary kept on by the new President, facilitated the sometimes arduous task of arriving at the Oval Office at the appointed time.

"Jason," the President greeted, rising from his comfortable chair behind the imposing desk. "Mr. President," Jason responded, looking him squarely in the eyes. Jason had rehearsed just what he wanted to say to the President, but the President was the one asking the questions. "My condolences for the Williams', and your Colonel Steinman," Harrison said. "The President and Carrie were dear friends of mine too, you know, but I had only met George a few times; I know you served together out at Pendleton," he said. "I also understand that you gave up a promising career in academia to help us here," he continued. "This tragedy has put the government in a difficult position, Jason, and I need your help a while longer," the President said.

Harrison Lipscombe asked Jason to take George Steinman's position, running the ABACUS project, with his two partners, Max McGurn and Brent Schultz to carry out their duties, with a sweetener added to their contracts, of course. Specifically, Jason and his crew were to gracefully archive all personal data securely, and then reconstruct exactly what took place on the project. The President told Jason that he knew that ABACUS had been sabotaged, but that he understood that, and felt they acted properly. He wanted to know about the blackballing of the Arizona Senator, and of any other untoward use of the system. He told Jason that he was considering giving ABACUS to the United Nations, for use in their crime control operations, and other tasks, but he wanted to talk to Jason and his lieutenants before he firmed up any plans.

Jason was visibly relieved, and was happy to report back to his sidekick back in Nevada. Jason had gone into his audience with the President with real fear and trepidation, uncertain whether he would be charged for his "crime", or if this would be the end of his career, or both. The President's calm manner and reassuring words eased his fears immediately. He felt like a ton of weight had been lifted off of him; and it was almost as if he were suddenly lighter than air. "Jamie, they have done it again, they made me an offer I can't refuse," he said into the phone, after checking in at one of his favorite hotels in Washington. He told her of his meeting with the President, and his appeal for help. And besides, with a hefty increase in his contract, they could retire in not too long.

***

The next morning, everyone was surprised to see him at the project. He and Jamie had said what everyone thought were their good-byes. His office was still vacant, but he moved right into the General's office, by way of telling everyone that he was now in charge of being in charge.

Patty Winthrope was still on an extended vacation, so Jason asked Suzie, Brent's secretary, to help him. He called a general meeting for 1:00 p.m. that day, and proceeded to try to get in touch with Brent and Max. Those two had very carefully blocked any attempts to get to them, and had secreted themselves away on some kind of sabbatical, so to speak. They had told their secretaries they would be gone for at least three weeks, or longer. It was now into the third week, so they might show up at any time.

Jason went ahead with his general meeting, which meant everyone on the project, at 1 p.m. sharp. It was a brief, stand-up meeting, which was appropriate, as he had very little to tell them. "This will be brief folks. I was called in to the White House yesterday, and I had about 10 minutes with the President. Here is what he said. First of all, he sends his condolences for our loss, and he wants to continue with the project. He asked me to head it up, taking the General's place. He wants us all to stay on for the time being, but he is also considering several alternate plans for the project. Until Brent and Max get back, I want to keep the system in a level 1 maintenance state, which will give us all a chance to catch up on our documentation. When I learn more, I will share as much as I can. Meanwhile, he sends his thanks for our past service, and hopes we will all continue the work," he concluded.

****** **The Pentagon:**
A week went by before Dr. McGurn and Dr. Schultz showed up at work. Jason immediately closeted himself with them, greeting them like the long-lost good friends they were. "The President is on to us," Jason began, and then paused, keeping them in suspense for a few moments.

"But all is forgiven," he continued. "Whew," they both exhaled, relaxing from the tension that the uncertainty of Jason's statement had generated.

Jason reviewed for them everything that had transpired since the death of the former President and his wife, and everyone on-board Air Force One. President Harrison Lipscombe had rapidly taken over the reins of government, continuing Grant and Carrie Williams' policies. Jason had begun to put together a presentation for the President; to summarize the history of just for what ABACUS had been used. "I have not heard from the White House, but we better be prepared to give him a summary of what was done with ABACUS, and maybe we ought to be prepared to tell him why we should keep it here, rather than give it to the U.N. I can't understand why the U.N. would ever need this much computer power, anyway," Jason continued. "As we have discussed before," Brent interrupted, "there is an abundance of good things ABACUS could do for the country."

After dividing up the work for the President's presentation, and setting stringent time lines, it became apparent to Brent and Max that under Jason's management, the three of them would continue to be a team of equals, largely. As soon as the three teams were launched, the three leaders began formulating their ideas about how and why ABACUS should be applied.

Max and his team briefly described how the Operating System managed the resources, their general approach to pipelining, and about the structure of the various data bases, both for the socioeconomic modeling, and the clandestine personal information which had the potential to destroy political enemies, as Carrie had done to destroy Senator Crzynski. Max's crew also briefly described the security measures used to preserve integrity and to protect the system from sabotage, both from inside and outside the project.

Brent and his crew described the development of the model, in its many stages, and the test procedures. Brent personally described the many applications, both legitimate and illegitimate. The authorization train for each was documented, as much as they could reconstruct.

Jason's team constructed a broad presentation of the history of the art, the TAT system, and the special applications dealing with Carrie Williams' attempt to rescind the 22nd Amendment. The leaders agreed that each of them should separately lobby for the applications each of them favored, leaving the choices up to the President, or his designees.

****** **The White House:**
"Caroline, get me Jason Phillips over at the Pentagon," the President ordered.

***

"Jason, when can you give your presentation on ABACUS?" he asked. "Mr. President, we can give our presentation to you as early as tomorrow morning, but we'd like a couple of days to polish it, however." "Good, be up here with a small crew Friday morning. What level of security should this be?" "We were planning on a level 4 classification," Jason said.

"Fine, Jason, Friday at 9 a.m. then!" the President said, and hung up, not waiting for a response.

****** U.N. Headquarters:

"Harrison, I'd like for my deputy, over at TAT to sit in with you," Avery Harrington said. "His name is Bill Sanders, and he already has his level 6 clearance on file at "State", and DOD! He will be there just to listen; he won't ask any questions." "Either way," The President responded, "your call." "Thanks, Harrison," Avery concluded.

****** The White House:

Present at the ABACUS presentation were three select members of the President's National Security Council, The Secretaries of State, Defense, Commerce, the Attorney General, Mr. Bill Sanders from Israel, and Mrs. Janet Simonson, the U.S. Ambassador to the United Nations. It was announced that Mr. Sanders represented Avery Harrington, the designated Secretary General of the U.N.

Jason was very nervous the morning of his big show for the President, but Jamie reminded him that no one understood ABACUS as well as he. The PowerPoint presentations were displayed on two large rear projection display screens. Most elements of the show were backed up with supporting detail, if it was necessary, which it was, occasionally.

The presentations went well and seemed to anticipate most of President Lipscombe's questions. The audience was clearly quite impressed, not only at the power and the fidelity of ABACUS, but of the obvious abuse to which the Williams' had put the system. At the same time, the audience was quite interested in the many ways that ABACUS could be applied to their many difficult problems.

Mr. Sanders took copious notes but never offered any comments or questions. But his body language and facial expressions displayed great interest and occasional amazement. He seemed surprised to learn that the ABACUS personnel knew so much about TAT.

***

"Jason, our thanks to you and your team. That was just what we needed. I would like for the three of you to show us your facilities next week. At that time we will try out some plans we have for ABACUS , and we'd like your reactions," said the President. Harrison Lipscombe took the time and effort to shake hands with and personally thank Doctors McGurn and Schultz, as well.

****** U.N. Headquarters:

"Are there any more questions we have for Mr. Harrington?" asked Anteres Jandi, as the time approached for the important vote confirming the nomination of Avery Harrington for the office of Secretary General of the United Nations. After a brief pause, and with no further questions, Anteres Jandi called for the vote, which was unanimous.

Chapter 18: COOKING THE BOOKS

In one of the major ghettos on the outskirts of Paris, the old enemy of Israel, one Mr. Malik Al Shafei, was holding forth among his inner circle. "Gentlemen, I am about to trust you all with the future of the whole Muslim world, the conquest of the entire world, and my life," he began. "We cannot wait on the random and sometimes regrettable vicissitudes of chance and circumstances. We need to accelerate the appearance of the Mahdi; we must strike while the opportunities are here. Now is the time, and you must all participate in this grand scheme."

Malik Al Shafei went on to tell them of his thoughts to magically produce their great Messiah, so clearly prophesied in the Muslim writings. His plan included the rebirth of his old network of great *movers*, reporting directly to him. His own makeover, the *correction* of various government records to verify the legitimacy of the *Promised One*, and the development of a huge arsenal of powerful weapons which would ensure the victory of the Muslim faith over the world. Malik Al Shafei was quite long on promising his underlings glory, riches, and honor, and special places in heaven, but short on the particulars.

****** **Alexandria, Egypt:**

Mohammed Aramuel, one of Malik Al Shafei's first tier of underlings, entered the great hall of records, one of the adjunct buildings on the campus of perhaps the world's greatest housings of antiquities. The clerk at the main desk carefully checked over his credentials, masterfully forged documents which proved he was an agent for the famous

229

Louvre in Paris. "So you too are looking forward to the soon coming of the great Mahdi," the clerk enthused. You will find the sacred charts showing the messianic line on the third floor, Section B, Row 8. May I examine the contents of your briefcase? Just following the rules, you know." "Certainly, of course," responded Mohammed. He had picked this day and this hour, knowing this particular clerk, a faithful and friendly Muslim, would be on duty. Mohammed had been here a month ago, taking photos of the old records housed here, carefully researching every reference to the lineage of the great and future Mahdi. After showing Malik Al Shafei himself, they had planned this exchange of doctored documents very carefully.

The section he was working was totally devoid of other visitors this hour, purposely coinciding with the afternoon prayer time. Mohammed surreptitiously exchanged the inside contents of the hidden section of his brief case with the contents of the large hand-written ledger with the peculiar leather and papyrus cover. The whole exchange took less than a minute to accomplish. He carefully cleaned the document of all hand and fingerprints, as a precaution.

This week he had been very busy, making similar exchanges in official records in London, Paris, Riyadh, Tehran, Damascus, and Jerusalem. There was great care taken in these other master repositories of the holy lineage prescription, but Malik Al Shafei knew that in the case of any dispute, or to verify the facts, the authorities of any stripe would go to Alexandria, as the records of greatest authority. Fortunately for Malik Al Shafei , he only needed a few subtle changes in the lineage names to bring these records into complete conformity with his own. But doctored *birthright certificates* were only one of several elements of the makeover.

****** **Paris:**

The plastic surgeon specialist Malik Al Shafei engaged for his makeover was a woman doctor from Sweden, who knew nothing of the prophesies of the great Mahdi. Malik Al Shafei went to his first appointment with her, equipped with sketches of profiles and detailed drawings of his mouth, nose, and eyes. "Doctor Hamming, I have been an admirer of yours since I first researched the possibility of my makeover, which I am requesting," Malik Al Shafei began. I need it for business purposes, and partly for my own vanity," he concluded. Svetla Hamming smiled, and almost laughed. Such candor about one's vanity was rare, indeed. "Well, Mr. Mohammed Barhuto (an alias he used for this occasion), we shall do our best. You say you are from Riyadh?" she asked. "Yes, I am here for an extended business conference, and I thought it would be well to get this done, from one of the best!" Malik Al Shafei answered.

Svetla Hamming looked at the drawings, and after thoroughly measuring Malik Al Shafei's head, and checking his general condition, showed him the extent she could match the desired "look". She brought in an associate to work on his front teeth, to finish the makeover. In fact, the braces required to force his front teeth apart would take longer to heal than the actual surgery by Dr. Hamming. After Malik Al Shafei set his special crew to their tasks, he went ahead with the surgery, paying for the operations in advance, with a bagful of cash.

***

Three assassins visited three different country homes on an early Saturday morning, in one of the rich suburbs of Paris, south and west of the city. A professional arsonist torched the whole medical facility where the makeover had taken place. The fire began in the records section of the offices, as was directed by Malik Al Shafei. There would be no records or witnesses to betray the birth of the new Mahdi, to be called the 12th Imam, and the modern day Caliph of the whole Muslim world.

Chapter 19: "STAR WARS" REDUX

Avery Harrington watched the demonstration of the newly minted *International Missile Defense System* (IMDS) from a special booth overlooking the control room installed at the World Headquarters of the United Nations, in New York. This day he was hosting the Ambassadors to the U.N. from all of the atomic club members, namely, the U.S., the United Kingdom, Russia, France, China, Israel, India, Pakistan, Indonesia, North Korea, and Iran.

The designated target sites at Brasilia, White Sands, the Gobi desert site, Sahara's Timbuktu, and Saskatoon, Canada, all signaled their readiness. The test was to be a demonstration of the flexibility of the IMDS, and to show that the U.N. had the capacity to withstand an overwhelming number of missile strikes from multiple sources at times unknown, from sites unknown. An elaborate radar defense network of eighty-seven sites around the world constantly scanned the skies, for the purpose of detecting missile launches and determining their trajectories within seconds of their detection. A compliment of 24 Spy satellites completed the surveillance network part of the IMDS.

Launch facilities were set up at forty sites worldwide, but only half of them were to be used in this test. The sites were selected only a few minutes before the demonstration began, and were known only to the designated base personnel, and the select members with Avery Harrington, watching the demonstration with him. "Missile launch out of Germany." was the first announcement. Ten minutes later, the military personnel in charge of the launch plan announced "Missile launch out of Australia." After another five minutes, there were four simultaneous launches from Egypt, The Philippines, India, and Jordan. Another thirty minutes later, a different set of simultaneous launches were conducted, all aiming at the target site in Canada. Altogether, there were one hundred and twenty missiles, launched from twenty sites. The maximum number of missiles in the air at one time was 68, which occurred twenty three minutes after the beginning of the demonstration. Of the 120 missiles fired, 92 were destroyed before their apogee, the rest shortly after the apogee of each missile. So the demonstration was pronounced 100 per cent successful. The levels of redundancy required to achieve this success was not known to the public, but was one of the tightly guarded secrets of the IMDS.

All of the club member representatives with Avery Harrington happily congratulated him for the dramatically successful test. The demonstration, of course, was conducted primarily as a sales ploy, for convincing all of the club members to accept the terms of the FAT, which provided for a gradual reduction of all atomic weapons over a ten year period, and as obsolescence rendered the arsenals useless.

****** **Tehran:**
Malik Al Shafei had been careful to place one of his operatives in the delegation supporting the U.N. in the IMDS demonstration. Shortly after, he convened a group of his technical lackeys to discuss the results. It was apparent to the group that Malik Al Shafei was primarily interested in determining how many land radar systems, and satellites should be disabled in order to defeat the system. He was already planning a demonstration of his own!

****** **U. N. Headquarters:**

A month after the IMDS demonstration, the issue of FAT was brought to a vote. In the meanwhile, Avery Harrington used his network to provide a massive public opinion war in favor of the treaty, especially in all of the *member* countries.

"Mr. Secretary General," announced the head of the Security Council, "the vote is unanimous to take the issue to the General Assembly," he beamed. It was rather pro forma from this point, as everyone knew. The Final Atomic Treaty was a done deal! Avery Harrington would monitor the progress of the prescribed dismantling and simultaneous testing and witnessing required by the treaty. Nothing would be left to chance. No nation would be allowed to back out of its commitment.

Part of the negotiations required to get the last club members to capitulate was to give all of them permanent seats on the Security Council, which Avery Harrington planned to dissolve anyway. But this concession, together with all of the carrots and sticks, and the massive opinion dynamics orchestrated by members of the *cause*, persuaded even the most reluctant of the hold outs, namely, the United States.

****** **Eastern Iran Desert Area:**

Four small trucks roared up the winding road to the entrance of what looked like a natural cave in the side of the hill. The first truck disgorged its load of men who quickly unloaded the very heavy cargo into the cave, where others took possession and stored all of the parts this convoy brought. The whole operation took less than twenty minutes. Still, overhead satellites saw the operation, and some took note; others checked the files on this particular site.

The place was near Bojnurd in Northeast Iran, in foothill country. Nomadic tribes grazed their sheep here, as they had for thousands of years. Barren and distant from everything, this is where Malik Al Shafei chose to store his cache of arms. A good cover had to be in place, as the whole area was under satellite surveillance almost continuously. The cover Malik Al Shafei devised was the construction of a mining operation, together with a cement plant. The proper licenses were procured, and elaborate, almost real, props provided the sky eyes what they wanted them to see. With the ruse of a false report generated by one of his faithful few, Malik Al Shafei arranged for a small U.N. inspection staff to visit the mining site early in the operation. With their Geiger counters constantly monitoring the area, and pictures providing the site background identification, the U.N. inspectors were able to check all of the boxes on their forms. Of course, once the site was visited, and tests, pictures and readings recorded, it would be listed in the U.N. inspection archives as *clean*, and no notice would be given it from that time onward. That was, of course, just what Malik Al Shafei had planned. Elaborate tunnels were then built at the "mine", with steel doors put in place to insure total security for his arsenal.

A big pre-fabricated steel building with a set of large doors provided storage space for the building supplies, and for the amenities of life. The partially complete cement plant provided plenty of smoke and steam in all directions, which covered their clandestine operations during daylight hours. Guards posted on the outward extents of the site kept sheep and shepherds alike a far distance from all of the operations. Only two of Malik Al Shafei's lieutenants at the site knew what was really going on. Local contractors were called in to do the welding, carpentry, and wiring for what was later to become a missile launch site.

Small tactical atomic warheads, launch railings, and almost antiquated delivery rockets were brought to the site in parts, and stored in the mine, awaiting the hour of their use. It appeared that dozens of barrels of paint were brought into the facility. In actuality, they were payload packages of anthrax and nerve gas, the use for which Malik Al Shafei had not yet decided. Not even his on-site flunkies knew what these sealed barrels contained, but were warned by Malik Al Shafei himself to not disturb, move, or open any of them without his being present. They all knew the consequences of disobedience, and no one had a curiosity greater than the fear of the terrible results to their person would be. After all of the weaponry was secured behind the steel doors, the compound settled into a routine of sparse but regular deliveries, simulated building activity, and of guarding the premises. The locals were let go, and the compound personnel were restricted to the site, and the place was rather forgotten, even by the surrounding population, sparse as it was, and rather distant from everything.

Other remote sites were equipped in a similar way, except all of the other sites were meant to simply flood the Israeli missile defenses, and to obscure the main launch site at

Bojnurd. None of the other sites had any nuclear warheads, or any chemical or germ warfare material, and were to be destroyed as soon as the planned demonstration was complete.

***

****** **Tehran:**

The Sheraton Plaza was no longer the finest hotel in the city, but that was where Malik Al Shafei held his reunion, so to speak, of his tetrarchs. Most of his appointed leaders were new, promoted from the ranks of his faithful. When Malik Al Shafei fled the country just three years earlier, he had the presence to take his laptop computer with him, and a couple of key storage disks. With all this vital information, and the supply of lots of cash he had cached, he was able to regroup his regime. It was now time to assemble the troops, and go into action.

Guards at every door to the intimate conference room they had acquired insured that there would be no press, hotel personnel, or strangers at the meeting. "Gentlemen, it is my pleasure to introduce to you our great leader who is Malik Al Shafei's successor, one who will lead us to great victories, after the consolidation of the Muslim Empire," Mr. Mohammed Aramuel began, after getting the undivided attention of the twelve princes assembled. "I give you Mahammed Hussan Kassim, soon to be the new Caliph of the whole Muslim world." The faithful held their collective breath, having never heard or seen this new phenomenon before. Mahammed Hussan Kassim entered from behind a curtain, dressed in the finest attire ever seen on any Imam. The group gasped at his splendor, and his appearance, and at his obvious command. All of them had seen the popular depiction of the prophesied Mahdi, with the unusual space between his two front teeth, and the man before them bore a very strong resemblance to that image. Although something about him reminded some of them of Malik Al Shafei, they had all been assured that Malik Al Shafei was officially declared dead, and buried.

"Gentlemen," Kassim opened. This man's voice was deep and commanding, and different from that of their former leader. Everyone was thinking 'who is this', but without exception, they were ready to resume the program started by Malik Al Shafei.

"Today we begin Mahammed's dream of world conquest for the sake of Allah!" Kassim continued. Everyone sat up, waiting expectantly. They wanted to believe everything this man had to say. "Your first assignment is to consolidate your base in every Muslim country. Be prepared for action by recruiting top men in each of your countries; men of authority, who can be trusted. Even as we speak, each of your personal accounts we have provided for you is being injected with an additional 40 million pounds. This will buy you the influence you need. After the infidels' atomic treaty has been implemented, and all of their atomic weapons have been destroyed, Allah's will is that we shall be provided with an exclusive arsenal of these powerful weapons. The infidels of the world shall then have to capitulate or die!" concluded Kassim. The assembled Tetrarchs stared at each other in disbelief.

Chapter 20: THE CHIEF BROTHER

****** The White House:

The new President continued his series of addresses to the nation, offered every Saturday morning. He had made presentations on the subjects of the national defense, the economy, world trade, the use of the United Nations as the favored peacekeeping agency, and the subject of atomic disarmament. This week, the announced subject was the ecumenical movement started by Carrie-Witherington-Williams.

"My fellow Americans, and God fearing people everywhere," he began, setting the tone of the morning's subject. "The Church of the Brotherhood of Man, so nobly begun by our former First Lady shall be supported on a continuing basis by my administration!" "The constraints of the 1st Amendment do not allow us to openly fund this activity, but we will and can continue to provide tax incentives for the many *Faith-Based* programs which so efficiently supplement our government social programs. Because the church activities have grown so much and because, as President, there are too many demands on my time to lead as well as Carrie-Witherington-Williams did, I will be appointing about two dozen church leaders from around the world to form an inter-faith council (IFC), to lead this effort. They, in turn shall select three church leaders to form a triumvirate to manage the activities on a worldwide basis.

The organization may fall under the sponsorship of the U.N. That is being studied, and a recommendation from the

IFC shall be forthcoming. It is our hope and expectation that every major theistic religion on earth shall be represented on this Council and it will be a peaceful and useful forum for religious leaders to share their ideas, concerns, and insights, with all people everywhere.

Please continue to support your local churches. Participation in this grand ecumenical movement will hopefully lead us all to accept the Fatherhood of God and the Brotherhood of man, and shall lead us all to respect and honor these principles."

After the President announced the appointment of an Ad Hoc committee to gather nominations for the IFC, he closed by again thanking the government leaders at all levels for supporting the transition of his government to power, in succession of the Williams' Administration.

***

In the following months, there was a strong ecumenical movement which was triggered by the President's initiation of the IFC. No one wanted to be left out of this powerful new organization. Strange things seemed to be afoot, including a large scale teaming of governments and clergy everywhere. There was room in this new form of religion for all beliefs, and all races. This seemed to be a good answer for the widespread anti-religion movement started in Europe. This movement argued that most wars were promulgated by religious bigotry, and the strong drives of most religions to proselytize others. It was seriously promoted that all religions be banned, upon pain of death or prison. Avery Harrington and his *cause* envisioned the world government as an alliance between civil and religious authorities, in control of a single world army, answering only to the world government. He promoted these ideas tirelessly among his colleagues in the *cause*.

The IFC promoted the most powerful leaders in their respective religions, including the Pope, the most powerful Imams, the various heads of the protestant sects, the Dahli Lama, the titular heads of the Hindus, and the Head Prophet of the LDS. The first meetings of the IFC were addressed by envoys from the U.N., and it was made clear that funding, and real power was to be shared with this new ecumenical body.

END OF PART V

PART VI
THE FINAL ATOMIC TREATY

"They will beat their swords into plowshares, and their spears into pruning hooks. Nation will not take up sword against nation, nor will they train for war anymore..."
The Holy Bible

Chapter 21: THE DEVIL in the DETAILS

The part of the negotiations required to get the last club members to capitulate, namely, to give all of them permanent seats on the Security Council, was formalized with great fanfare.

Mrs. Janet Simonson, the United States Ambassador to the United Nations, was quite reluctant to give up such a large piece of the sovereignty of the country to any international body. Her position was reinforced by the Secretary of Defense, and all of the Joint Chiefs of Staff.

****** **The White House:**
At a special called meeting of the National Security Council, to which all of the relevant players were invited, President Harrison Lipscombe addressed the group. "Ladies and Gentlemen, we live in a very dangerous world. The threat of a global holocaust, ignited by some rogue dictator, or by some misguided or misunderstood actions by one of the club members, grows heavier by the year. Already, we have eleven members in the club, and our intelligence has uncovered an additional six 'wannabes'. We have the wherewithal now to detect and destroy missile launches from anywhere, and our international naval inspectors, and our port and border defenses are reducing the overall probability of attack by atomic weapons to an acceptable very low probability. Now, let us address your objections to the implementation of FAT."

The Secretary of Defense jumped to his feet. "Mr. President, we have studied the inspection problem, and we conclude that there is a very *high* probability that one or more club members will withhold some of their weapons!" "Mr. Strauss, as usual, you have gone straight for the heart," the President responded. "My sources have come to the same conclusion! That **IS** the weakest point in the plan. Therefore, we have already initiated plans to back up the inspection activities with intelligence surveillance of all of the members and wannabes."

The President went on to introduce Mr. Glen Brookstrier, an intelligence specialist in atomic weaponry, who presented their tentative plans for extensive efforts in this area. The presentation and accompanying discussions used up the remainder of the scheduled two hours, but at the conclusion of the meeting, there seemed to be a consensus to go ahead with the FAT, with the assurance that the surveillance plan would be implemented in full force.

The world of experts on atomic weapons agreed that the shelf life of all weapons was about twenty years. Since earlier treaties had halted all refurbishment over ten years ago, it was felt that over the next ten years, all atomic weapons would become totally obsolete, and should be scrapped. The issue, of course, was whether they would be replaced, in violation of the existing treaties.

Because of this situation, one of the first actions of the FAT was to document the history of all fissionable material, starting with the exploration and mining operations, and through the refinement processes, and including the recycling efforts practiced by breeder reactors, and the older fission reactor generating facilities in the world.

****** **The Pentagon:**

"Gentlemen," Jason began, ensconced in his big office, inherited from his friend and mentor, the late General George Steinman. "We finally have some marching orders. The President is not going to give us away to the U.N. just now." Brent Schultz and Max McGurn seemed pleased at that turn of events. "Our primary assignment now is to support the implementation of the Final Atomic Treaty. The liaison official from the U.N. shall be Mr. Sanders, whom you met at our presentation at the White House. We shall house him in my old office, unless one of you wants to move there and give him your office."

So ABACUS had a new life, important, secretive, and challenging. Administratively, they were to report to the Secretary of Homeland Security, Dr. Eugene Giuliano, who just happened to be an atomic physicist, with a strong background in intelligence and weaponry. Their first task was to design a software system which would integrate all of the existing data bases for the various existing national systems, the IMDS, and the intelligence networks to show the ever-changing conditions relating to atomic weapons, the inspection processes, the disposal functions, and any violations developing contrary to the FAT.

In the months that followed, the ABACUS team developed a fantastic data base for this new application. They started by designing the display systems first, as had become the practice of most interactive software development. Three major design presentations were made, with all user agencies represented. The final show had the President in attendance, and he was most impressed. The displays looked so realistic, that the team had to keep reminding the user community that what they were seeing was merely a dummy set of data, and that the first step was to confirm the efficacy of the displays and the implied data requirements.

Upon the ratification of the FAT by all of the club members, and the General Assembly of the United Nations, the inspections began. All of the wannabes were pressured into ratifying the treaty, formally, and without reservations. ABACUS, which was the repository of the sum of all of the related information, provided regular briefings for the international press, together with written reports and high quality still shots of the graphic displays. The old catch phrase *transparency* was evident, and served notice to all parties wanting to keep their own information secret. Reading between the lines, it was obvious that the inspection process was supplemented with lots of intelligence work, in a cooperative manner.

****** U.N. Headquarters:

All means of possible delivery methods were included in the treaty, including all hard and portable missile launch mechanisms, all aircraft systems, all naval vessels, both above and below the surface, particularly the *boomer* submarines which carried up to 32 atomic missiles each, to be launched from under the surface. By volume, the greatest task was inspecting cargo ships, with their hundreds of thousands of containers shipped every year, to and from even the smallest port facility, anywhere in the world. By manpower, the extensive national borders were a great burden.

In the previous 60 years, drug smuggling had greatly increased across borders, but with the U.N. taking over the task, with sovereign rights to police drug traffic worldwide, the traffic had reduced the movement of drugs across all borders to an absolute minimum. In some countries, and in some states, home-grown manufacturing and growth of drugs was allowed, under license, and thereby controlled, making a tidy profit for local government entities, although the extra costs of the increased rehabilitation programs used up most of this income. The extra costs of the social programs used up more than the rest of the government income. The net savings and extra security across borders was thought to be worth it.

****** **The Pentagon:**

"Ladies and gentlemen, may I direct your attention to the large screen on the left," began the Secretary of Homeland Security, Dr. Eugene Giuliano. Usually an Undersecretary or their press spokesman would give the demonstration, but this time, they had numerous dignitaries, as well as the press present. "Displayed here you can see our network of surveillance satellites, and their overlapping coverage, displayed as ground patterns. As you can see, the network has full coverage over the earth, at all times, whether night or day. The Secretary resisted the impulse to say "24/7". "On the large screen to your right is displayed all of the radar systems belonging to the IMDS. Again, all views of the atmosphere are redundantly covered at all times. Dr. Giuliani paused for questions regarding the first two screens. "Now, on the left screen, we are displaying all of the previous launch facilities for all missiles with a range of more than 100 miles. As you can see, color codes distinguish those fixed rather than hard sites, the range, the height at apogee, and those circled in green indicate which have been removed or disabled. These data are updated daily, as our inspection teams personally witness those actions. The data is further verified by surveillance satellites, aircraft flights-over, intelligence reports, and formal reports from the governments involved.

To your right, we are now displaying all but the most primitive airfields in existence. As you know, all public and private aircraft are required to continuously use transponders, for the purpose of locating aircraft by our satellite network. Any aircraft flying on a path deviating from its approved flight plan is immediately identified, and a simultaneous launch of armed high speed aircraft by the relevant tactical air command is initiated. So all aircraft traffic worldwide is constantly monitored, and interceptor aircraft are available to any deviations from approved flight plans. Any suspicious aircraft or personnel is subject to rigorous ground inspection before takeoff is approved. All major airports are equipped with especially sensitive monitors which will detect almost any level of radiation. Luminous dials on personal wrist watches have even been detected occasionally. The system also keeps track of all sea and river traffic, and of the surveillance craft of the IMDS. This information cannot be shown for obvious security reasons, but you can rest assured that all traffic on or below the oceans' surface is strictly accounted, and inspected at both the departure and destination points. Are there questions?" After exhausting all of the press' questions, the regular handouts were given, consisting of the latest textual and graphic material. Many questions were turned away because of possible security issues, but almost everyone went away satisfied that things were under total control.

Observing one of these briefings, Jason wondered about how much extra effort would be required for ABACUS to additionally track individuals from the surveillance satellites, and the network of ground transceivers used by government. Being knowledgeable of the end-time prophesies, he found it interesting that ABACUS could be expanded to monitor all financial transactions, worldwide, on an almost real-time basis. He wondered whether this had occurred to those leaders at the United Nations, who obviously were directing the world toward a single government, or so it seemed to him.

Chapter 22: THE PROGRAM in HIGH GEAR

****** **U.N. Headquarters:**

The scene was billed as a summit, for all of the *club* members to report the progress each of the eleven nations had made, their plans for the further disarmament, and a chance for the nations of the world to applaud the progress. It was all of this, but Avery Harrington had a primary goal of accelerating the program as much as logistics could allow.

"Citizens of the world," Avery Harrington began. "We have heard the wonderful news of great progress with the implementation of the Final Atomic Treaty, by all of the nations which currently hold atomic weapon arsenals, and those other nations in partial development of such weapons. I want to recognize the great humanitarian gesture for peace and prosperity advanced so nobly by the governments of China, France, Israel, India, Iran, Indonesia, North Korea, Russia, Pakistan, The United Kingdom, and The United States!" "The people of the world thank you, and history will record that this is the single most important undertaking by all of mankind in their evolution toward lasting peace and universal prosperity," Avery Harrington enthused. "Additionally, we need to especially thank the governments of Egypt, Japan, Germany, Canada, Italy, and Spain for their unselfish restraint in finishing their efforts toward the development of their own atomic arsenals," Avery Harrington continued. "These nations are here listed in the order of their stepping forward to volunteer to make this very noble sacrifice," Avery Harrington concluded. Waves of applause followed, led even by the heads of state in attendance.

"Again, citizens of the world, thanks from all of us," Avery Harrington said. "And now, I have even better news. The administrators of the program have told me that improved logistics now make it possible to shorten the program schedule by three years. As you know, the treaty allows, even anticipates this, and it is our hope and desire to accelerate the program accordingly." Thunderous applause again rocked the hall, with a standing ovation for their beloved leader, the Secretary General, Avery Harrington. Noticed by some was the rather lackluster response by the leaders of the Russian and U.S. delegations.

****** **Rome:**

The Final Atomic Treaty was not the only program moving ahead rapidly. The drive toward a total ecumenism (otherwise known as a world religion) was also hurtling headlong toward some kind of finality. The scene was the massive new conference center just off The Vatican, where the IFC presented their new Council to the public. His Eminence, Pope Alexander IX was getting ready to address the assembled dignitaries.

"Men and women of faith, welcome to Rome, the Vatican, and the first formal conference of the Interfaith Council," he began. "We are here assembled to introduce to the world the permanent members of the Council, and the leaders they have selected. Every major faith is here represented, and a true spirit of brotherhood prevails. It is our intent to promote a greater tolerance of our various views, and further promote those programs where we can join forces for the common good, especially in areas of strife or natural disaster."

"We want to especially thank the Secretary General of the United Nations, Avery Harrington, for his tireless support and the total financial support of this great cause. Some have said that our religions have been a root cause for most of the problems of the world, particularly as the driving forces for wars and territorial ambitions, but we refuse that premise and are organizing the IFC for the goal of defusing any territorial, racial, or cultural dispute based on religious differences."

The Pope soon turned the meeting over to the interim president, the Most Reverend Archbishop Boris Ivelski of St. Petersburg. The permanent members of the IFC were introduced with great fanfare. Next, the forty-two limited-term members were announced. Between these seventy-two members, virtually all of the world religions were represented, with some of the best leaders of each major religion taking active roles in the IFC. Finally, the Triumvirate of the IFC was announced. The three were announced in alphabetical order; Pope Alexander IX, Imam Keradine, and His Most High Priest Lannartes. The three represented the Christians, the Muslims, and the Buddhists.

The selection of the Triumvirate was almost pro forma, and surprised no one. The headlines coming out of the conference was that the IFC had unanimously agreed on a resolution which stated that all religions, races, and cultures had a right to exist and to live within their current boundaries, in peace and protection. The resolution did not condemn the violence and persecution of minority religions, but it was a definite beginning, and engendered new levels of support for the IFC.

Chapter 23: THE DOMINOES FALL

Over the next year the disarmament continued under the accelerated schedule. Extra pressure was applied to the two nations who seemed to show a new reluctance toward the execution of the terms of the treaty. Russia and the United States, the major adversaries of the Cold War were, not surprisingly, the reluctant ones.

Avery Harrington dealt with this issue by providing extra publicity with every small step each of the two nations made, and working behind the scenes in both countries, countering the factions in both of these nations which opposed the treaty.

During this year, Harrison Lipscombe led his country toward giving up more sovereignty through the process of new international treaties, which gave various agencies of the United Nations authority to monitor and oversee many aspects of life in the United States.

****** **Smith Valley, Nevada:**
A certain wise lady residing in Smith Valley, Nevada, watched these developments with grave concern. She still had her unique secure telephone system developed and implemented by her brilliant computer geek of a son, one Jason Phillips. "Son, who is driving these latest efforts to give up our country? Is this the POTUS just trying to continue the previous incumbent's policies, or are other pressures being brought to bear on him, or what?" she said, rather exasperated. "Aunt Jane, (there was no Aunt Jane), I don't know. My *machine* isn't being used to manipulate anyone, or I would

know it. I will work on that question, and get back with you."
Jason shared his mother's concerns with his two special
friends, and they began meeting again at Hot Dog Heaven.

***

At the end of the second year after the program was
accelerated, both Russia and the United States gave up the last
of their arsenals on the same day, accompanied with fanfare
and great rejoicing. This development was quickly followed
by the monitored dismantling and disposal of the last 200
missiles each country had left in their arsenals. A collective
sigh of relief went up in cities all over the world. Universal
peace and prosperity seemed like a possibility more than ever
before.

****** **Bojnurd, Iran:**
Mahammed Hussan Kassim wore the uniform of an
army colonel, a wig, and a false beard this day, and arrived
unexpectedly by helicopter, with three of his top lieutenants in
tow. "Ali Mohr, go alert the keepers for my inspection, while
I look over the main office facility, would you?" Kassim
commanded. Ali Mohr soon emerged from the main building
with most of the resident crew, and led them up the short road
to the cave entrance. Kassim and his two other lackeys
walked up to the main building and inspected the facilities, the
stores, the vehicles, and the two residents left to man the
building. One of the residents was doing a radio check with
the perimeter guards when the inspection party arrived, but
snapped to attention when they entered his area. "Please show
us your visitor log," asked one of the inspectors. The
paperwork was in order, the facilities in the usual disarray, but
the secure areas remained secure, and Kassim was pleased that

all of the equipment that he had ordered delivered here had arrived, and was well secured. The inventory included 28 tactical nuclear warheads, 120 Scud VII missiles, dismantled, and ten launch rails, also dismantled. The estimate of the time required to assemble the weapons and be ready for launching was 12 hours, working with an expert crew of 16 technicians.

Mahammed Hussan Kassim was quite satisfied with the storage and launch site, but had yet to solve the problem of the spy satellites. The options he was considering were to somehow blind the satellites or to create a diversion away from the area. Finally, he decided on the option of creating a visual diversion, well away from the base near Bojnurd, and the other sites.

END OF PART VI

PART VII

TIMES OF DISTRESS

"...There will be a time of distress such as has not happened since the beginning of nations until then. But at that time your people-everyone whose name is found written in the book-will be delivered."
The Holy Bible

Chapter 24: PREPARATIONS for LAUNCH

Six months after the FAT had been executed, and the last of the atomic arsenals were destroyed, people were having second thoughts. In the United States, Harrison Lipscombe's poll numbers had fallen precipitously. A third party, "The Conservative Cause" had emerged and threatened to divide the Republican vote, which would almost certainly put the Democrats back in power. The agenda of the Conservative Cause party was to restore the sovereignty of the country, restore freedom, and expel all illegal aliens, lower taxes, and drastically cut government spending.

Rumors abounded that several countries had cheated with their atomic arsenals, and still held a significant part of their weapons. On the other hand, due to the new optimism of the IFC, and the almost total reduction of military budgets, prosperity was being restored to previous high levels for each country, albeit taxes remained high. The rumors of remaining atomic arsenals always triggered a new round of inspections, which helped allay the worst fears.

****** **Bojnurd, Iran:**
The unveiling began. First, massive new prefabricated camouflage covering was set in place, under cover of darkness, using only the moonlight, and small spots directed away from the sky. Next, even before morning, parts for a dozen launch railings were bolted together and fastened to heavy concrete footings installed much earlier. Finally the Scud VII missiles were assembled and armed with small, very light conventional warheads. Signal and power cables were plugged into place, tested, and then turned off.

****** **Tehran:**

"Uncle John, this is your nephew. The city lights continue to burn brightly," was all that Kassim's agent at the U.N. said. It was the message he expected and hoped for, as it told him that the spy satellites had not detected the activities of the previous two days and nights at his missile launch sites.

Everything was prepared for his own big show, and awaited only the announcements he wanted made to the special people who would be privileged to know about the coming holocaust. Kassim called his 12 Tetrarchs personally, and instructed them to give a warning to those important people that an attack on Haifa was eminent, and they would know that they (his Tetrarchs), represented great power, which was behind the new movement of their new Caliph. They were cautioned not to use the term "Mahdi" with anyone.

All this time, the Israeli government had continued to financially support all of the underdeveloped countries of the world, including some Muslim nations, but this did not particularly endear them to many of them, especially the Muslims. In spite of their massive aid programs, the Israelis continued to become very wealthy, with their power sales, their agriculture sales, and their middleman operations with the various trading groups. Most Muslim nations continued to teach hatred of the Jews.

****** **U.N. Headquarters:**

Mr. Mahammed Hussan Kassim called the Secretary General. "I am calling to make your acquaintance, sir, and to also make you an ally," he continued. "Is this a secure line? I have an extremely urgent and important matter to discuss with you," Kassim continued. After a few seconds, while Avery Harrington signaled his secretary to trace and record the message, he responded. "It is now secure, please go ahead. With whom am I speaking?" Avery Harrington said. "I will be introducing myself with a demonstration of the power that I control. After that, we can meet at a neutral site, and we can negotiate," he said. Having already alerted his private secretary with hand signals, Avery Harrington knew that the call came from somewhere in Iran. "Please listen carefully, Mr. Secretary General," Kassim commenced. "Some time within the next 3 days, I shall be firing rockets on Haifa. One of the rockets will have an atomic warhead. This will be my calling card," Kassim said. He then hung up abruptly.

Avery Harrington instructed his private secretary to cancel or postpone his next few appointments. He closed his office doors, and replayed the taped call. His first thought was that this must be a crank call, given that the FAT had been concluded months ago, and the U.N. inspection teams had been unhindered in their efforts to carefully ferret out all traces of atomic weapons and all fissionable material, including the history of all shipments of raw material from every mine which produced Uranium, whether it was primary or a by-product of lead or copper mining.

Harrington then summoned his two most capable aids into his office and played the tape for them. "Gentlemen, who is our most capable and trusted member of the U.N. inspection team?" he addressed to Jim Thornton and Hugh Watson. The two of them responded as one: "Jack McGinty," they said. "Where is he at this moment?" Avery Harrington said. "He is

260

in Beijing," responded Watson. "Please help Mrs. Davis get ahold of him, if you can. What time is it there?" Avery Harrington said.

***

"Mr. Jack McGinty is on line three, sir," Sarah Davis announced over the intercom. "Thanks," responded Avery Harrington. "Jack, this is Avery Harrington. I am putting you on the speaker. Jim Thornton and Hugh Watson are here with me," Avery Harrington said. The four of them discussed the situation for some thirty minutes. At that time, Avery Harrington excused himself and asked the three to continue to assess the probabilities.

Harrington asked his personal secretary to call the new Prime Minister of Israel over a level 6 security line ASAP. Avery Harrington then advised the PM of his recorded call, and even played the tape for him. Next, Harrington called the chief U.N. military commander, and gave him the same information, then ordered him to put his forces on full alert, particularly the forces in and around Israel. This was to be coordinated with the *Israeli Defense Forces (IDF),* which were already putting their entire Arrow and improved Patriot missiles on imminent attack status.

****** **Israel:**
The *demonstration* began at dusk the next day. The IDF had time to put extra defense systems in place, including the latest Doppler and phased-array radar systems, and even an AWACs (Airborne Warning and Control system) patrol, using a four hour cycle of replacement.

The first missile alert came from a Doppler radar set placed on the eastern border of Israel. "Missile launch detected in sector 40, azimuth 315 degrees from base," the operator reported, excitedly. The early detection allowed the IDF to provide a primary and a back up missile defense assignments. The primary defense missile destroyed the incoming shortly after apogee, somewhere over Iraq. A formal protest from the Iraqi government would be initiated days later. After another three missiles and another three successful intercepts, the mass attack came.

Five different sites, each launching a dozen missiles in very rapid succession, flooded the IDF network, and Haifa suffered the impact of eight missiles which got through the defense systems. The warheads each contained twenty pounds of high explosives. Three buildings were demolished, two cars were destroyed, and three large craters were dug into the streets of Haifa. In the midst of this holocaust of missiles, the real demonstration took place. In the basement of a warehouse, in a somewhat secluded industrial area of Haifa, a real fission bomb was ignited by shaped charges blowing two little hemispheres of prepared plutonium together. The tactical-sized bomb yielded a mere 1000 pounds of equivalent TNT explosives. This was enough however, to dig a crater fifty feet deep and two hundred feet across, and to level an area about the size of four city blocks. More importantly for the perpetrator, however, was the residual radiation, proving that it was a full-blown atomic device. Missile shrapnel had been placed in the warehouse to complete the illusion that the device had been delivered by missile. No one suspected otherwise. The attack ended abruptly, shortly after the *real* bomb was detonated.

****** Tehran:

A phone message was immediately initiated to Avery Harrington's office, to the point that the demonstration had been delivered, as promised. Mahammed Hussan Kassim next advised the upper echelons of his hierarchy of the successful execution of the demonstration, telling them to immediately advise the important people in their respective countries of the event before they heard it on the news.

As the network news agencies had already discovered the fact of the extra defense missiles deployment, some of Mahammed Hussan Kassim's vassals were just a tad late in spreading the word. But the demonstration which they had promised had the nerve-shattering effect desired, and national leaders everywhere were in a panic.

****** U.N. Headquarters:

The panic was pervasive in Avery Harrington's office. It was the U.N., after all, which had assured the nations of the world that: 1. All atomic arsenals extant had been proven to be eliminated, and 2. That the IMDS was capable of taking out any possible missile attack launched anywhere, against any nation. Who the perpetrators were was the biggest question. Given the target, a large group of Muslim nations suggested itself.

****** Ankara, Turkey:

Mahammed Hussan Kassim arranged with one of his top level underlings to host a very secure and clandestine meeting at the neutral site of Ankara, Turkey, to be held in one of the small conference rooms in one of their better hotels.

"Mr. Secretary General," Kassim greeted, walking across the modest sized room, hand outstretched in a gesture of Western friendship. "Your Eminence," Avery Harrington responded, rather casually and without much excitement in his voice. Avery Harrington had worn dark glasses, and a Turkish Fez, which together, provided sufficient disguise for this part of the world. A modest sized table and two comfortable chairs were provided by the hotel, at Kassim's request, through his agent. "May we begin," said Kassim, gesturing toward the table. They both set their brief cases on the table and sat down. Avery Harrington waited for Mahammed Hussan Kassim to initiate the conversation. And although Kassim's English was heavily accented, he was quite understandable to Harrington.

"Let us get right to it, Mr. Secretary General," Kassim began. "As you know, my forces bombed Haifa, as I told you we would. And I must say that given the warning we gave you, your IMDS and the Israeli Defense Forces were rather easy to penetrate. However, we are not here to gloat or to make demands. I want to offer myself and my forces to you as allies! We are willing to deliver to you all of our nuclear weapons, and allow your inspectors and disposal teams full access to our several sites, and we will become a full partner in the FAT." Harrington was almost incredulous, but he waited for the other shoe. Kassim paused before he went on. "In return, we require that I and my fellow Imams of the faith be given a dominant role in the Inter Faith Council. We envision a partnership between governments at all levels, and the church," Kassim said. "This can be justified by the fact that over three billions of our earth's population subscribe to the Muslim faith. As you know, this is significantly more than for any other faith. I have prepared papers for this agreement, which are provided for you in both paper and magnetic media, here in this smaller briefcase." With that, he opened his large briefcase, pulled out a small valise, and opened it for Harrington to examine.

"A considerable effort will be required to negotiate this with your various memberships. We are hopeful that thirty days should suffice. We can meet again, to sign such an agreement, at a place of your choosing," Kassim concluded.

"Very well, Your Eminence," Avery Harrington responded. The Secretary General looked tired, and he felt defeated. However, there were words of hope in the demands this strange new player had laid on the table. Mahammed Hussan Kassim certainly looked imposing, had supreme confidence, and seemed to have real power. "How can we contact you," Avery Harrington asked. "My agents shall be contacting you regularly," Kassim responded.

The two of them discussed travel plans, and then left separately. Kassim had arranged for an armored limousine to take the Secretary General to the airport. The limousine was sandwiched between two city police vehicles, providing the security proper for his high station.

Chapter 25: WHOOPS!

"General Fleischman, have you figured out where the missiles were launched yet?" Israel's new Prime Minister Jacob Weinstein said into his special military phone system. "Yes, Mr. Prime Minister, we have been given a copy of all the surveillance satellite tapes taken during the attack, and recordings from all of the IMDS radar, and our own AWACS data. We fed all of this data into our TAT computer and have identified five sites from which the missiles have been launched, but high-altitude RPV over-flights have shown us that all but one of them have been evacuated already. Other over-flights, verified by satellite surveillance have indicated that this last site, located in eastern Iran, must be their storage facility, as well as a launch site."

"So what are we going to do about that?" the Prime Minister responded. "With your permission sir, we would like to use our new laser guided bunker buster bombs to wipe out their supply of atomic warheads," the General responded. "General, I'll poll my military advisors, and get right back with you."

Prime Minister Weinstein immediately ordered up a secure communications network conference call to his three close military advisors. He explained the situation to them and without any hesitation they all endorsed quick action, as requested.

***

****** **High over Northeastern Iran:**

"Charlie-3, this is Fox-1. We are at station and are painting the target for you. There will be no G/A (ground to air) defense, as far as we can see." "Fox-1, this is Charlie-3; that matches all of our surveillance data. We are about 30 seconds from launch," the flight leader, Lt. Colonel Cyrial Isaiah said. "Roger that, Charlie-3."   Moments later, three huge bunker buster bombs were launched in careful succession. The first one was locked on to the entrance of the complex. The second and third bombs blew deep and deeper into the storage complex, causing a great mushroom cloud to form and rise very high into the air. The bombs had ignited considerable explosives and fuel storage tanks, to cause a giant conflagration visible for 5o miles. "Charlie-3, I have my cameras rolling, over." "We're out of here, Fox-1; get some high altitude shots if you can, over and out." The recce/spotter aircraft got his photos and headed home, shortly after.

****** **Tehran:**

Mahammed Hussan Kassim let his visitor wait for a full 30 minutes, as was his habit. His inner office had been installed with an 8 inch platform and a raised office chair, specifically to intimidate his guests, no matter who they were.

"Welcome, my brother," Kassim enthused, welcoming the great Mullah of Iraq, Ayatollah Keradine, nominal leader of the Muslim world, recently elected to the ruling triumvirate of the IFC. "Thank you for coming here. I want to share with you my plans, and ally myself with you if I can," Kassim said, forthrightly. "And I with you," responded Ayatollah Keradine. "My people suspect it was you who orchestrated the raid on Haifa. Is that

267

true?" "That was a demonstration for the world, but especially for Mr. Avery Harrington," Kassim said. He tried to read Ayatollah Keradine's expression, but he appeared to be totally unconcerned. "I am currently negotiating with him on our behalf, to give us more authority in the United Nations Security Council, and to get **you** elected as the titular head of your IFC," Kassim informed him. "**Have** you?" the Ayatollah Keradine said. Kassim was not sure whether he was being sarcastic, or was truly impressed.

The truth was that he was in awe of Mahammed Hussan Kassim, who had him brought here in his private jet, to this palace on the outskirts of Tehran. All of the people surrounding the man also seemed to be in awe of him, as well. Kassim's appearance, his confidence, his charm, his strong sense of command said to one and all that this man was in charge, and should be obeyed. "We are the only ones left with atomic and biological and chemical weapons, now that they have implemented the FAT," Kassim continued. "I expect that will give us the authority to bring our faith to all people, Allah willing," Kassim concluded.

Ayatollah Keradine was overwhelmed, and truly in amazement of this magnificent leader before him. He was somewhat reminded of his erstwhile acquaintance, one Ayatollah Al Shafei, but of course he was dead. "Allah be praised; what can I do?" he asked. Mahammed Hussan Kassim spent the rest of the day explaining to this powerful new ally his strategic plans, detailing his strategy, and how he (Ayatollah Keradine) would share in the coming glory.

Ayatollah Keradine returned to Rome the next day in Kassim's jet, having been sent off as the dignitary he was. The Ayatollah Keradine still felt overwhelmed by Kassim's plans, his wherewithal, his demeanor, and his recent accomplishments. Yet the man seemed to come from nowhere. He was Mahammed Hussan Kassim's instant ally, although he somehow felt subordinate; perhaps it was his looks. He was reminded of the pictures he had seen years before of the prophesied Mahdi. *Could he be the one?*

****** **United Nations Headquarters**

"Yes, Harrison, I understand," Avery Harrington concluded after a long and strained conversation with the POTUS. Avery Harrington had informed him of his ongoing negotiations with Mahammed Hussan Kassim, hoping to correct the one glaring error of the FAT, that being of not eradicating *all* of the atomic arsenals. The situation might yet be saved!

Chapter 26:   HOT DESERT WINDS

****** **The Sayetvet AF Base outside Moscow:**

A surveillance aircraft called the base. "Sayetvet Base, this is Sayetvet Runner 2. I have taken the air samples as ordered, over the region of Kazakhstan, but I want to report that I have observed what appears to be a large herd of dead sheep, about 300 kilometers north of the site of the big explosion. I recommend you send up a photo reconnaissance aircraft over the area I flew today." And it was done. The pilot's message also evoked extra caution in the lab where the air samples were tested.

****** **Moscow:**

"Yes Mr. President, our labs indicate a strong lethal concentration of airborne anthrax from the site of the Israeli bombing, northward for 600 kilometers," said General Markeloff, head of the Moscow Military Region. "And our best weather information indicates strong winds continuing North, and then West, at about 40 kilometers per hour. I strongly recommend that we alert the citizens of Moscow and the surrounding suburbs, or perhaps initiate our evacuation plans, sir," the General concluded.

Vasily Kerinskov paled, his legs weakened, and suddenly he lost his voice. He stared out of his window, looking over the city, as if to reassure himself that it was still there. "Get me the head of the Moscow Civil Defense," he shouted at the nearest secretary.

"Sergi, what defenses have we against airborne anthrax?" the President snapped. "We can only issue gas masks," Sergi responded. "But we don't have enough for the whole city." "Sergi, issue an immediate alert for airborne anthrax; suggest voluntary evacuation to the West and South, then supply all government employees with your gas masks, and offer everyone else simple face masks. Do it *now*!" the President ordered.

Barely 10% of the city had been evacuated when the white, deadly clouds reached the southeast edge of Moscow. Fortunately for the residents of Moscow, the clouds moved more northerly, rather than to the northwest, as had been predicted. The city almost escaped; still, more than 350 thousand Muscovites died over the three days following the terrible scourge.

The citizens of Uzbekistan and Kazakhstan fared less well. Closer to the source of the pestilence and with no defense or evacuation plans, some one million people died of the dreaded anthrax. What with the normal west to east winds carrying fewer and fewer residual spores, the devastation was dissipated fairly rapidly. Still, what with the logistics of developing the specific vaccines, and the delays in distribution, uncounted additional thousands of people died of this catastrophe, worldwide.

****** **Tehran:**
"What?... When?... How?" Mahammed Hussan Kassim demanded. He saw his dream of world dominion again fade, because of his eternal tormentors, the Israelis. But as before, he almost immediately saw how this terrible event could work out to his advantage and to the final destruction of the Jews.

***

"Mr. Harrington, if we are to achieve world peace we must get rid of the state of Israel! If you don't do it with your United Nations Forces, we shall make every one of their towns and cities so radioactive that it cannot be populated for a thousand years," Mahammed Hussan Kassim almost screamed.

Kassim knew that Avery Harrington would not have the U.N. attack his homeland. His expectation was to simply neutralize him, so he could carry out his own plans.

Kassim had learned well from one of his early heroes, the late and infamous Saddam Hussein. So at this time he used his paid network of news media to arouse the world against the heinous crime the Israelis had committed, unleashing the airborne anthrax. The Israelis denied it all of course, but their voices were drowned out by the worldwide network inclined to blame the Jews for everything, at any opportunity. Casualties of every nation, race, and creed were paraded for the TV audiences everywhere. In almost every news segment, the Jews were cited as the aggressor.

****** U. N. Headquarters Security Council Chamber:
"Ambassador Maroni, Will you respond to these charges?" said Mr. Chea Il Lee, the temporary Chairman. "Thank you Mr. Chairman," responded Mr. Mordicai Maroni. "Thank…" was all that was heard in the chamber, or on the network feeds. The Ambassador's words were downed out by a cacophony of shrill cries, a chorus of guttural epithets in a dozen languages, and foot stomping. Every time the noise

272

abated, and the Ambassador tried again to speak, the noise began again. The Ambassador threw up his hands in disgust, gathered his papers, and walked out of the chamber, accompanied by guards, who were fearful of an attack on his person.

When resolution 3841, condemning Israel, came to a vote, it was vetoed by Israel, having recently become a permanent member of the Council by virtue of their cooperation in the FAT negotiations and implementation. The General Assembly, meeting in plenary session, voted on the resolution, taking advantage of the new rules. The measure passed by 78 to 8, the rest abstaining. The resolution called for a total blockade, total trade barriers, seizure of all of their assets outside their country, onerous reparations and strong condemnation of their action.

But inside the Kremlin, this was considered totally inadequate!

Chapter 27:   A NATION with no FRIENDS

****** **The Capitol, Washington, D.C.:**

Mr. Speaker, the bombing of the port of Haifa was a tragic and ill-considered attack on the sovereignty of Israel, but her over-reaction and reckless attack using germ warfare on a rather harmless remote desert site in Iran was equally inexcusable! I therefore intend to vote for this resolution and I urge all fair-minded Americans to call their congressmen and urge them to strongly support it as well," intoned the congressman from Nevada.

And so it was, that in legislative bodies all over the world, as they passed resolutions supporting the U.N. condemnation of Israel. Every Israeli embassy in the world, save two, was fire-bombed and gutted.

***

Meanwhile, Jewish citizens of Arabic descent fled Israel in every direction, sensing the inevitable slaughter that was about to begin. Jewish citizens wanted to leave, but all flights were cancelled, and all of their port facilities were blockaded by European navies.   Primarily, all of their border crossings were turned into heavily armed defensive fortifications, and travelers trying to escape from Israel were fired upon when they got within the range of their guns.

Having seen the futility of trying to leave Israel, most of its citizens simply retreated toward its major cities. Optimism was in very short supply. Protestors marched in most of the capital cities worldwide. The question everyone was asking was *Can war be averted, and how?*

The Russians, Iranians, Syrians, Saudis, Palestinians, Jordanians, and the Egyptians did not wait for the formality of a declaration of war. It was a mob scene of gigantic proportions, as army units, terrorist groups, and even irate citizens marched en mass toward Jerusalem from every direction. The hatred against the Jews, taught in most Muslim schools, bottled up over the years, finally had the support of the world and was not to be denied. Israel, with almost undefendable borders, and inadequate conventional weapons, had just been stripped of their only real deterrent, their small cache of atomic weapons, which were, it turned out, very few. They had relied on the protection of the United States and England, ever since their birth in 1948. With the influx of so many Muslims into England, support from that quarter had disappeared. In America, their only strong support came from the conservative Evangelicals, and their strength had been diminished severely by the emergence of the IFC, and the drive toward a world religion.

****** The Israeli-Syrian Border:**
Syrian tanks rumbled down the road, headed south. The Kibbutz just inside Israel had been abandoned within hours of the undeclared war. "Let's stop here and make this our temporary headquarters," spoke the Syrian Lt. Colonel in the lead tank. They were anxious to kill their first Jews, but a good supper and rest would equip them well right now, and the massacre could wait until tomorrow!

****** Israel, Southeast of Hebron:

In this whole quadrant, the Jordanians were the first to cross over the border into Israel. The Jews had retreated from the borders and Israeli Army Units were not to be found. Unknown to the Jordanian Army units, Saudi tanks and Iraqi armored vehicles, and others, were moving in the same direction, about a day behind them.

***

****** South of the Golan Heights:

"Vasily, those dumb Jews have all of their tanks nicely parked in front of that commune down there. Their camouflage is so pathetic! Company 8, there is a cluster of enemy tanks parked about 300 meters distant and about 20 degrees east of that water tower in front of us. Prepare to fire, using standard firing sequence from formation! We can take them out before they can escape. Fire when you see my green flare. Over and out." The twilight made it rather impossible for the Syrian troops to see the formation of Russian tanks to their north. The bright green flare caught the attention of the Syrian guards. The next moment however, bright flashes north of them told them they were under fire, and they all dashed for cover. It was too late for most of them, as incoming shells found their targets and the air was filled with shrapnel from exploding tanks, ammunition and fuel.

"How did the Israelis get in back of us that way?" shouted the Syrian commander. He ordered his units to return fire, together with the artillery pieces he had placed for their protection. The final score was Syria: 15 tanks and 322 men lost; Russia: 24 tanks and 126 men lost; Israelis: no losses.

The news of this mishap reached their respective upper commands 18 hours later; too late to keep the event from being repeated many times over.

****** **Israel, Near the Gaza Strip:**

From the Southwest, Palestinian units were the first to cross the border into Israel, and set up defensive positions. Then Egyptian units appeared, ready to blast anyone who got in their way. All these many disparate units from so many nations and tongues, **and there was no coordination!**

****** **United Nations Headquarters:**

Avery Harrington was alone. Recently the most respected and powerful world leader, credited with almost achieving the dreams of world peace and universal prosperity, his stock had sunk to the *pink sheets* status.

"Mr. President, our IMDS surveillance satellites show us that several of your armored units are headed toward Israel. Are you taking plunder; can't you wait for the U.N. to do this peacefully?" Avery Harrington asked of the President of Russia. The line went dead. In terms of foot soldiers and tanks, Russia still had a sizeable army, and the U.N. really only had a navy.

Streams of trucks and tanks and heavy artillery pieces flooded south, through Turkey and Syria. Russian aircraft were being prepared to support ground operations. Already massive air raids over Israel had taken out the bulk of the Israeli Air Force while their aircraft were still on the ground.

****** Jerusalem:

"Major Matthews, this is General Garth. We need some manpower to finish erecting our defense lines north of the city. How many troops can you send, and can you deliver any bulldozers?" "General, I need a third of my men and women to help maintain order in my quadrant, but you can have the rest. I can send 2800 people, but we only have about 40 trucks and buses, and we have no *dozers*." "Fine, Major; please do so as soon as possible. I will send down some buses and I will try our engineers and your fire departments for the heavy equipment."

***

Gail and David Shively sat in their basement, glued to the TV, watching this disastrous scene unfold. "Darling, it has been 20 years, but I can still fire a rifle. In the morning I'm going to volunteer for the City Defense Forces," David said. "I know, my darling. It looks hopeless, but we must all try to survive as our leaders have told us. I will volunteer at the hospital; God knows we are going to have casualties," responded Gail Shively. They, as most of the Israelis, were resigned to their fate. This young nation, less than 100 years old, had struggled for their survival its entire life, and they were stoic and tough. However, this time was different. The end seemed near, but they at least could die defending themselves.

END OF PART VII

PART VIII

THE BLESSED HOPE

"For the Lord Himself will come down from Heaven, with a loud command, with the voice of the archangel and with the trumpet call of God, and the dead in Christ will rise first. After that, we who are still alive and are left will be caught up together with them in the clouds to meet the Lord in the air. And so we will be with the Lord forever."
The Holy Bible.

Chapter 28: EVERYTHING GOES WRONG

Russian, Turkish, and Syrian tanks were driving south toward the valley of Megiddo. Iranian, Iraqi, Saudi, and Jordanian forces were rolling westward toward Jerusalem. Egyptian, Sudanese, and Libyan vehicles were driving north through the Negev and Gaza toward Tel-Aviv. The movements were largely uncoordinated, but they had at least stopped shooting at each other. The Israelis were hunkering down, resigned to their doom, probably death.

The problems for the invaders began with a series of massive earthquakes so coincidental that the instruments were incapable of pinpointing any epicenters. The whole region rocked and undulated in relatively slow motion, accompanied by low rumblings, like the groaning of an earth grown weary of wars and the ways of man. Ear-splitting internal high-pitched explosions told of great cracks opening, and huge granite structures splitting and being torn asunder.

The sun turned blood red, perhaps from the dust, but then it seemed to suddenly go dark. Whole mountainsides gave way, burying convoys of vehicles on every major road leading to and inside Israel, and generating thick clouds of dust and debris, hundreds of feet into the air. Most shocking of all however, they all were being bombarded by storms of meteors, and huge hailstones, as burning rocks, and sulpherous debris and huge chunks of ice came down on them all, burying and burning everything in sight. To some it seemed like being at the foot of a massive volcano, except it was everywhere!

The invading armies had no defenses for this holocaust from the sky, and they were all stopped dead in their tracks.

The Israelis had largely congregated back into their major population centers in Jerusalem and on the coast. They were merely spectators, who couldn't really see what was going on, but were as fearful as the invaders were of all of the natural or perhaps supernatural activity.

Movement ceased on all of the roads into and around Israel. Feeble calls for medical assistance went unheeded. Everyone within hearing had their own horrific holocaust to deal with. Eventually, the whole area grew quiet, except for the groans of men dying, and machinery exploding, collapsing and burning.

The scene just before the dawning evoked thoughts of Dante's "Inferno", and memories of great battles of the past. There seemed to be only one group of protagonists, albeit a rag-tag agglomeration of a dozen nationalities with a common purpose, and now a common ending.

******The Capital Cities of the World:
The news was very sketchy. Those forces attacking Israel were careful to impose a strict news blackout; only the U.N.-controlled satellites had any inkling of what was happening. Avery Harrington imposed his own news blackout, except for a few of his top allies, such as Harrison Lipscombe, and Jacob Weinstein. Even for these few, the battlefields were so occluded that they could only wait for

more information before doing anything, except putting their defenses on high alert.

Washington had gone to bed about the time rumors started seeping through official sources, so the crew at ABACUS and their families were oblivious of the unfolding disaster. The soon to be Mahdi was in close contact with his allies in Moscow, but none of them had any hard information, even from their own troops. It would be late the next day before the scope of the disaster would be widely known, but by then, these events didn't even rate the headlines.

The second cataclysmic event, not entirely unrelated, occurred that next fateful morning.

Chapter 29: THE TWINKLING

****** **Everywhere, Worldwide:**

It happened just as the sun rose east of Jerusalem, turning the ghastly, ghostly grim predawn into a new day. In less than a twinkling of an eye, actually less than a millisecond, the bodies of millions of people worldwide, both living and dead, were transformed. A simultaneous new transfiguration occurred with each of Christ's followers, living or dead. Taken together, they constituted His Church, His Bride to be. God's creative power had never, since the original creation, been exhibited so powerfully, as this gathering of His Church, and in the transforming of corporeal bodies to pure energy, light, and Spirit. In studies of the Holy Scriptures, this event has been called the *Rapture*, or the *Blessed Hope*.

Subjectively, those raptured felt an elation transcending their most joyous moments in life. They all *knew* what was happening, and they all *knew* that they were going *home* to be with the Lord.   In their new bodies, there was no sense of forces or mass; no sense of acceleration or restrictions of movement. Their first event was hearing a great shout, or perhaps two, and the sounding of a golden-voiced trumpet. The compelling shout was heard by each person as his or her own favorite given name.

The first thing everyone saw was a great gathering of friends and relatives, even those long dead. The joy was universal, and there were warm embraces, and visual examinations of the new incorruptible bodies they each inhabited. Everyone was amazed and delighted at what they saw, and at the reactions of all of their loved ones.

Time seemed to be frozen, and there was sufficient opportunity to speak to everyone you knew, and to exchange histories, which brought back memories, and insight, and new knowledge and appreciation of all of your loved ones.

Then that time for re-acquaintance was over, everyone sensed, and everyone looked up, and moved toward their King and God, their Lord Jesus.

****** McLean, Virginia:

The Phillips' bed was unmade, with their bedclothes still under the covers. All of the lights, except two night lights were turned off. The doors and windows were locked, except for the openings in their bedroom windows they almost always left open for fresh air. Jason and Jamie Phillips were gone!

One moment they had been asleep, the next moment they were more than awake. Together they moved towards a group of their friends and relative who had "fallen asleep" in the Biblical sense. All of their parents were there. There were no tears of joy, just pure joy.

****** A Washington Suburb:

Patricia Winthrope had stayed out quite late the evening before. She had drunk too much, and had fallen asleep watching late-night TV. Her bed was turned down, but was still neat. On the couch was the pile of clothes she had worn at the party she had attended. She too had vanished, although her apartment lights were still ablaze, and the TV was blaring.

****** A Country Mission School in Australia:

A small, country mission school housed thirty orphaned girls. The main hall where they took their meals was bustling, as they were eating their lunch. When *it* happened, instantly twelve of the girls and three of the staff disappeared, their clothes falling to the floor or on the benches where they sat. The other girls, and the remaining staff who had witnessed this, began screaming, in panic. No one seemed to know what had happened, but a cold chill came over them all. In the subsequent hours and days, there would be endless speculation about this event, which apparently was worldwide.

****** A California Highway Patrol Office:

Officer Henry Gonzales had been on duty for over thirteen hours; strictly against regulations. The outlook was not good for his relief. Of the thirty-eight officers and sixteen support staff assigned to the district, twelve had somehow disappeared, including Chief Investigator Morrison. Communications were not in order, power was out almost everywhere, and crazies seemed to be having their way. It was worse than the combined effects of a full moon, Friday the 13th, and payday for the sailors.

In his twelve years with the Highway Patrol, Officer Gonzales had never seen so many things go so wrong all at once before. There were apparent homicides, over 400 automobile accidents reported, and strangest of all, the lines were jammed with reports of missing persons.

It had all begun the previous evening, many hours ago. At the moment, Officer Gonzales thought nothing much of it.

A brilliant flash of light, warm and scattered, not like lightning. A sudden unease had gripped him. Fear, uncertainty, foreboding! Everything was in balance; then, in an instant, things were askew. Officer Jones, his partner, was there in the office, filing one of the interminable reports for the DWI arrest they had made the hour before. Gonzales had glanced over to see if Jones had noticed something too, but Jones wasn't there! Gonzales looked around, instinctively, yet unbelieving. He was just there. *Was his mind failing?* he thought. The room was too small for him to not notice his partner leaving, his peripheral vision too good, his highly trained awareness and practiced observation skills too keen. He quickly stepped into the inner office to see if Jones had indeed slipped past him. Carla and Charise weren't there! Their equipment was live, and buzzing, but no traffic seemed to be on the air just then. But they would not have both left their post...

"George," Gonzales opened, when he was finally able to reach a senior staff member over the public phone. "What in *bleep* is happening?" Gonzales demanded, as if the Assistant Chief, who was in the middle of his four days off, would possibly know what was happening at the station. "You tell me, Gonzales" George Schmidt responded, seeming unusually irritated. "The Duty Sergeant, our dispatcher, and our comm clerk have all vanished," Gonzales almost shouted, "and oh yeah, my partner, Jones is gone too."

As Henry Gonzales contemplated it now, he remembered feeling disoriented, out of breath, and fearful, all at once. In that instant, time had somehow changed things. But it kept on; life continued. The earth rolled on, smooth in its quiet sweep through space, dragging the moon with it. The stars were all in place, it seemed. Unknown to most, however, an eternal hour glass had just dropped its final grain of sand. The inexorable pulse of fate and providence had run its course. Wave sweeping over endless wave swirled and frothed and sighed, playing out their assigned role. Some greater plan was ended. Invisible beings could rest now; the day was done. Night had fallen, finally. The players had completed the second act; it was time for curtain calls, and for masks to be removed. The play was over.

Henry Gonzales stayed on duty at the station. For a while he had to serve as dispatcher, communications clerk, desk sergeant, and even Chief. Finally, an irritated George Schultz arrived, half dressed, and without breakfast. "It seems to be this way all over the country," Schmidt remarked in the direction of the crew, which now consisted of a full complement of substitutes, plus Gonzales.

Henry wanted to go searching for his partner, although he had not an inkling of where to start looking. Instead, he was pressed into duty by Schmidt to help with the 'paperwork', which was becoming a blizzard, what with all of the *missing person* reports.

Another curious thing which fascinated Henry Gonzales was the amazingly huge number of abandoned vehicle reports they were receiving. If you were to believe John Q, there were hundreds of folks out there who just left their cars in the streets and freeways, and proceeded to disappear! Henry found the folder of blank forms for reporting abandoned vehicles, picked up the huge sheath of memos from the Comm, and began the forced labor that was the generation of the reports. This particular report form required the owner's name, the VIN, automobile make and model, color, the location, the time and date of the report, the name of the person reporting the abandoned car, the name of the property owner if it were on private property, the condition of the car, and the mileage. *This is crazy* Henry thought. People just don't abandon good cars like this; especially on the freeway! He pored over the data, looking for some correlation. He could find nothing. The drivers were young and old, alone and with friends, male and female. There were Mercedes' cars and Ford trucks, ages and colors of the full range of possible values.

Then he noticed something very strange. He looked up and down the column several times to verify the data. "This can't be true," Henry said, to no one in particular. Every one of the reports listed the mileage as either blank or ending in the number 3! Henry Gonzales methodically searched the whole stack of reports that he himself had just generated. It showed without exception that the last digit was a three! Frantically, he went over to the filing cabinets, and pulled out the previous two days' reports. The mileage on those reports seemed to be perfectly random!

A compelling urge required Henry Gonzales to walk out of the office, down the corridor, and outside, to the parking lot. There in the front row of reserved spaces were the cars of yesterday's crew. Henry snapped on his big flashlight, so he could see the odometer readings through the closed windows. First the Chief's car, then his Partner's, then Carla's, and Charise's. The last digit on each of the odometers was three! Almost as an afterthought, he walked over to his own car, a white Taurus. The odometer read 46786!

Instinctively, Henry Gonzales suspected what had happened. During several of the sermons by a Pastor Ott, he had heard of a strange phenomenon such as this, as written in Biblical prophecy. He was almost glad his wife had dragged him to those sermons now. Without hearing the Network News, he was sure this was worldwide. He could hardly wait to hear the explanations.

***

The following description of our new selves is imagined, drawn from scripture, science, and the author's insight. As Paul said, so many years ago: "When we were children we thought as a child, and …. Then we shall see face to face…"

Our new bodies shall be incorruptible. In less than a millisecond, the tent we wore shall be shuffled off, replaced with a fixture of light. There shall be a massive transcendent metamorphosis of each individual, taking us into dimensions never experienced before!

Our forms shall be fixed from our original blueprint (our DNA), perfected by a healing force which will correct all of the weakened or missing genes. Our selves, our memories, and our reason shall be intact. We shall recognize each other, and our voices shall sound about the same. Some things shall be changed. Our vision shall be better than the best birds' vision; our strength won't matter, because our new self will be able to cohabit matter, and other light. We will be able to travel with a thought; we can walk through walls, if we want.

We will learn, I think, that the matter we all perceived when we wore our corruptible bodies, is an illusion, both of mass, and of sight. The physicists have known that matter is almost entirely empty. We shall learn that the Spirit is the most *real* thing. And we shall be spirits, dressed in light, able to operate in, and with, and through the substance of matter. And we shall know as we are known, and we will come to know others we have never known before. Most importantly, we shall instantly know Our Lord.

EPILOG

In a sermon I once heard, the minister talked about the message written in Revelation 20. The sermon was entitled "When warnings are ignored, people often suffer". He used several stories to illustrate his point.

He spoke of the Titanic, where over a dozen phone messages were received, warning of icebergs nearby, much further south than usual. One of the owners claimed "Even God could not sink the Titanic!" They should have studied their mythology before they named the ship; the Titans were destroyed when *they* defied the gods. The real reason for the disaster seemed to be the reckless disregard for danger; the owners were anxious to cross the Atlantic in record time.

The small town of Cameron, Louisiana lost about half of their population, as they ignored clear and repeated warnings of an approaching hurricane. The year was 1957; the name of the hurricane was "Audrey" The national warning system had just been completed the year before, but had not yet established its reputation for reliability. Just two years prior, local forecasters had warned the area of an impending hurricane, but it was largely dissipated by the time it got near Cameron. At that time there were skeptics, and many in the town held a hurricane party in sheer ignorant defiance. No lives were lost then, and there was very little property damage. This time almost half of the population of about 1000 residents died in the storm.

The details of the space shuttle Challenger tragedy were investigated in great, agonizing detail. Investigators reported that several authorities from various engineering groups had presented grim warnings, formally, and in writing.

In the Holy Scriptures, everyone is warned of a great Judgment, called the "Great White Throne" judgment. "And I saw the dead, great and small, standing before the throne,… and books were opened." No one will be too important or too insignificant to be excused. All who ignore the good news of the Gospel shall have to answer to God Himself. "..*tormented day and night forever and ever*" is not to be desired.

The preponderance of Biblical scholars have told us that we are probably living in the last days. The specific references to these prophesies are given in the following table.

***

SELECTED END-TIME PROPHESIES

Advances in science and travel: Daniel 12:4

*"But you, Daniel, close up and seal the words of the scroll until **the time of the end**. Many will go here and there to increase knowledge."*

Great Apostasy in the last days: Romans 1: 29-31.

"They have become filled with every kind of wickedness, evil, greed and depravity. They are full of envy, murder, strife, deceit and malice. They are gossips, slanderers, God-haters, insolent, arrogant and boastful; they invent ways of doing evil; they disobey their parents; they are senseless, faithless, heartless, and ruthless."

The return of the Jews to Israel: Ezekiel 37: 12

"I will bring you back to the land of Israel. Then you, my people, will know that I am the Lord..."

Israel attacked by many nations: Ezekiel 38: 8

"In future years you will invade a land that has recovered from war, whose people were gathered from many nations..."

The "Blessed Event" (Rapture):   1Thes. 4:17

"After that, we who are still alive and are left will be caught up together with them in the clouds to meet the Lord in the air. And so we will be with the Lord forever."

Titus 1: 14

"*...awaiting our **blessed hope**, the appearing of the glory of our great God, Savior Jesus Christ...*"

The Tribulation (7 years):   Daniel 12: 26

"*The end will come like a flood: War will continue until the end, and desolations have been decreed. He (the antichrist) will confirm a covenant with many (Israel) for one 'seven'...*"

Christ's 2nd Coming: Revelation 19: 11

"*I saw heaven standing open and there before me was a white horse, whose rider is called Faithful and True. With justice he judges and makes war...*"

The Great Judgment: Revelation 20: 11

"*Then I saw a great white throne... and books were opened...*"

***

I would add to this list the *Gospel*, succinctly summarized in ***John 3***.

This passage tells us how to avoid the impending doom of the Tribulation, and the Judgment which follows. Find a Christian friend, and ask to study the Bible with him or her. May God bless your search!

T. Steven Brown: tomBrown3080@gmail.com   (Write me)

Made in the USA
Charleston, SC
13 July 2010